Novels by Sherman Smith:

Poets Can't Sing
The Honeysuckle Rose Hotel
Silencing the Blues Man
Golden City on Fire
Sausalito Night Music

For information on the author and all his writings go to:
Shermansmithauthor.com

Special thanks to the team at FPW Media for the cover
design and irreplaceable editing support.

SAUSALITO
Night Music

SHERMAN SMITH

Earl Crier was in rare form, his fingers gliding magically across the piano keys in a way that you could practically see the notes rise from the ivories as a flight of scarlet chested sunbirds. The bass, moody, reaching out for her lover in the middle of the night – secretive and lustful. Imogene, the beautiful lyrical songbird of the Earl Crier quintet parted her lips to sing 'Good Morning Heartache' with such heart and soul that the raindrops falling outside The Honeysuckle Rose Hotel hung in mid-air hypnotized by her purity of heart – the blues. Then, as she faded, the voice of a tenor saxophone filled the room. There is no one sound to a tenor saxophone, it is the heart and soul of the musician that makes the music.

Michael O'Dea transcended his music making it more powerful than he was. His sound was dark, fat, lush, masculine, wallowing in the heart and the pain that made up the man's soul. A man of flesh and blood, Michael O'Dea was an ugly man, hard to look at, hard to forget. His physical appearance made you uncomfortable – his music was unforgettable.

Chapter One

No one wants to go there - to hell - but sometimes in life we are given no choice but to suffer a personal trek to that dreaded place. There you are stuck in the muck knee deep, only you went in head first. Digging your way out is not easy, for some it is a one-way trip. For others, if you are lucky, you find your way back to mortal ground and hopefully you are a little wiser, kinder, patient, and compassionate for the experience.

Going into hell head first is often caused by sins of our own volition, the heartbreak of the loss of a loved one, a tragic illness, an accident, drowning in financial quicksand, poverty, prejudice, or in Michael O'Dea's case, for just being remarkably ugly.

Michael was born ugly, and as the years passed he did not grow out of it. The sad truth is that he became uglier. He grew up in an orphanage and told as a child that he was the devil's progeny, only he was so ugly the devil wouldn't have him. Loneliness his constant companion, he managed to lift himself out of hell's muck by putting his heart, and his pain, into his music. The beauty that no one else could see he shared through is a tenor saxophone.

More than once he had contemplated ending his life, but suicide is a sin, he had already been to hell, and knew that he wasn't wanted there, and so he trudged on one day at a time. There was a tune that stuck in his head that he could never shake. Where he heard it, or when, it didn't really matter, he would just start humming it. He never played it on his saxophone,he just couldn't.

When a child is born

They possess a gift or two

One of them is this

That they have it within them to make a wish come true.

Michael gave up on wishing, that was until the day Mollie entered his life. She was a small-town girl who had brought with her to the big city the ability to see beauty where others did not. The first time she saw Michael she saw beauty.

This morning he looked in the mirror, as he had done each day for almost forty-two years. The face that mocked him was his own. He was five feet seven, with large ears and a long stretched out leprechaun-like face that ended with a sharp lantern jaw. The smallpox he had had as a boy had left his face scarred, making some places hard to shave. His skin lacked any dramatic color, causing these scars and the little blue veins that appeared with every movement of his facial muscles to stand out glaringly. He was mostly bald except for an auburn patch that he greased and combed into a ludicrous quaff. His eyes seemed void of color, though if one looked closely they were an anemic grey, the same color as the lonely space in which he had lived for so long.

Mollie stepped behind him, wrapping her arms around him as she kissed his neck and smiled at his refection in the mirror. "Good morning," she whispered, the lightness of her breath a gentle breeze that teased the grey, turning bits and pieces to various shades of blue, that allowed the warmth of the sun and her love to touch him.

When looking in that same mirror Mollie saw beauty in the man she now knew to be her husband. When looking at Mollie, Michael saw all the colors in the rainbow, heard all the good sounds that lighten the heart, and for the first time he felt his loneliness slipping away. He had yet to find words that could come close to possibly describing his Mollie.

When he picked up his saxophone and began to play Mollie heard his heart sing, and when she looked at him she saw beauty.

* * * * *

February 6, 1952

The grand old ballroom tucked beneath the Honeysuckle Rose Hotel felt cold as a crypt as Stella entered for the last time. There were so many wonderful memories that echoed across the semi-darkened room. Stella's Grotto had been home to an amazing experiment that had forever changed the music scene in San Francisco. Here for the first-time musicians of color had dared to challenge the musician's union's closed-door policy for colored musicians, Asians, and women outside of the classical field. Here, white, black, brown, yellow, and red dined, danced, and performed together honoring the vision of Earl Crier, her husband, who started and conducted The Earl Crier Orchestra.

Earl had always been a musician, jazz on the keyboard, and at his best crooning hot smoky blues. He had been terrified of the dark since being trapped in a well cave-in as a small boy. After losing his vision during a ship explosion while serving in the Merchant Marine during the war, he struggled to overcome his terror by singing the blues as only a man who is terrified of the dark, while being trapped in the same, can. He also developed a knack for attracting extraordinary musicians who struggled with their own demons. He understood Michael's pain allowing his soul to soar through the saxophone that was as much part of him as an arm or a leg.

While close to the same age, they developed a father-son relationship that blossomed until there had been an unfortunate confrontation with the police. Les Moore, a black trombonist, perhaps the best musician at the Rose, was saved from a call-up to Korea by a broken leg. Earl suffered a concussion followed by a series of strokes that led to the death of the bluesman.

Three months ticked quickly by and the Honeysuckle

Rose Hotel died for the want of money the bill and tax collectors demanded, and the fading audience that left Stella's Grotto all too silent.

Chain smoking most of the morning, Stella lit another as she took her place at Earl's piano as she savored the memories. In a few moments her family would arrive to share this moment and to say good-bye to The Rose.

When looking at Mollie, Michael saw all the colors in the rainbow, her beauty the music that lightened his heart. Love was something he had never experienced and was woefully unprepared to understand. He had thought that *love* was something he did not deserve, a punishment for a sin he must have committed in another life. Thus, his feelings for Mollie were foreign, and very much a learning process.

"Are you ready?" Mollie asked.

Michael nodded.

Their bags were packed, they hadn't much more than the memories of their home – The Honeysuckle Rose Hotel – where they had first met. Where Earl Crier's music had brought them all together, redefining their lives.

The elevator took them down to Stella's Grotto where for the last time Earl's family would share their music as they said good-bye to *The Rose*, Stella, and to friendships they knew that no matter how far the miles that distanced them, how many the years that passed, they would always be more than friends, for they had all grown together at The

Honeysuckle Rose.

As Stella entered The Grotto it lit up as if it were a Saturday night, the orchestra in full swing, the dance floor bustling, cigarette smoke and laughter filling the air, inter-mixed with clink of glassware as the guests forgot all their troubles and tribulations, delighting themselves to an evening brought to you by the one and only Earl Crier; a fading memory. Only this morning the orchestra boxes were empty, the Grotto quiet where only the family gathered for one last dance. Cigarette smoke rose from an ashtray adding a slight haze as Stella she sat alone, her fingers softly caressing the piano's keys.

Everyone turned to Stella, as Rusty Mayer brought the mallets down rapid-fire on the marimba with a bright, Sunny rythme. Followed by Henry on the clarinet, Les Moore on the trombone, and Michael on his hauntingly beautiful tenor saxophone. This was all that was left of the Earl Crier Orchestra. The drums, violin, cello, slap bass, trumpet, guitar - Earl's piano with his rich bluesy voice, all fleeting ghosts in this once grand ballroom.

Everyone rose as Imogene, their gifted songbird, stepped to the microphone and began to sing Stella's Song, while the house poet Oscar, who was blind as Earl had been, neither seeing eye to eye on anything, escorted Stella to the dance floor. When Michael picked up his saxophone and began to play, tears glistened in her eyes as Earl's recorded voice joined Imogene's for one last dance.

One by one she danced with her boys, her men, her family until Imogene fell silent, the last words coming from a vinyl recording.

Tiny lights, like so many twinkling stars, lit the ceiling as Stella looked up and blew his memory a kiss. She touched a hand to her cheek as she felt what must have been Earl returning hers. To her surprise, she remembered the sound of Sy's voice, along with the sweet sound of Elsie, his violin. "Blow Gabriel, Blow," she whispered, knowing that Earl would never be silent as he now played and sang his blues at Gabriel's side.

Stella was the last to leave The Rose. With Stub at her side, she pulled the door shut and turned the key. The key she dropped through the mail slot along with a note:

May God bless whoever unlocks these doors.

Chapter Two

Bags in hand, Michael and Mollie, walked away from The Rose. The goodbyes had been said with nothing left to do but find what tomorrow would bring. They had each other, in truth that was the scary part, finding a roof and a warm bed had become a daunting challenge. Michael's ugliness did not make it any easier.

Les Moore had easily found a home in the Fillmore District with a regular gig at The Black Cat, where thanks to Earl Crier, he already had a following. The city was steeped in prejudice and it stunk like the humid bogs and sharecropper's miserable cabins that Les had grown up in Broussard, Louisiana. The Fillmore was a colored com-munity - a modern-day ghetto - from its stores, churches, unemployment, to the bars and their music. In a white city, the Fillmore was Black. Michael was white, exceptions were made where talent was concerned, but he was also outstandingly ugly - and that was a double strike against him. Ugly was not contagious, still he was treated as if he were a leper.

Michael and Mollie stepped aboard the Powell & Mason Street cable car and deposited their ten cents each as they endured the stares that were always present whenever they went out in public. It wasn't just Michael's appearance that drew the whispered comments and stares. Mollie was twenty-three, twenty years younger than her husband. At five feet two she could easily be mistaken for the actress June Allyson. The youthful contours of her round face was accentuated by her short page-boy bob. The wave lift, above the forehead, gave her face added height. Her curly hair is fine textured with a medium thickness that accented her innocent Iowa farm girl face, her smile shy; always curious. Her robin-egg blue eyes flecked with gold, welcoming and honest. With her beauty and Michael's disfigurement they were a freak show, the comments only silenced by Mollie when she returned their stares with a smile that suggested: Don't worry, he's my husband, and it was I who asked him to marry me . . . and the only thing that would make me happier would be for you to stop staring.

The clanging cable car took them to the waterfront and fisherman's wharf where a fish monger who had provided fresh fish for the Rose would take them on an old fishing boat across the bay to Sausalito.

The ferry to Sausalito had stopped running in 1941 leaving the only access to the smaller village a one point-seven-mile drive across the Golden Gate Bridge. After the shipyards had closed towards the end of World War II regular bus service had also been cancelled as Sausalito was forced to become a sleepy backwater to its bigger sister across the bay. It was a working-class town where former mill and shipyard workers struggled with post-war unemployment. The colored workers had moved to the Fillmore, or across the way to Oakland and Alameda where the navy base still offered employment. Sausalito was a place where men reached their calloused hands into empty pockets as they looked across the dark waters at night to the city's lights, the foghorn's calling enviously into the night.

Michael and Mollie had struggled to find an apartment, even a room, in San Francisco where they found nothing but closed doors. It was improper for a young lady to rent an apartment by herself. Though married, when Michael and Mollie inquired about an apartment or room for rent the landlords only stammered and stuttered, their unspoken comments about the unusual couple bordering on the obscene. "I'm sorry, but we currently have no vacancies;" their excuse as the doors slammed shut, the For-Rent signs visible in the window left untouched. It had been a Catholic Sister, that had seen Mollie's tear-stained face and hurting eyes, that had told Mollie about a small boarding house in Sausalito that would not turn them away.

Sausalito seemed terribly far away, like Portland, Maine, or some nameless mining town in the Ozarks. With one phone call the decision was made.

"Welcome, you must be Michael and Mollie O'Dea, please come in," said Betty McPheters, a wide-eyed, gracious, and welcoming woman, a moment after they had rung the front doorbell. The Sister had told Mollie that the manager of the boarding house was a survivor of two recent tragedies. Her husband, Reginald McPheters, had lost his life when his ship, a Fletcher Class Destroyer, was hit and sunk by a Kamikaze Japanese aircraft. There had been no survivors. One Japanese pilot in exchange for 329 officers and crewmen was not a fair trade. Within the last year, during a ferocious windstorm, they had lost power and she had fallen down a flight of stairs in the dark resulting in a back injury that now bound her to a wheelchair. While Mollie knew about the wheelchair, seeing it for the first time struck her momentarily speechless.

The Bayview House, a twelve room, yellow, wind and rain weathered three story structure, perched on the side of a hill just above the backwater village of Sausalito. It looked out over the bay towards Alcatraz Island, and the lights of the Bay Bridge, the East Bay beyond, and downtown San Francisco. She let out eight rooms and on the day Mollie called she had a vacancy.

Moving her wheelchair aside to let them in she reached out her hand in greeting to Michael, never taking her eyes and a warm smile away. Michael tried to smile, failing to say thank-you.

In that first moment Michael and Mollie felt as if they had found a home, one in which they were not made to feel as if they were outcasts or charity cases. However, this did not lighten their load because they had left the music behind in San Francisco. Getting to and from San Francisco was nigh impossible without a car. In Sausalito there were no night clubs or possible places of employment for Michael the musician. Buying a car, even an old beater, would not be in the cards until employment was found and they were able to save enough to make getting a car possible.

Michael had never earned any real money back at The Honeysuckle Rose Hotel. Free room and board had been part of the deal for all the musicians in the Earl Crier Quintet. No one anticipated the closure of *The Rose* following Earl's untimely passing. Michael certainly had not foreseen Mollie asking him to marry her - thank you, God - which did not make it any easier now that he had no job, and nothing in his pocket to take care of his new bride the way a man ought to.

Mollie paid a full month's rent in advance but now she had not much more in her purse than Michael had in his wallet. If there was a bright side it was that Betty needed some help at the boarding house and had halved their rent in exchange for Mollie's part time work. Mollie had asked about full time and quickly learned that Betty had a fond loyalty for Renata Vazzali, her one full time employee.

Unpacking their bags, they both knew that it would be some time before Michael's gifts as a musician would be little more than a memory of how happy they had been. Having a roof over their heads was shallow gratification as friends and family seemed farther away than the Statin Island Ferry. The lights across San Francisco Bay might as well have been Manhattan instead of San Francisco.

Happier days settled into a distant memory as they sat down to their first communal dinner. The boarding house seemed well kept, but it was not the home they had had at *the Rose.* The Honeysuckle Rose may have been a cold old hotel that had seen better days, its interior had been warmed by the heart and soul of good friends and family, its blood their music that flowed through its very foundations.

The first moment they sat down there was a tension in the air that suggested trouble simmering like bad wiring in the attic. To Michael the air smelled of mold and corruption, the man-made kind he knew rooted itself in prejudice and contemptuous ignorance. Michael had learned long ago to not trust nor judge people, his experience a long rocky road of disappointments. Mollie touched his wrist sensing what he was thinking. When caught in stormy weather he often played music in his head to deafen hurtful words. She wondered what he was about to play - the first words around the dining table yet unspoken.

Betty smiled. "Gentlemen, Ms. Brandt, we have new residents with us tonight, Mr. and Mrs. Michael O'Day. They come to us from San Francisco where I am told that Michael has quite a following as a jazz musician." Betty announced this as if Michael and Mollie's presence at the dining room table was a glamorous event, the welcoming of royalty perhaps.

Most nights, the dinner conversation at The Bayview House was inane, hostility breathing nearby. Tonight, their faces were sullen - silent - sucking stale air that might have as well have seeped out from an Egyptian tomb. Everyone knew that Sarah Brandt was not going to tolerate a freak at her table. The redness in her face was a sure sign that she was ready to explode. The fragrance of fresh baked bread, salad, a pot roast with roasted vegetables steaming at the table's center filled the air as the residents sat, stone cold, staring at Michael, each expecting the other to speak, none willing to part their lips least they be embarrassed by what might come out.

Michael understood, he was used to dining alone at a crowded table. Usually he would nod slightly, while playing his head music, acknowledging their unspoken somber prejudice. He would fill his plate without waiting for anything to be passed, and excuse himself to dine in a dark corner where his presence would not ruin their meal. Now he had Mollie and felt his rage build at her mistreatment. He slowly glanced around the table as the music gave way to the insipid silence.

"Michael plays the tenor saxophone," Mollie said. Her face beamed with the pride that comes from a new bride.

"Oh, really," said Sarah Brandt as she shook her head with displeasure. I don't cotton to jazz, it's too noisy, and the saxophone, well . . . I can tell you that it sounds like so many monkey's screeching in the jungle." She glared a Michael. "Monkeys." She deliberately repeated. The word harsh and blaming.

There was no hiding the punishing look Betty gave Sarah that strongly suggested that she was being rude - which she was. The heavyset spinster, with dry, ratty, spaghetti-like gray hair that she obviously cut herself, had an opinion on everything. This included religion, sex, and politics, which she would loudly declare "One doesn't discuss such things over a meal, it's bad for the digestion," whenever someone dared broach the subject at the table. If asked, and no one dared, everyone at the table could tell you that Sarah did not bathe often enough, which she masked with too much talcum powder, rose cream and rose water.

Mollie, who had the misfortune of sitting next to the woman, did not have to guess that her seat was avoided by most. Betty sat on her other side, at the head of the table where her wheelchair fit the best. "Michael's music," she responded, "is very mellow, thoughtful perhaps."

"Monkeys," the woman grumbled as she stuffed a buttered dinner roll in her face, her cheeks filling out as she chewed like a greedy Billy Goat.

This is going to be fun, Mollie thought, as she patted Michael's knee. Michael slowly ate the pot roast, the best he had ever eaten, appreciating the food, ignoring the company the best he could.

Well, well, ...well, ain't this one a beauty, thought Patrick Doyle. Doyle had been the schoolyard bully in his youth. Having been kicked out of the Boston Public School system, he had grown up with fast fists and a quick temper. As a union man by necessity, he was contemptuous of management, Jews, Catholics, niggers, women who stepped out of their proper place in the world, and those that deserved his caustic eye because he deemed so. Now, with the shipyard closed, he met his needs through larceny, and a petty protection racket he ran along the waterfront. While he was often behind in the rent, he never lacked for a Guinness. He immediately saw Michael as someone he and his boys would have to put a scare into, then tighten the screws for every dime they could squeeze out of him. Putting a fist or two into Michael's ugly puss would be a pleasure. As for his little missus, well there's more than one way to pay the piper.

"Harvey, Harvey Freed, pleased tah meet yah." The smallish man sitting next to Michael introduced himself.

Sarah's owl-like eyes went up at the mere sound of Harvey's voice, which was high, sounding much like a young boy's going through testosterone changes, and fast spoken.

While he did not offer his hand to Michael, he leaned forward enough to give Mollie a welcoming smile. Harvey was a smallish man in his mid-forties. He was scrawny, his coat drooping over his boney frame. He had dark brown beagle-like eyes that looked as if he were about to cry. His receding hairline brought that much more attention to his remarkable eyes, as did the fact that he had almost no eyebrows. Harvey liked to talk; ad nauseum. Whenever Sarah's dark personality silenced the dinner conversation it was Harvey who lightened the meal, often causing Sarah to take her plate and stomp off to her room.

The other members of the dining table introduced themselves without much fanfare.

"Pierre McBeth, most folks call me Scotty." The behemoth Scotsman, who if put side by side with a redwood lumberman would make the lumberman look like a ram compared to a bull, introduced himself. His full crop of red hair, and flushed cheeks made him look as if he had just come off the north slope of Alaska. He gave a nod to the man sitting to his right. "This here is Doyle."

Mollie was surprised with the short words of the Scotsman, most Scotsmen – and women – she had met were long of the tongue and tight with the coin. The one he had introduced simply as Doyle caught her off guard in a disquieting way. When she had been growing up on the farm there had been a salesman who came by once a month, regular as clockwork, with an old pickup truck filled with all sorts of assorted, useless junk. Mama said that he wore an actor's mask with a wide forced grin that expressed a mean streak hidden behind a smugness, delighting in doing something contemptable or noxious to others. Papa usually chased him away with a shotgun telling the salesman to get that shit-eating grin off his face. The man named Doyle had that same smug grin as he sat at the table a fork in one hand while holding an unlit Camel cigarette in the other. His gray hair was perfectly cut, well-maintained, with not a single hair out of place. She could not fix an age on him, he was neither young nor old, though the creases in his skin suggested that he had lived through the kind of trouble that drew most men silent. He was pale, with an unsettling quiver beneath a three-inch scar to his left cheek. There were beads of sweat on his brow as his dark brown eyes searched her, then Michael, with that god-awful grin that suggested the thoughts behind it were not very polite.

The man scared her, and she had to look away.

"Oswaldo Rafael Cammano." The next man said. His voice was gentle, his speech rough and accented, a muscular man with large scarred workingman's hands, and a large nose that had seen too much wind, sun, and rum.

"Mr. Cammano comes to us from Ecuador," Betty offered. He's a fisherman, and I might add, has a beautiful singing voice. While everything he sings is in his native tongue, I do so love to hear him sing."

"Hello, Rafael." Mollie said adding a friendly smile.

"Oswaldo, please," the man said, his accent heavy, his heart open as he extended a hand across the table to Michael. " It is the name my mother called me by." His kind welcome hit Michael with a feeling he rarely enjoyed; acceptance - for who he was as a human being with no preconditions regarding his disability.

Sarah Brandt, a Baptist, did not like foreigners, people of color, Catholics, unionists, most everyone at the dining table – especially Patrick Doyle - or anyone else who did not fit into her vision of how the world ought to be. With the exchange of hands between the foreign fisherman and the freak, she let out a pronounced sigh of disapproval, reached in front of Mollie taking the last two dinner rolls from the basket as she screeched her chair back, and then taking her plate, she stomped off to her room.

The exact second that her ponderous ass passed through the doorway Scotty struck a wooden match to Doyle's unfiltered cigarette, setting an open pack of Camels on the table between them. Despite the addition of the tobacco smoke, everyone relaxed with her departure.

Mollie thought about the singular significance of that cigarette and wondered why the very scary Patrick Doyle was afraid of Sarah Brandt. He hadn't spoken the entire time she had been at the table. Doyle blew a weak smoke-ring in Michael's direction. "Were you in an accident," he asked?"

Without looking up, Michael answered. "Nope, I was

born this way."

"I keep saying that God don't exist, but if there is one, He's got a crappy sense of humor." The cigarette tucked into his grin insinuated that laugh behind his words.

"Crappy would be one word for it." Michael answered. "And friend, please blow your smoke in another direction, you are ruining my wife's meal."

"Father Palazzeschi isn't here" Betty jumped in. "He rarely joins us for dinner, I always keep a warm plate in the kitchen for the dear man," she said motioning towards the vacant chair at the end of the table. "Mass? Are you Catholic? No?" She politely did not delve any further. "Michelangelo, Father Palazzeschi, is always with us for breakfast." She looked around the table to see if anything else was needed. "I see that we a need more rolls," she said as she wheeled herself towards the kitchen.

Mollie helped Michael to more pot roast as the serving plate was passed quietly around by an elfish old woman. Renata was all of four feet six, her face an ocean of age spots and wrinkles, her thin hair covered with a linen hand-kerchief. Her chicken bone wrists and arms, barely hidden beneath aged-parchment paper skin, shook as she held the heavy dinner plate up to serve.

As the sun set on that first day, after they had met and shared an uncomfortable meal with the other tenants, Michael found his way up to the second-floor roof where he found a spot of solitude. It was a good spot, with a small flat roof that tucked itself on one side beneath the perpetual shadow from a steep hillside which broke the wind, while a small raised attic protected him from prying eyes. Above, the second floor rose to a third. Nothing was said about the third floor, whatever it was, it appeared to be small, an attic perhaps. An old wobbly wooden chair provided all he needed as he raised his saxophone finding melancholy memories which soon drifted towards the lights of the city across the bay.

Mollie listened through an open window in their apartment as her husband cried the only way he knew how. She knew and whispered the sad words to his song as she remembered how he had come to *The Honeysuckle Rose Hotel*. She had not thought about it until now, but it was in that moment of condemnation and disparagement when he had truly been at his lowest that she had begun to fall in love. She listened, trying to understand the pain he felt, his loneliness, that with the loss of his music there would be no light in the sky; no hope. In their life back at The Rose every second of every day evolved around the music and the musicians that brought the place to life. Here, in Sausalito, the only place he had to play was out on that small roof. In her woman's heart she knew that the sun would rise tomorrow, and the day after that, each brighter as they found their way forward as man and wife. That was Mollie, always finding the positive. Tonight, she listened, her tears real because the loneliness within his music was stealing her heart away.

Betty sat in her chair with a dish towel in hand while Renata stood on a milk crate doing the dishes - their usual routine. The old woman was not a talker unless queried. "What do you think?" Betty asked.

"About what?" The old woman was being coy.

And Betty knew it. "Mollie and her husband, of course."

"Mollie seems like a nice young woman. It will be nice to have another woman - besides Sarah - as a guest."

"Yes, it will." She had not told Renata yet that she had hired Mollie part time to help with the general cleaning and laundry. Renata's duties were exclusively in the kitchen.

"And her husband?" Betty asked as she whipped a plate dry and placed it on the counter.

The old woman laughed, showing three front teeth, then said something in Tabarchino, a local Italian dialect spoken on the island of Sant'Antioco where she had lived until the age of eight when her parents had immigrated to America. If it was possible for the old woman to blush through her sea of wrinkles she did.

"Well."

The old woman cackled. "I say . . . They are going to have a very interesting marriage. He must be *molto buono a letto,* she said in Italian, *very good in bed.*"

Betty almost dropped a plate. "Perhaps," she said. "One has to wonder."

Chapter Three

Sitting on the roof top, looking out towards the lights of the city Michael played his saxophone, his soul echoing for the first time around the hamlet of Sausalito. It was an unfamiliar sound to those who first heard it – mysterious, pleasant, haunting . . . night music.

Mollie listened, marveling to herself the things she was discovering about her husband – and about herself. They were married now for a short three months and so much had changed. She sat on the fire escape, just down the hall from their room, listening, as she remembered the day Michael had first bared his soul.

* * * * *

The elevator door opened. Mollie had never seen someone so ugly, so unnerving that she, Rosemary, and Stella stepped back afraid of what dreadful plague, what evil this creature had brought to the warm sanctity of the Honeysuckle Rose. It wasn't long before they learned of his betrayal and judged his intent.

Earl knew that he was about to put Michael O'Dea on the hot seat. Michael had two choices, sink or swim, with no other options. It was only fair, he had come into their midst with deceit, a thief in the night out to steal their dreams, a spy, and for what it was worth still might be one.

Michael – "Beauty" – had turned against his bosses asking for sanctuary if he confessed his sins, swearing to fight alongside the residents of the Honeysuckle Rose Hotel in their battle against the musician's union. Their music had moved his soul, or so he said. If he did not get that sanctuary Earl suspected that his life expectancy wouldn't allow him to get much beyond the hotel's front doors. His betrayal of the union was unforgivable, and the President of the Musician's Union, Frank Cambria, was a very unforgiving man. Michael had made a tough decision, and now he had to lay it on the line, because he was asking those who were about to judge him for both forgiveness and acceptance. When his name was called Michael did not step up as Earl had expected him to.

Michael did not like to be in the spotlight and that spotlight was about to shine down on him hot and heavy. He desperately needed to be accepted by these people, strangers all; except the cop. Between his looks and his deeds, he wasn't going to get much sympathy.

"Michael, if you are not standing, then do so." Earl said as he tapped out a repetitive D - major on the keyboard. The single note grated on everyone's nerves as they

*waited in silence for Michael to speak. They had no idea
what he had done, nor why he was on the hot seat. Earl
had never done this before; the meanness wasn't part of the
man's character. Everything that had been said this morning sounded urgent and dire regarding their deteriorating
situation with the union. Those that didn't know guessed
that this curious trial had to do with that. Now they were
growing impatient. Earl spoke again, the tone in his voice
clear that he was not going to call on Michael a third time.
"You have all heard Michael on the saxophone. He is a
gifted musician who has come to our door and I welcomed
him. Michael, you and I have talked about this, if you are
to be allowed to stay it must be by a unanimous vote of
everyone in this room. My vote is yes. Detective Hoyt, Sam,
you each have a vote here because whichever way the vote
goes it will have a significant impact regarding our battle
with the union. Okay Michael, here's your chance - you
won't get a second offer."*

*Michael felt the overwhelming burden weighing him
down as he stood as straight as he could. He slowly looked
around the room, taking in each face, allowing each in turn
to see his. Knowing that he was about to be judged not just
for his deeds but for being ugly – and ugly always brought
harsh judgements. He held his sax as if he intended to play
rather than say anything. 'Well, here goes nothing.' He
thought as he opened his mouth to speak. "I'm not much
for talking," he said apologetically. "The truth is I don't
have much to say that would be of much interest to anyone
once you know the truth. This here saxophone is how I
speak with most folks. She says what I can't, so if you don't
mind I'll mix words with a few notes . . . otherwise I might*

as well leave now."

He looked at Thaddeus. "When I checked in to the hotel I lied, not about being a musician, but my intent. I don't have a sainted mother near death's door waiting for me. I was dumped at an orphanage because I was born an ugly bastard, so ugly my own mother would not have me. I checked into the hotel as a spy for the union, with orders to find out whatever I could that would open the doors of this place, so the union could bring you down. I didn't know anything about you except for the few dollars I was paid to do this evil thing. Why the union boss has made you his personal target I don't know, nor do I know anything about what they are planning. Whatever it is, it's not good."

Everyone's reaction, exempt for Sam, Stella, and Earl, was exactly what Michael thought it would be. When deceived and threatened, most folks would rather run you out of town on a rail than bake you a cake. As he listened to the angry murmurs being exchanged he brought up his sax and played a hauntingly sad original piece that expressed his sorrow.

After Michael had finished Earl tapped that same D-major key a couple of times to get everyone's attention. "Go on, you're doing fine."

"Last night I was casing the joint and found myself down here. While you were playing I hid in the kitchen. Whatever good there may be left in me screamed at me to come out in the open. I never wanted to play so much in my poor miserable life. But I couldn't, I had my orders, and that was to report back to boss Cambria what I had found out, so he could do you all harm."

"This morning I went to the cafe next door where I was supposed to meet with a guy who goes by the name Harry the Hammer. When I saw that sonofabitch, I knew I couldn't betray you folks, though all I know about you is your music. In this town the Musician's Union has a lot of clout. They say who can play where, and if you don't dance to their tune, you're black-listed, if not worse. You are already on Cambria's black-list. Whatever he has in mind for you will be bad, and I cannot be part of that. So, I turned my back on Harry and introduced myself to Stella, Earl, and the cop they were sitting with. When Harry saw that I was also talking to a cop I just signed my own death sentence." Michael said that with a level of certainty.

The room held a deep silence as everyone registered what he had said. "All my life folks have thought me to be ugly. They're right, you're right, I am. I'm no beauty, which is why I've been saddled with the nickname Beauty."

Mollie remembered the bitter salt of her first tear over Michael.

"Earl, it's been so long since I have been called Michael I almost forgot it's my name. I thank you for that." He played more of the melodic tune he had played earlier, then finished. *"I'm asking your forgiveness for coming here the way I did. I hope my actions show you where my heart is. I'd like nothing more than to stay, I'll stand beside you against the union. I ask for nothing more than your forgiveness and to play alongside some of the best musicians I've ever done heard."* This time Michael didn't play. With tears in his eyes he searched the faces around him as if his life depended on it.

"That includes Michael volunteering to help with the music upstairs in the lounge." Earl said. "That takes some courage, the union thugs most likely will take that personally. The windows give a clear view to the street."

Les, who had an ear for music, remembered much of the tune Michael had played. He voted by picking up his trombone and playing it. On her bass, Rosemary added her own interpretation of Michael's heart rendering piece.

"I . . .I say yah . . yes." Stub stuttered. Stub, everyone's favorite uncle, vote had influence.

Stella voted yes, then motioned to Stub that it was time to for them to pick up Brooks. She heard all yes votes as they left and expected that when they returned Michael O'Dea will have been added to her problematic family.

One by one everyone voted yes, accept for Ivory who remained silent. "Ivory," asked Earl, "I said that Michael's fate depends on a unanimous vote if he is to be allowed to stay. A non-vote is the same as a no."

Mollie bit her knuckles as she waited for Ivory to have his say.

Ivory remained silent.

"Mr. Ivory, I'm . . ." Michael said, trying not to sound as if he were begging - but he was. "I'm told that you are head of security around here. That you were once a proud United States Marine who has served his country well. That you won't take crap from no one. I'm guessing that if you vote for me to stay you'll be watching my every move, like a cat watches a canary bird, for some time to come. If I go out that door they'll shoot me down sure as night follows day. If I betray your trust you have my permission to shoot me down the same."

"Whew." Responded Imogene, her eyes doing the begging that Michael had fought so hard to avoid.

It was tough for Earl not to intercede.

"Mr. C," Ivory said loud and clear so there was no mistaking his words. "I'm going to come off sounding like one hard-assed gunny sergeant; so be it. You gave us the right to vote our conscience and I'm going to do just that. When I was in the Corps, in China, and in the Jap prison camps, not one marine turned traitor, each man preferring death to dishonor. It meant something to put one's life on line for character and honor. The boss man of this here musician's union paid O'Dea here a few lousy bucks to lie his way into the Honeysuckle Rose, spy on us, and report back with whatever dirt he could find to do us grievous harm. If a marine had gone over to the Japs, for whatever reason, and then came back saying: 'I was wrong fellas, will you forgive me, and take me back. I promise not to do it again.' No sir, once that line is crossed a traitor is a traitor and can never be trusted again. My vote is no." He paused for a moment giving O'Dea a long hard look then repeated his answer directly to him. "No."

Imogene, Mollie and Rosemary all let out a surprised gasp with the words - No, you can't do this - buried within.

Otherwise there was stone cold silence.

The sentence was harsh as Michael O'Dea stood convicted, condemned, and unforgiven before them. He had no words left to say, he had gotten himself into this mess, and had a hard time forgiving himself. All he had wanted was some acceptance and to play some music without being looked down upon. After a moment he took the saxophone, his voice silenced, and laid it on the piano in front of Earl. He knew what faced him once he walked out of the hotel. There would be no sanctuary. Cambria was not the forgiving kind. He doubted that they would shoot him - more likely he would be killed by a speeding car or beaten to death by thugs in a dark alleyway.

The door to the stairway slowly closed behind him.

The dull glint of light on his saxophone's brass radiated like a failing match in a darkened coal mine telling Mollie that Michael had accepted his fate; his music left behind as he went to surrender his life.

What happened next Mollie did not pretend to understand.

Michael held a broom stick as a defensive weapon as he sat on the couch in the lobby gathering up the courage to go out and say howdy to the union men. Mollie did not know which looked worse the fear written across his already horrific face, or the hate agitating in the eyes of the union men who lusted for violence just outside. The lobby clock ticked away as both images waited for the other to blink.

Then . . .

Then, Stub and Stella returned in Stella's car. Stub seeing the picket line that now blocked the front door sped up, stopping the car at the base of the steps, as close to the front door as he could get, the passenger door closest to the hotel's entrance.

The car's sudden arrival galvanized the union goons, already in a surely mood, into immediate action. They had orders to let no one into the hotel and had been looking for an easy target. It didn't matter that one of the people trying to bust through their lines was a woman. Hidden partially by the car no one saw that Brooks was blind. Like hunting dogs following the scent of blood they moved towards the car with raised fists and malicious intent. These men thrived on violence, it was their calling card, a drug that moved through their veins.

Michael did not have time to think. He saw that Stella was in trouble. He also knew how vicious these goons could be. With no thought to his own safety he clutched the broom handle tight, threw open the doors to the hotel and flung himself out as a human shield to protect this wonderful woman who had treated him with such kindness. She and Earl had given him his name back and if he died here he would go out as Michael O'Dea and not as the pitiful Beauty.

For a moment he was startled by the well-dressed man whose head was entirely covered by a silk hood, who was floundering, confused as to what direction he needed to go. Stella and the guy everyone called Stub were losing precious seconds in trying to get this guy pointed towards the door.

Sam, a retired policeman who had joined them in their fight against the union, held the door to the hotel open.

The goons swarmed the car.

One, a big swarthy man with long ill-kept dark red hair and a full beard, jumped up on the hood. Sam knew the man as a lumper down at the fisherman's market. He had a list of assault and battery charges long as the picket sign he wielded, the sign reversed so the handle could be used as a club. He raised it towards Stella, his club coming down was a powerful sweeping motion.

Michael was a fraction of a second faster. His broken broom stick struck the man in the knee, causing his aim to be off just enough for Stella to escape being hit by inches. The goon's second swing hit Michael in the shoulder. Michael heard a crack, felt a sharp pain as a numbness slide down his arm like an electric shock. The crack had come from the picket sign's sturdy handle - not sturdy enough - it was the handle that had cracked, not his shoulder. Michael was going to have one hell of a bruise, but at least his arm was still operational. He switched his grip to his other hand, swinging the broom stick painfully into the goon's groin, causing him to fall backwards from the hood of the car. Michael's forward lunge put him off balance, causing him to fall to one knee, his weapon rolling beneath the car.

Another goon rounded the rear of the car, the open door hindering his reach as Sam reached out and caught Stella's hand, pulling her inside the hotel. She in turn pulled

Brooks. Stub stopped just long enough to help Michael to his feet. Two of the goons coming around the rear of the car had truncheons and were just short of being able to bring one down on the back of Stub's head. "Hey, it's Beauty," one called out, "that SOB is mine." He raised the truncheon and . . .

A powerful and well-aimed stream of water blasted the closest of the assailants back while others tried to climb over the car. From the roof of the hotel, Ivory and a second retired policeman, Marty, held them at bay with a powerful stream from a fire hose. The hose barely reached the edge of the roof, limiting their aim.

Sam slammed and locked the front door as Stub and Michael sprinted inside.

* * * * *

Mollie's memory, selective to the events as they unfolded, was that Michael had come close to losing his life that day, not because of deeds he would have a hard time making up for, but to rescue Stella, a woman whose simple kindness had touched his heart.

Ivory changed his vote with a thumb's up, his smile giving a new respect for Beauty's courage; although he would always keep a cautious eye out.

Scotty and Doyle did not waste time sitting around the table. When the food was gone so were they. If there was a need to speak – *pass the potatoes* - it was Scotty who did so for both. Scotty spoke because Doyle had too much to say, easy to explode into bursts of violent rage, the line between words and fists always dangerously thin. Theirs was a unique relationship, Scotty protecting Doyle from himself like an older brother protecting the younger from the violent impulses he could barely control. When that beast breaks out, demanding to be fed, rage and hatred all consuming, Scotty helped to feed that beast until finally it calms, returning his best friend to him.

No women or booze in the rooms was the house rule. Scotty and Patrick Doyle had their own rule: *What the house didn't know, the house doesn't know.* Doyle's room was on the second floor. With Betty in her wheelchair and Sarah the bitch's room on the first floor, they were usually free to enjoy their chosen liquor - Famous Grouse Irish Scotch Whiskey - without too much concern. Doyle's room was next to the new couple's, whose sudden arrival was their object of conversation over two-finger pours.

"I don't believe I've ever heard a saxophone before, it does put out a nice sound; kind of melancholy, haunting, a lot of passion to it." Scotty said in a low voice, unsure how Doyle would respond to talking about artsy stuff. They did not know how the couple would take to the men drinking on a nightly basis in the room just next door to theirs. They didn't care.

Scotty watched his friend.

He had seen the beads of sweat on Doyle's forehead and

could foresee an attack coming. Sometimes it passed, other times it did not. On the way up to the room he had dropped a dime in the pay phone letting the crew know that tonight the boss would be needing some fresh air.

"He's out on the roof?" Doyle asked. Alone, with Scotty. Doyle made up for his quiet times – often with a dry sense of humor.

"That he is."

"Hope he doesn't fall off." Doyle mused as he lit a filterless Camel cigarette.

"The man is sober, at least I think he is." Scotty raised his glass. "Here's to us that do our best to avoid sobriety. Should we invite, . . what is his name? I don't recall."

"Montgomery, I think." Doyle suggested.

"No, that's not it." Scotty raised his glass again.

"It'll come to us in time," Doyle added, "but I'd rather not drink with the man, lord knows he's hard enough to look at. I once knew ah bloke back in Boston who had a dog almost as ugly. He put the bitch in a potato bag and dropped it into the river. It was the merciful thing to do." He enjoyed laughing at his own jokes, rarely at others. "Besides we don't know what the woman will think. It will be trouble for sure if she's against a man having a simple drink now and then and finds her husband gee-eyed just next door."

"That we don't. And to tell the truth, Michael gives me the willies, with his looks and all."

"That's his name."

"Willie?"

"No, you . . . ignorant jack-ass. Michael, his name is Michael."

"You sure it isn't Willie?" They laughed. "He is one ugly . . ."

Scotty had seen it one too many times before. They both fell silent as Doyle slipped into one of his black moods, back to that moment in May 1945 on the bloody hillside known as Sugar Loaf Hill on Okinawa where he cracked.

＊ ＊ ＊ ＊ ＊

They had been told what to expect when they went up that hill - the inner-locked machine guns firing and mortars would be murderous. The thunder of artillery shells that exploded to soften the enemies' defenses shredded their nerves as if they were listening to their own obituaries, their landing craft already crossing the River Styx. Sargent Patrick Doyle, United States Marines, part of the combined Army & Marine 10th Army, given the task of taking the island of Okinawa, blinked the fear-sweat from his eyes as his bowel told him that he needed to go a different direction.

When they had landed on Okinawa on April 1, his squad was well trained and combat hardened having survived bloody Tarawa, seventeen months prior. It had been at

Tarawa that Doyle had been promoted to Sergeant. He had been one of seven survivors out of the original forty-eight that had made up his platoon.

"When you go up that hill, many of you will not be coming back," he heard an officer say. "Thanks, I feel one hell of a lot better you telling us that." He looked at the officer wanting to turn his M-1 Carbine in his direction and pull the trigger. The painful pressure in his ears tightened as the last of the bombardment intensified. Word went up the line that it was time to go. The sergeants, up and down the line, chocked back their own fear as they rose, raising an arm as they beckoned their men forward.

When they reached the first crest the Japanese opened fire. Four well-hidden machine guns cut them down before anyone in his squad had a chance to return fire. A second later a Jap mortar obliterated the pile of dead or dying marines throwing Doyle like a rag doll into a still smoking shell hole littered with bits and pieces of some other sergeant's squad that had met the same fate as his. Dazed, and wounded with a dozen pieces of shrapnel, none serious, Doyle spent three hours in the blood, gore, and stench, before a marine corpsman discovered the one lone survivor.

That night, resting on a cot, waiting for the shrapnel to be removed, the only emotion, the only thought in his head was rage. His men had all died uselessly, their bodies chewed into unrecognizable rat fodder. The field hospital, located in and around an abandoned farm house overflowed with the wounded, their cries drowning out the sound of the surf that roared at the base of a sixty-foot cliff.

The perimeter to the hospital came under a Japanese

counterattack. With their backs to the sea all walking wounded were ordered into the fight. Doyle looked around for his M-1. A moment later a mortar hit a nearby surgical tent killing everyone inside. Doyle's rage exploded into a blinding madness where all he wanted to do was kill the enemy regardless of any threat to himself. As he found a carbine with fixed bayonet a group of women and children pushed aside a thick bush that had covered a hidden tunnel. In front of them was an elderly Okinawan. The women, holding the children's hands, some carrying infants, ran towards the cliff committing suicide without hesitation. Doyle screamed, "NO!!!", as he ran towards them. The old man pulled a gun from his robe, his thin wire-framed glasses catching the light just right, so Doyle could see his aged rheumy eyes. He turned the gun on Doyle but was not fast enough as the bayonet pierced his chest leaving a look of peace, horror, and agony in the old man's eyes; his last sight the rage in Doyle's.

The women and children had all gone over the cliff.

By the time someone found Sergeant Doyle only the old man's white beard – more red than white – remained of what had once been a head - after having been pulverized by that bloody bayonet.

* * * * *

No one except for Doyle knew what agonized memories occupied his dark moods whether it be waiting with the blood and gore in that shell hole, or the old man's face as it dissolved under Doyle's mindless attack. Scotty suspected both.

Scotty knew that tonight he and the boys would be going hunting. Doyle's rage was always there, slowly building until finally there had to be a release. Tonight, they would be hunting for an old white-haired, bearded, man. It did not matter if he was Jap, Chink, or Korean. A lot of veterans of the Okinawan conflict came back with disabling memories of that experience. Doyle was one of 27,000.

Doyle's crew relished a good fight, they were more than adept at giving a brutal ass-kicking. Doyle was the only one who got to taste the kill.

Scotty was no boy scout, he had killed before, but compared to Doyle he might make scout master.

The boys, Hector, Smitty, and Smokestack were dumb, young, and mean with a cruel streak - not likely to improve with age. In Sausalito they looked as out of place as a pack of Jackals – dirty street predators, mangy, evil laughing mutts, to most of the folks in this sleepy seaside town down-right scary. The generation that had fought and won the second world war were lucky not to have these three punks fighting by their sides - none were registered to become Korea bait- the world no safer with them walking upright.

They got new tattoos after each arrest, their numerous graphics telltale of their crimes. Each time one was arrested a new tattoo appeared somewhere on their torso, which was not too bright on their part, an easy read for Doyle to know that they had been in trouble with the law – which might bring the cops in his direction. None had been arrested in Sausalito, their fear of Doyle's wrath keeping them on the straight and narrow. He had told them that if any one of them were to bring the cops sniffing in his direction they would disappear; that was not a threat, it was a promise. They might be dumb, but they were not stupid. That, and a couple of the local cops on Doyle's payroll kept his protection racket off the District Attorney's radar.

Scotty was a big man whose size dwarfed a lumberjack, solid as a redwood, he was no one to push around – accepting Doyle. Scotty kept his hair Marine Sergeant buzzcut short and bore only one tattoo visible on his left forearm; *MOTHER*. More than one shipyard worker had made the mistake of commenting about his tattoo to quickly learn from his quick jack-hammer fists who was the toughest mother in the shipyard.

It was at the end of WWII when the Marinship's Sausalito Yard was winding down that Scotty and Doyle met. Doyle did not work at the shipyard, he worked the shift change with a numbers racket. He usually did not hit up big men like Scotty, they tended to get upset when their numbers never seemed to win. He had been impressed when he witnessed Scotty flatten a man equal his size with one punch after a wisecrack. With the shipyard closing he knew that the big Scotsman would be needing a job, and he needed some muscle to protect him from the poor losers.

Doyle soon learned that Scotty lacked the mean streak that ran through his own backbone. He was a quiet-spoken man who at first glance seemed a bit apologetic about his immense size. He liked kids and showed little evidence of superiority when it came to Niggers, Jews, Japs, Chinks, Pollocks, and the like. With the shipyard closing Doyle was energetically building his protection racket and Scotty's muscle was equal to that of four men. But Scotty had a conscience, while not afraid of a fight, he did not want to hurt people. How to control his prodigious new friend became a challenge – that was until he found out after Scotty had one too many whiskey shots that the mild-mannered giant was wanted for murder.

Scotty had been working at a shipyard in Oakland. It was a little after one in the morning, raining buckets with winds strong enough to cause the drunken Scotsman to bend against its force. He had missed the last bus, and cabbies were too intimidated to pick him up as a fare. He stole a pick-up truck whose engine had been left running in front of a late-night liquor store. Five minutes later he side-swiped a cab killing the cabbie and a woman who had been getting out of the rear passenger door. The gruesome accident had been all over the newspapers, but the case remained unsolved as no one had seen who had stolen the truck, or staggered away, leaving no evidence. He left his job and room in Oakland finding a job in Long Beach. Once again drink got him into trouble and he migrated back from Southern California to find another shipyard job in Sausalito. There he found a new friend, a mentor, who managed to keep him from losing his temper. Sometimes – Pat – no one could call Doyle by his first name other than Scotty -needed him to rough someone up, that was okay because Pat was his best friend, and whatever he said was okay by Scotty; except the times Doyle showed his bad side, then that was okay by Doyle. But Scotty could hear, and what he heard tore at his soul.

A car horn blared two short and one long bleep from two blocks down the hill on the waterfront. Doyle did not allow Hector's 1937 Ford 'Woodie' Wagon anywhere near the boarding house. The 'Woodie' was strictly used when Doyle, Scotty, and the crew went to San Francisco to play. Play meant that Doyle was hungry and after chain smoking a dozen cigarettes, and drinking some Irish Whiskey, they went hunting – usually for a good for nothing street bum, a nigger, a chink, or anyone the cops wouldn't worry themselves much about catching whoever had killed them; even though the murders were often brutal in a sick way. Doyle allowed his boys to kick and punch their victims to the ground, but it was Doyle who did the killing. It was at times like this that Scotty wanted to up and run away, but like Smitty, Hector, and Smokestack, he was not about to do anything that drew Doyle's wrath. When Doyle was not on the hunt or conducting business, he was not just Scotty's boss – Pat was his best friend.

Father Michelangelo Palazzeschi entered the kitchen as quietly as if he were wearing the Pope's very own slippers. While the hour was late, he was almost on time. His eyes looked tired, his Sinatra blue eyes hidden beneath a brow furrowed from a day trying to mend souls.

"Will you be going back for Mass, later?" Betty asked as she pulled his dinner plate out from the cooling oven.

"No not tonight," he sighed, taking his plate and satting in his usual chair by a small table.

"Coffee?" Renata asked, holding up a half-filled pot. The coffee was what was usually left from the morning's breakfast.

Michelangelo shook his head as he tasted the pot roast, pushing the now over-done vegetables to defensive positions on the side of the plate. He was hungry, but had no appetite, an ailment that chased him on a daily-basis since the shipyard closed.

"Here, perhaps this will suit you better," Renata said as she poured him a glass of Italian red wine.

"Grazie, si, si prega di lasciare cio che resta deila bottiglia." The priest answered as he tasted the wine while eying the bottle to see how much was left.

"Long day?" Betty asked. This was meant as an open-ended question allowing for the priest to ease into his own confession.

"Yes, a long day, but I knew it would be." He tasted a small bite of the roast than pushed the plate away. "Grazie." Half of the glass of wine went down with ease. "Since the shipyard closed the Parish has suffered. Attendance is the lowest it has ever been. As the parish has shrunk so has the money needed to keep the doors open. The Archbishop has suggested that it might be time to close it and write off the loss."

"But where will you go?"

He nodded towards a window and the lights of San Francisco beyond. "I'm not a big city priest," His voice soft enough that his words were barely heard.

Renata opened a cabinet, found another bottle of the wine, pulled the cork and poured herself a glass.

Betty watched with amazement as Renata's scrawny old arms muscled the cork from the bottle. She had yet to figure out how the octogenarian did it, always making it look so easy. She turned down the first offer of wine.

"We are not there, yet, the Archdiocese has given us a little more time." His ears almost fluttered as he caught the sound of Michael's saxophone.

"That, Father, is Michael O'Dea. He and his wife Mollie have taken the vacant room upstairs near next to the fire-escape. They come to us from San Francisco where he was a musician of some renown. Hard times, now they can barely afford us."

The Priest gave Betty that look that said *do 'I have to say it again. Please call me'*. . . "Michelangelo, please." He waved a finger upward. "He likes the roof?"

"Where else can he play?" Renata said, then answered her own question. "Perhaps on Saturday nights you could open the church as a jazz club, splitting the offerings basket. You might need more wine though."

"Now there is a possibility. It may come to that - our little community needs something bright and lively." He laughed as he thought about what was coming out of his mouth. Opening his hands wide in offering, "It could be a jazz club every day of the week, but Sunday - of course. It would have to close by eleven," his right hand and pointer finger moved as if he were about to give a benediction, "we must not forget Midnight Mass."

They laughed, a second glass of wine poured. This time a tiny sip for Betty. "There's more?" Meaning bad news, she asked.

"I've been reminded of my vow of poverty as a priest. To help keep my parish doors open I am gifting back to the church most of my salary. Which means I must give up my room here."

"I won't hear anything of the kind," Betty said with a touch of alarm to her voice.

"No," Renata answered vehemently. "There is a curse upon this house and it is growing bolder like a poisonous snake. When your hands touch these walls, your feet the stairs and creaky floorboards, you are a man of God who breaths the air here. The serpent knows that you are here, and it is afraid. God will not allow this evil to grow. If you leave . . ." The old woman stopped, her lips quivering, with a spot of spittle trapped while her last words remained ensnared as she studied the priest's eyes. She saw his sadness and sincerity, turning her own towards Betty. "When Father Michelangelo Palazzeschi leaves so do I."

While not superstitious, Betty was beginning to believe that there might be a curse, an evil spirit, amongst them. There had been times at night where she thought that she could hear a child crying, things that had gone missing, footsteps, the sound of someone running when she could see that no one was there; all nonsense of course. At this moment she wished she could pack up her bags and do the same. She had not spoken to anyone, including Renata, about it, but she was certain that something or someone had pushed her down the stairs. And Mary Griffin, the tenant whose room Michael and Mollie, now occupied, had mysteriously disappeared in the middle of the night. No sign of a struggle, no-one heard anything, she just disappeared leaving not one clue for the police to work with. "If it will help, you can have the room for nothing, for as long as you need it?" There was a tinge of hope in her voice.

"The Archbishop has said that it is not good for the church's doors to be locked at night. I have a cot in the rectory that is quite comfortable, thank you."

Up on the roof top, they could hear Michael play: I'll be seeing you in all the familiar places. "There is always enough food. I will put a hot plate aside for you for breakfast and supper. A hot shower, the use of the bath whenever you need it." She raised her eyebrows just enough for Michelangelo to know that it would be unwise to decline. "When will you be leaving?"

She looked at Renata. "Please, give me some time. I can't do everything needed from this chair."

Despite their friendship, her long years of service – Renata had been in the kitchen long before Betty had taken up residence – the old woman said "I am sorry, I am old and vulnerable, if I stay the evil will come for me. I will help with breakfast and prepare some lasagna for your supper. Perhaps, Mollie can be of help?"

Three glasses filled with wine, no further words adequate to say goodbye.

Michael played for another hour until Mollie called up to him that it was late, and they had had a long day. He said that he would be down in a few minutes stalling for as long as he could. He had seen Scotty and Doyle leave and had wondered why the car that had summoned them had parked so far away.

When Michael was one with his saxophone his mind was free of troublesome thoughts and life's distractions – of which he had plenty with a whole pile of new ones since he had started the day. Leaving the Honeysuckle Rose topped his heartache. Each step they had taken towards Sausalito was a coffin nail for the place the Rose held in his heart. Not being alone made being alone more difficult. There was a time when it was easy to turn inwards from life's cruelty and hardships. He could hide from the derision, ridicule, and pain in his music. Now Mollie's voice constantly whispered in his ears - deformed as they are – that she was now part of his life, and he could not hide from her.

Their first day in Sausalito had not made a good impression. It was cold, windy, and the foghorns were off–key. The boarding house was old, weather-worn, and creaked with the wind. The house itself had an unpleasant smell human or rat made, it was unpleasant.

Their first dinner experience had been a foreshadowed warning of unpleasantries to come. The food was good but shared with the kind of people he had taught himself to shut out. The woman Sarah Brandt was bossy, one who meddled in everyone else's business, self-appointed bigot, who most likely was a man hater. Why not, she hated everyone else. That was too many points against him for life to ever be comfortable in such proximity.

Harvey might prove to be a nice guy, but he was too damned talkative and hyper. Michael knew all too well that he was in no position to be picky,but the guy was annoying. He sensed that Harvey was desperate for attention, a dog chasing its own tail in search of a friend. The big fisherman sang, that was a good thing. Still, he had always been nervous around bear-sized men having been bullied far too many times growing up in the orphanage. That brought him to Scotty. He sensed there might be a little kindness hidden within the man, however his friendship with Patrick Doyle put up a big red warning flag. He couldn't put a finger on it, but Patrick Doyle was a dangerous man. He would have to warn Mollie about him. How, he didn't know. She is always so optimistic about the goodness in people, sometimes he thought that she did not have a clue about the real world. As for Betty McPheters, she was nice enough. He knew better than to prejudge anyone with a handicap – the mirror too close -however, from the first moment he met her he had the feeling that the poor woman, tied to her wheel-chair, was over her head when it came to be managing the boarding house.

Moving to Sausalito had been a bad decision, if he didn't have Mollie to worry about, there is no way he would have done it. There were always some single room occupancy hotels that rented on an hourly basis to anyone. He had been there, and done that, and now he had made the foolish decision to go along with Mollie about moving to Sausalito because he knew she would not be able to handle one day in one of those low-down hotels. She would be afraid for her life, and rightly so.

He looked out across the bay towards the lights of the city wishing he was there. The one thing he did like was his little perch on the roof. It was his, no one would bother him there, even Mollie, who had a fear of heights. With a sigh, he stood, his feet not feeling secure on the steepness of the roof's slope. For a moment tears crossed his eyes as he cursed Earl Crier for dying. With Earl's passing Michael had quickly been reminded that his ugliness was forever holding him down like an anvil weight in deep water.

As he climbed back down the fire-escape he suddenly was confronted by . . . by his *man* problem. They had been married for three months now and had not consummated their marriage. He was forty-two years of age and had never been with a woman. He never thought he would. Now, he wondered if he could. Prior to Mollie he had never kissed, or been kissed, let alone allow himself to think that a woman would ever want him. Mollie did, and it scared the hell out of him. When they cuddled, and she touched him in the right ways, teased and fondled his penis, he had stiffened, but when he tried to enter her, he softened, the desire in his loins running away like a scared rabbit. Each night as he prepared to share their bed he felt ashamed, if not helpless. Tonight, he hoped that he would not have to confront it again. It had been a long day, he was tired, and his frustration level was bleeding dark red blood. He hoped that he had waited long enough for her to slip beneath the sheets, being the late hour,and be asleep before he got there.

Her eyes were closed, her breathing sounded of sleep as Michael quietly slipped beneath the sheets next to her. She was not asleep, choosing to leave her husband alone for the moment. She knew how much he was hurting but did not know how to lift him from his emotional morass. She was learning how intelligent her husband was, how he had survived his loneliness she did not understand – but was trying.

Michael listened to the mournful foghorns across the bay, solitary guardians, not sirens ready to steal one's dreams away. There was no music within them.

Mollie heard the night music that called from across the bay, wondering how long it would be until her husband succumbed to their siren's song.

Chapter Four

Sarah Brandt heard the deep mournful cries of the foghorns as if they were the long steady ticks of her old grandfather's clock. She hated them. God had placed them across San Francisco Bay for the sheer purpose of tormenting her – it was a personal thing.

She had few pleasant memories of her childhood. She never dwelled in the past, especially when it came to the old man whose memory lived in dark storm clouds that she pushed away day after day. How many nights had she lay in her bed listening to that damned clock as she waited for him to beckon her to his bedroom. Grandma had her own room, the door locked to keep away unwanted visits which weren't likely, the old man preferring his dominance of a child no longer innocent.

She hated her grandfather, never knew her father, tried not to think about her once upon a time alcoholic lover - husband - from whose seed she had birthed a son who had died early in the war. Her husband a cruel beast of a man she prayed not to love – but had.

Her secret.

Michael wasn't a breakfast person, especially if he had to share it with people who insisted on ruining it with their stares and rude comments. Mollie tried to make the boarding house, their small room, their home. They had only been there one day. He knew when he wasn't wanted. If home is where the heart is, his heart was far astray.

Mollie brought him a cup of coffee and a bagel, and off he went to his roof top perch to think. Up there he felt like a bird in a cage, isolated, with a desperate need to fly, yet the thought of venturing beyond this safe perch was daunting – the more he thought about escaping the more his feet stuck to the roof shingles that were weathered and in need of repair.

When Mollie woke this morning, she saw the new day as a fresh start, their day to figure things out. She did not worry about Michael isolating himself up on the roof - that was just his way. He would spend the day lost in his music and when he came down he would wear a goofy smile and tell her that everything would be alright – that moving to Sausalito was a good thing. A girl had the right to dream, didn't she? Today she would start her new job, part time, helping out around the boarding house. Perhaps she would get a chance to meet their neighbors, find a way for them to begin to like her husband – just a little.

Sarah Brandt sat alone at the breakfast table, a stack of pancakes swimming in butter and maple syrup sitting in front of her. Plates of scrambled eggs, toast, crisp bacon, and steaming grits sat otherwise untouched on the table. Betty, Harvey, Rafael, and Father Palazzeschi, who usually breakfasted were all absent. Mollie started to sit, but one look at Sarah's unpleasant morning face advised her that there was a reason this morning that she ate alone. Mollie did not know that this had been the usual breakfast situation for the last several weeks. Piles of food going to waste while the matron of the breakfast table glared at anyone who even thought about joining her.

Sarah Brandt knew of the rumor that the house was cursed and did not want to get caught into a so-called polite conversation with Father Palazzeschi regarding the validity of a curse, or any of the other dark incidents that had recently occurred. The hospitable priest enjoyed a family table which Sarah disrupted with zeal.

"Good morning," Mollie said as she took a small plate in which she placed two meager strips of bacon, her eyes on the bowl of steaming grits.

Sarah intensified her glare as she pulled the bacon platter closer to her. She did the same with the grits. The fork in her hand suggesting that trying for the scrambled eggs would be at her on risk.

"That was rude," Mollie couldn't help but respond.

"Go away, you . . . impertinent trollop." The older woman curled one lip with contempt as she scooped most of the eggs into a mountainous blob onto her plate.

"That will be quite enough," decried Betty who had overheard everything from the kitchen door. "I have grown weary of your disrespectful behavior towards everyone in this house – enough is enough. Your rent is paid until the end of the month, at which time I expect that you will have found other accommodations."

Father Palazzeschi, looking oh-so-handsome dressed in his black cassock, and clerical collar, a cup of steaming tea in hand, appeared in the doorway immediately behind Betty. His Sinatra eyes all but twinkling at Betty's decisive, if not proper stand, against the rude, all powerful Ms. Brandt.

"You wouldn't dare . . ." Sarah hissed, while caught off guard she gave no indication of surprise nor acceptance of her notice of eviction. She did not turn her eyes away from Mollie as she responded. "Perhaps, it is you who should be leaving," she said, delivering the words as a curse, "and take your hideous Ogre with you."

"Now, see here!" Boomed Father Palazzeschi, his fore-head turning red as his temper reached the tip of his tongue.

Stunned, over-whelmed, Mollie burst into tears. The small plate of bacon shattered unnoticed as it struck the floor. Her tears nearly blinding as she ran for the protection of her room upstairs.

A hollow, midnight museum silence, encased the next few seconds in ice as Sarah held the moment as her victory, Betty and Michelangelo too thunderstruck to find any words suffice for the moment.

Renata came into the room, her eyes locked on Sarah's

as she approached the table purposely taking her plate of pancakes smothered beneath the yellow mound of scrambled eggs, along with that of the bacon, and grits away. "Per voi, la prima colazione è terminata – for you breakfast is finished."

It did not matter that Sarah did not understand Italian - the message was clear. Not one more word was said as the door to the kitchen swung shut leaving the breakfast table bare, the room empty except for Sarah, who still owned the empty moment, refused to budge. Five minutes passed before the sound of Sarah's chair scrapping the floor was heard in the kitchen as she left the room.

No one heard her quietly take the stairs.

The truth was that Betty wouldn't dare evict Sarah Brandt because she couldn't. After Betty had fallen down the stairs, Jacob Fisher, Attorney-at-Law, Trustee of a Trust which owned the property, told her that he had been instructed to keep Betty on as the boarding house's host and manager. He left her with a carefully wrapped hint – calling it a threat would be more correct. "A woman in a wheelchair is hard placed to manage a two- story boarding house. Ms. Brandt has a room for as long as she wishes. Just so there will be no misunderstandings, her rent will be paid monthly through my office. If you do not like her attitude, you will look the other way, is that understood? This is not a job for the handicapped. Being that your accident occurred in the house your new limitations are being overlooked for the moment. With no family, or resources – with no job, you have no future."

That she might have rendered herself homeless a few moments ago crossed her mind as Betty sat quietly for a moment trying to compose herself.

"That woman is the curse of this house." Renata said as she poured Betty a cup of coffee.

Betty shook her head saying that she did not want any. She was almost sick to her stomach as it was.

Renata tsk-tsked the house's evil spirits, the waste of food, as well as the sad events of the morning as she reached for the remaining wine from the prior evening and poured three glasses handing the first to Betty, the next to Father Michelangelo Palazzeschi, the third for herself. "She is evil, Father." Draining the glass, she leaned into the wheelchair giving Betty a farewell hug. She then hung her kitchen apron on its proper hook, slipped into her winter coat, and left the kitchen she had for so long treated as her own. The events of the morning had occurred so abruptly that Renata had failed to prepare a lasagna for the boarder's dinner, a task not impossible, but difficult for a woman bound to a wheelchair.

Father Palazzeschi set his untouched wine on the kitchen counter. "Will you be alright?" He asked, patting Betty's hand. "I think I should pay young Mrs. O'Dea a visit."

Betty nodded. "Yes, of course, I would, but . . ." She looked at Michelangelo with tear glistened eyes. She had not been up the stairs since she had fallen. "I didn't fall, I was pushed," she whispered, the tremble to her voice suggesting her deepfelt fear.

"Are you sure?"

The look in her eyes told him so. She listened to the priest's footsteps as he slowly mounted the stairs. Alone in the kitchen she stared for a long moment at the glass of wine in her hand as if it had somehow magically appeared there. "What now?" She whispered as she downed half of the wine, then held onto the glass so tightly she almost broke the glass. She sat alone, weeping deeply troubled tears as she remembered the horror of that push.

Up on the roof Michael sipped at his coffee, finding it too hot, he sat it down near the edge of the roof where it was flattest. There was a pleasant morning breeze just in off the bay. Over the waterfront seagulls challenged each other over morsels of food and bait fisherman flung over the side of their small fishing boats. Here and there the dinging of small ship's bells as they rode a mild harborside surf. It was a peaceful start to what might become a nice day.

Mollie's Pollyanna -like attitude was beginning to wear-off on him. He remembered when he woke this morning their closeness, the sweet smell of her hair – her lovely eyebrows. He did love her, or did he? He had trouble loving himself. He did love his music; his saxophone was his life. He had never been loved or loved anyone in his entire life until Mollie. What did he know? Mollie . . . she was different. He had never felt about someone as he did her. He began to dwell on his impotence when it came to making love with her. He wondered how she put up with him. It hurt to think about what she must be thinking when he tried and failed. Perhaps, it was time to admit the truth and . . . angry at himself for even thinking that he forced himself to think of something positive.

The breeze tossed his ridiculous tuft of hair as he looked around at the amazing view around him and thought he might be able to make something out of this beautiful day. He nudged his invisible birdcage door open just enough to let the sense of freedom ebb through. Perhaps - no promises made - he might take a walk down to the boatyard he had seen and see if they were doing any hiring. If nothing else, he hadn't had the chance to scare the hell out of the neighborhood kids yet. His momentary self-deprecating humor caused him to chuckle. Had Mollie heard it would have given her a good laugh.

Then, the sun dropped out of the sky, a good day gone suddenly bad, when he heard the door to their room slam shut, the way only an emotionally overwrought woman can deliver. Mollie was crying! He jumped to his feet, jarring his saxophone causing it to slide towards the edge of the roof. He would rather go over himself then loose his saxophone. The roof was steep - he leaned too far forward as he reached for it, sure that at that moment he would fall to his death. He grabbed hold of a heat-vent as he watched his beautiful horn go over the edge. Time slowed, the next two seconds an eternity as he watched the coffee cup, its steam hanging in the air, the cup oveturning as it dropped from sight, at almost the same anguished moment he caught the last glimpse of his horn. He started to let go, willing to let himself fall if he could cushion his horn, protect it from crumpling on the hard earth below.

"Please, go away!" He heard Mollie's voice, anxious

and tearful, and knew in his heart what – who – was more important as he grasped the heat-vent, straightening himself as he turned back in her direction. He did not hear the angry cry that rose up as the hot coffee rained down. Afraid that he might scare Mollie on top of whatever else had upset her, he swallowed his cry – *Mollie, I'm coming!* He had forgotten to put the wooden block in the window sill. Without it the window slid shut, becoming awkward, if not impossible to open from the outside. He knocked on the window, their room just down the hall, but with her crying she couldn't hear him.

Doyle was in a foul mood. It had taken them most of the night to find just the right victim. An old Chinaman had just come out of an all-night Fan Tan gaming room. The old man was dressed in his best Sunday-come-to-meeting clothes, which hung on his lean scarecrow frame like a well-tailored potato sack. His western dress suggested that he was the patriarch of a respected clan – that he was not escorted suggested that he lived very and always under the watchful eyes of the clan which made the opportunity all that more appetizing to Doyle.

The old man made a foolish move stopping beneath a streetlight to count a roll of dollar bills. "Yes sir, his number has truly come in," Doyle said, speaking of his own luck in finding such a prize. The *Woodie* slowed to a crawl as Doyle's three hoodlums quietly got out. As Doyle surveyed the windows and surrounding doorways for watchful eyes *the noise* in his head began to build as did his stress and anticipation. "Take him over there, in the alley. Darken that streetlight." Doyle ordered as he took out a sharp pocket knife. "He doesn't have much of a scalp, but I want the beard and his ponytail. The ponytail – tail of a Chinaman –queue – was worn by Chinese men since the days of the Manchurian takeover of the Ming Dynasty. Most Chinese in modern day San Francisco did not wear a queue anymore. This old man did, signifying that he was a proud patriarch of a Han clan whose ancestors had once been feared warriors.

The only warning the old man heard was that of a rock shattering the streetlight overhead. An arm quickly wrapped tightly around his throat as he was dragged, feet kicking, into the gloom of the alley. Scotty kept the car idling while Doyle's boys took the old man's money. The ponytail, and the wizened long white beard, were brutally cut from the old man's chin, then tossed through a car window as Doyle pulled a baseball bat from the truck. The boys backed off as Doyle entered the darkened alley and raised the bat. The look on Doyle's face just before a kill never failed to frighten his boys.

The old man screamed.

A light came on and a window opened just above them in the alley.

The old man shrieked.

"That you Uncle Yang? What's going on? OH . . ." the man yelled in Han Chinese that beloved Uncle Yang was being attacked in the alley. Lights came on all along the alley and the street across the way. Young Chinamen appeared in many doorways as Doyle and his blood splattered crew jumped into the car leaving a threatening mob of Chinese behind them.

The voice coming from the open window was enough to save the old man's life. He lost his money, queue, and chin whiskers, along with a great deal of dignity. He had taken a few good kicks from the young hoodlums, but fortunately only one painful strike from the white man's bat that had broken his wrist. The old man would live, his honor more damaged than his wrist and bloodied chin.

Doyle did not have his kill. A man in heat, he needed more than a cold shower to cool down. They drove the rest of the night knowing the cops would be looking for a *Woodie* with four to five white male suspects unwilling to quit until they found a dead man walking to put out Doyle's fire.

There was a long history of prejudice and animosity regarding San Francisco's Chinese population. There was a day, not that long ago, when the public murder of a Chinaman was ignored by the police – sometimes it was the police who were behind the dreaded act. The attack of Uncle Yang enraged a community as it was learned that this was the third known attack on a Chinese resident within the last seven months. The first two had died.

The sun rose, and it wasn't going to happen. The queue and bloody chin whiskers were tossed out the window. No kill, no souvenirs wanted. It was time for the night predators to go home.

Doyle and Scotty had just reached the front steps of the boarding house when scalding hot coffee rained down on them. A ceramic coffee cup clipped Doyle on the forehead drawing a small half-inch cut that bled just enough to cause him to see red as he roared with unhinged rage.

Father Palazzeschi knocked lightly on the door.

Mollie, who was lying face down on the bed turned at the sound. "Michael?" She glanced at their dresser top where she saw that he had left his wallet and keys, a frequent problem when they had lived at The Rose.

"Mrs. O'Dea, its Father Michelangelo Palazzeschi, may I come in?"

Mollie, who knew of the Priest by name only, was suddenly flustered at the thought of letting the clergyman in. Her eyes were blood-shot from her tears, mascara had stained her cheeks with dark streaks, her hair was a mess. She looked at the mirror, embarrassed by what she saw. "Ohhhh! Not now." Quickly finding a damp facecloth, which she kept next to a rinsing bowl, she only managed to smear the mascara, - making it worse. "Ahhh, one moment please. I'm not decent."

"I saw what happened downstairs. May I speak with you?"

The mascara was now mostly on the washcloth. She fluffed her hair with her hands the best she could. "One moment."

The window to Michael and Mollie's window was

open allowing for Michael to hear that Mollie was talking to someone only seconds after he had heard her crying. While he could not overhear the conversation, it sounded like she was upset, trying to tell someone to "go away." Unable to open the window by the fire-escape, he fumbled in his pocket for his keys. Remembering that he had left them on the dresser his next option was to climb down the fire escape, run completely around the house, through the kitchen, then up the stairs – which would take too long. His eyes caught on a narrow decorative ledge that ran along the face of the house just below the second-floor windows. The ledge was significantly narrow, the risk of falling greater than that of reaching their open window. But, that was the fastest way to get to Mollie.

Looking up to where the scalding coffee had come from Scotty was the first to see someone reach out for a hand hold as he started out onto the ledge. The nearest window was Doyle's. With only his backside exposed neither he nor Doyle could see that the intruder was Michael. As far as they were concerned they had been assaulted by a stranger who had just crawled out of Doyle's window headed towards the fire-escape when he gave himself away by accidentally knocking over a coffee cup that had been left in the open window.

"You there, what the hell do you think you're doing?" Doyle roared as he pushed Scotty towards the lower end of the fire-escape."Don't let him off the fire escape in one piece. I'll go inside we'll trap him between us."

"Hey, I think it's what's his name, Mendel, the ugly

guy." Scotty yelled back.

Doyle did not hear him as his head quickly filled with *the noise* as blind rage took over. Veteran's distressed by extreme combat often had psychotic episodes where they reheard the sounds of battle, these memories as vivid as the real event had been. The army psychiatrists who interviewed Doyle at his discharge were unable to determine whether the noise he heard when stressed were the voices of his dead or dying buddies, or shells exploding among a storm of violent combat memories. Regardless of the cause, when threatened or highly stressed *the noise* took over its roar all-powerful until the threat was removed, usually by Doyle killing whoever or whatever threatened him. Then, there would be a popping sound, much like one experienced during a high-altitude change. POP! Whoosh, *the noise* – the pressure in his head - left as suddenly as if it had been sucked out by a vacuum.

Once Scotty determined that it was Michael trying to reach his own window, his focus was no longer on stopping an unknown intruder, he climbed up the fire escape, forced open the jammed window with a pocket knife and climbed through.

Mollie opened the door, patting her hair, straightening her dress back into place, as she sheepishly greeted the concerned Priest. She wasn't sure how she should behave; should she curtsy? She had grown up in a small farmhouse near Lenox, Iowa, a Presbyterian. The nearest Catholic Church was in Des Moines. She had visited the bigger city once with her parents and had seen a Catholic Church, but until this moment she had never met a Catholic Priest. Michael had gone to a Catholic Orphanage and did not speak kindly of the Nuns who had so often verbally abused him – and worse.

"Please come in," she said demurely.

"I could not help to see and hear the shameful behavior you unfortunately were subjected to downstairs. I wanted to assure you that your neighbors are not like Ms. Brandt."

The Priest's eyes were kind, his words reassuring, nevertheless, she shivered and self-consciously stepped back as he reached out to her.

Michael reached their window, stepping in with his left leg he was relieved to see that Mollie's visitor was a Priest.

"Jesus, Joseph, and Mary," Father Palazzeschi swore in surprise at his first sight of Michael's face. While he did not put a name to it, his first impression was that a gargoyle was entering the second story room. Is the Lord God about to challenge me with the fearful task of performing an exorcism because I have begun to question my faith? He reached for his cross as he stepped in front of Mollie to shield her from the beast.

"Michael why are you . . .?"

Her husband looked at her suddenly with alarm.

The noise controlling his every move and thought, Doyle bypassed his own closed door, charging directly towards Michael and Mollie's. There he saw Mollie cringing fearfully behind a man in black as the intruder came in through the window. All the way up the stairs his only thought was to kill the intruder. His hands reaching out to strangle his victim, he heard only the noise.

Father Palazzeschi turned as Mollie screamed. Because of Mollie he did not see who shoved him violently through the window. Off balance he had no time to protect himself.

Mollie screamed "Michael, watch out . . . NO!!"

Father Palazzeschi was suddenly shoved through the open window taking Michael out with him. For the next five seconds Mollie remained transfixed on the shattered window frame for the moment not comprehending what had happened. When she blinked she was alone in the room, her husband and the priest somewhere down below.

The noise popped and hissed away as Doyle gripped his stomach in agony. He had experienced pain like this before and knew that if he did not get to the bathroom in seconds he would explode in a most painful and embarrassing way. One doctor had called it Crohn's disease – regardless of what it was called it struck him when he was highly stressed. Hell, yes - not getting to the god-damned toilet in time is about as stressful as it gets. His desire for murder and revenge no longer mattered.

Sarah was a snoop. One of her favorite pastimes was to quietly go door to door throughout the rooming house

and listen. If she knew the occupant was out, and not due
to return, she would use a master-key to see what someone
might have reason to hide. The rooms on the second floor
were always of interest. Doyle's was to the left of the
O'Dea's, and to the right a vacant room. Across the hall
was Scotty's, the shared bath, stairs, Mary Griffith's room,
then Harvey Freedman's room. She dearly wanted to get
something on Harvey, so she could blackmail him to move
the hell out. She never went into the Ecuadorian's room,
thinking an unemployed fisherman would have little of
value, including secrets worth knowing.

Sarah had followed Mollie up the stairs and entered
Mary's room across the hall. She had done her best to upset
the young woman and wanted to listen - women in tears say
the most surprising things.

Harvey had slept in. He wasn't hungry and hadn't a
job he had to rush off to. Sometimes it was fun to be lazy,
although he kept telling himself that it was time to find
some meaningful work. That was the problem, there wasn't
any in Sausalito. He fretted about having to move to the
big city. Bullies always seemed to find him. Here there
was only Sarah and Doyle to worry about. So far, he had
kept Sarah Brandt at bay by being deliberately obnoxious.
Doyle, he paid protection money to leave him alone. It
frightened him that Doyle might arbitrarily raise the price,
which he could not afford. If he didn't pay he would be
beaten, and he had a low threshold for pain.

He had heard Sarah's conniption from downstairs,
followed by Mollie running to her room in tears. A moment

later he heard the door open to Mary's room. *Who, besides Betty had a key? And she could not climb the stairs.*

Mollie's scream penetrated every nook and cranny in the house.

Chapter Five

Detective Ralph Schmidt, San Francisco Police Department – Homicide, reached his desk a little bit fuzzy and hungover, having taken a rare night off to chase a tall red-haired skirt he had met at Malone's, a popular police hangout. He had been working on Janet for a couple of weeks, anticipating that tonight was the night he would be getting laid. He hadn't. It seemed that all he ever did was anticipate, while the other guy scored. When he arrived, he found her giving an officer with brand new shiny Lieutenant bars a spectacular view of her cleavage as she whispered sweet somethings in his ear. She left with the eager Lieutenant.

He laid a saw buck on the bar and watched its value shrink to nothing as he drained a bottle of Rye Whiskey. He should have drunk bourbon, the Rye got him every time.

The Night Shift Captain waved him towards his office.

Trouble?

Captain Francis Savoy didn't like Schmidt. In his mind

the Sergeant did not deserve his rank, would be better shut-
tled off to traffic control, then to rest his drunken ass-end
in Homicide. He was the most incompetent cop under his
command. He stared at him. The guy did not even look like
a cop. Early forties, medium height, thin with little muscle.
He was pale skinned, and always wore black from head to
toe. When he sweated you could almost see the shoe polish
drip down from his perfectly coiffured black hair. The
Captain once loaned him out to Vice as bait for perverts in
public restrooms. That didn't last long, even the bathroom
he-she's didn't want him.

Trouble; Schmidt knew that the Captain was just
waiting for him to screw up to bust him down to desk
duty taking missing dog reports. He brought his palm to
his mouth just before entering the Captain's office. He
reeked of cheap rye and there was no hiding it. *The hell
with it, he'd been on his own time.* "You need something,
Captain?" He stood just inside the doorway, as far away as
he could from his frowning boss.

"You like Chinese, Sergeant? A little Chop Suey, some
Moo Goo slop perhaps." Captain Savoy asked humorously
as he tossed Schmidt a stained brown paper bag. "This was
found around four a.m. out in the Richmond. Some guy
was out walking his dog and found it lying in the middle of
a sidewalk."

Sergeant Schmidt opened the bag dumping the contents
on a small table near the door.

The Captain shook his head. *Idiot!* "Those belonged
to an elderly chink who was robbed, mugged, and almost
beaten to death in an alley in Chinatown last night. That is

the old man's ponytail and his beard which was cut away like an Indian scalp. The Chinks have been burning the phone to the Mayor's office all day."

Schmidt held up what remained of the mangled beard.

"Almost killed?" Meaning, why is this in Homicide if the old guy survived?

"The attack matches the MO of two similar assaults that have happened over the last seven months. Both were Chinese, both scalped, both died. Serial killers are of special interest to this department, even if the victims are all chinks. Knowing how you like that Moo Goo crap I thought you might like the case."

"Ahh, thanks Captain, but shouldn't this go to an officer who speaks Chinese?" Schmidt asked as he gingerly picked up the evidence placing it back in the bag, taking an extra second to examine the beard.

"The guy who found it had a hard time taking the beard away from his mutt, thought it was a chew toy." The Captain said as he gave Schmidt an exhausted smile. "You've got the case because I don't want to waste the valuable time of a real policeman on it. I don't expect you to solve it - why start now. The victims are Chinese for gods-sake – no one gives a damn. But . . . just in case this possible serial killer gets a hankering to start knocking off some Eskimos, a Greek Orthodox Priest, or God-forbid some white people, someone needs to pretend we're doing some real police work here. The report is on your desk." He sniffed, detected the Rye. "And Sergeant . . . go take a shower."

Chapter Six

Mollie shrieked, ran to the window where tree branches and ground shrubs blocked her view. All she could see of Father Palazzeschi was one of his legs. She couldn't find her husband. "Michael," she screamed as she ran for the stairs.

Sarah opened the door to see Mollie fly down the stairs. The look on the young woman's face told her everything she needed to know. A moment later she leaned out the broken window where she could see the Priest's feet, one most likely broken. She couldn't see if there was anyone else. She smiled just a tinge, when she spotted the saxophone wedged in a tree branch, slightly bent, a valve missing.

"Michael." It was Mollie's voice, as she appeared on the lawn below, finding her husband whose landing had been softened by some shrubbery where he now hung like a string puppet.

Scotty bounded down the fire escape. Rafael, who had been walking up the street in time to see the two men explode through the second-floor window, dashed the rest of the way to help.

Harvey, still in his PJ's, arrived, venturing only as far as the wheelchair ramp, full of ridiculous theories on what must have happened, which he spouted like a chattering squirrel.

"What's happened? Betty called as she wheeled herself down the handicap ramp off the kitchen.

Sausalito did not have a hospital nor an ambulance – the ambulance having been sold when the shipyard closed. The nearest ambulance had to come from either Mill Valley, or San Francisco. Both men they made comfortable on the grass, it would be some time before they got any medical attention. Father Michelangelo Palazzeschi lay unconscious with a compound fracture to his left leg, his right not looking much better. Michael had a piece of glass embedded in his right thigh, his wrist on the same side broken.

"Sweetheart, are you all right?" One look told Mollie differently. At least he wasn't as injured as the Priest. "Someone help me get him out of there." Her tears were on top of her words as she started to pull on the shrubbery to get to her husband.

"I'm all right, Mollie dear. Just leave me be until help comes. What happened?" Michael looked around, all anyone knew was that they both had come crashing through the window.

Mollie shook her head. "It all happened so fast. Someone must have pushed Father Palazzeschi, I didn't see who." She reached into the shrubbery finding his hand.

"Ouch!"

The broken one.

"Just leave me be, sweet-pea." Michael knew that she wasn't about to stop. As Betty wheeled up he gave her a smile. "I was just telling Mollie that I'll be fine. I'd prefer to be left alone until the ambulance comes." With that he began to sing an old Irving Berlin song that he remembered from the Great Depression:

It's a lovely day tomorrow

Tomorrow is a lovely day

Come and feast your tear dimmed eyes . . .

"Oh dear," flustered Betty, as she turned her chair. "I'd best call the ambulance, hadn't I." She looked with grave concern at Father Palazzeschi, who Rafael and Scotty were about to move. "No, No, don't move him. He's got a badly broken leg. Rafael, use your belt to make a tourniquet just above where the bone is coming out. I'll bring a blanket soon as I call the ambulance."

If today your heart is weary

If ev'ry little thing looks gray

Just forget your troubles and learn to say

Tomorrow is a lovely day . . .

Mollie listened as he sang to her, her eyes following

his as he found his saxophone. Between his wrist and the damaged horn, he would not be playing it for some time.

Chapter Seven

Renata crossed herself when she heard about Father Palazzeschi and Michael's accident by the priest who was filling in for Palazzeschi. "Accident, my eye, it's the curse," she spoke aloud. "Hurting the Father in such a cruel way is evil doing." She cocked an eye a she looked up towards the Cross of Jesus she had so often prayed to in the little parish church. "Perhaps, Holy Mother Mary, it is time for you to intercede, if you are not too busy." This last part was spoken as if it were a private joke between two old women. "Help Michelangelo out, he's a good boy."

The Archbishop visited with Father Palazzeschi in the hospital with the news that because of the sad finances of the church, and the Father's injuries, the Archdiocese would close his Parish. He made it sound as if he had no hand in the decision-making process, that it was the bureaucracy of the church that had taken the church away from him. The way he inserted the well-spoken word *WE* might have suggested that Jesus, Joseph, or Mary had closed the real estate deal. Because the parish was small it had no curates, or assistant pastors, no one to step in during what looked like a long healing period for its pastor. The coffers had bleak promises, the Archbishop making the point that "the entire Archdiocese was struggling through challenging economic times, with so many worthy causes, there was no choice but to close the church's doors - the property to be sold. "We are sorry." The Parish was part of the Archdiocese of San Francisco, members of what remained of the Sausalito Parish given to the care of the San Rafael Parish, a larger, older, well-established Parish fifteen miles to the North.

The Archbishop, along with his enclave, stood just outside the church's doors enjoying the views that Sausalito offered. Renata was the last to pay her last respects to her church, and she was not about to give the time of day to the Archbishop whom had determined its cruel fate. She did, however, turn at the sound of the door's final closing towards the great man dressed in amaranth red, looked him straight in the eye and said: "The Devil has come to Sausalito, with his eye on a greater price – beware your own backyard."

Mollie barely had a chance to breathe since Michael's fall and her Pollyanna outlook on the world was beginning to tarnish. If it wasn't for Michael she could easily find herself swimming in a pool of self-pity. She hadn't been this uncertain or unhappy since her best friend Rosemary had tuned on her like a rabid skunk blowing all her stink towards her because she was quaint and uninteresting and treated her as such. That was a painful time, one in which she almost decided to return to the family farm – the one she had sworn she never would - shortly after Rosemary had turned to the dark-side and arrested for attempted murder. There had been the unsuspected suicide of the Earl Crier's Quintet's drummer. The police beatings of Henry, Les, and Earl which ultimately led to Earl's death and the closure of the Honeysuckle Rose Hotel. Emotionally hard times, she wondered how she got through it all. Through all the confusion and heart-ache she had found an anchor, who had become the love of her life.

Life would be easier if Michael wasn't perhaps the ugliest man on earth. *And those were the good old days one looks back on so fondly.* Now she looked across San Francisco Bay with a yearning, almost as self-destructive as Michael had been when he had stood alone against the dark storm that surrounded the image of his face. Only Michael wasn't self-destructive these days – and that was confusing.

Betty depended on Mollie more and more each day.

Until Renata had left, she hadn't realized how close they had become. Renata had been her barrier, her comic relief, against the daily shit storm that was Sarah Brandt and Doyle's unspoken threat. Now she spent most of her time in the kitchen, including meals, keeping as much distance between her and Sarah as she could.

Renata had been a jewel in the kitchen, her meals appreciated by the residents, her reputation as a cook known throughout the community where there had been more than one offer to steal her away over the years. Betty's skills in

the kitchen were limited by her handicap, and not having
a very good palate, her food coming out both simple and
bland.

Mollie's help in the kitchen neither improved the quality
or the taste - the kitchen stove, the pots and pans crying
from their loss of Renata's magic. If she had any shortcomings, Mollie was a lousy cook. The poor dear could barely
boil an egg – Swedish Meatballs or Chicken Cacciatore
well beyond her reach. Her strength, she never quit trying
and was willing to learn. Now, if only the residents would
be more patient with her. Her job description now included
the general day to day housekeeping which left Betty alone
in the kitchen for much of the day. Mollie also spent a
great deal of her time sitting by Michelangelo's bedside
and seeing to her husband's needs - his broken wrist, and
damaged saxophone, keeping his music beyond his reach.

Unfortunately, Sarah Brandt saw Mollie's weaknesses
and used them against her like a hard-squeezing nutcracker
against a nut with a very soft shell.

A week after the accident the brown chunky stuff hit
the fan as Sarah set her up for a big fall. Mollie had spent
the day trying to make her first meat lasagna. Her third try
was finally pronounced by Betty as fit to be served – if one
did not linger over its visual feature. "You can be proud
of that dear, it may not be the prettiest pasta dish ever
made, but neither of us is a Renata. Get it out to the dining
room while it's still hot. It's okay by me if you serve your
husband first."

Michael was proud of Mollie. He knew that she was not
a good cook. When they first married she could barely boil

an egg. Thank God all their meals were provided for them back at the Honeysuckle Rose. He eyed the other tenants seeing that each was enjoying the chicken carbonara as much as he was. How had Mollie done it, even Sarah Brandt, who did not enjoy anything was woofing the pasta down.

Mollie pushed open the kitchen door, lasagna in hand. Her smile fell like a gut-shot duck when she saw that dinner had already been served. It smelled wonderful, what was left of it. Mollie did not have to look farther than Sarah's face to know that it had been her that had done it. In fact; it smelled wonderful. "You . . . you, conniving, evil, bovine, old crow. How could . . .?" She looked around the table seeing everyone with forks raised, mouths full, pasta stains on their chins and napkins – including her husband. "For now on, all you will get from me is burnt toast with runny cheese sandwiches" - which was the way her last attempt at grilled cheese sandwiches had turned out.

The last thing Mollie heard besides her own sobs as she ran into the kitchen was "Don't run away mad, dearie, there's enough left for you." Sarah bleated with pride at the level of her nastiness.

If Michael was capable of giving the evil eye, he would have. Pushing the chicken carbonara away he rose and followed his wife to the kitchen.

Betty had overheard everything. "Enough is enough, I'm giving that awful woman notice to get out tomorrow. I don't care if that buttinski lawyer does fire me." Mad she was, but she also knew that she hadn't the authority.

Michael pulled Mollie into a meaningful supportive hug as she drained her tears on his shirtsleeve. "Oh Michael, we can't stay here, its unbearable."

Michael kissed the tip of her nose, picked up the lasagna from where she had placed it on the counter and turned back towards the dining room. On the way out, he used the serving spoon to loosen up the pasta from its dish. He spotted the delivery bag from Valencia, an Italian restaurant in Mill Valley. He remembered that it had been Sarah's doing that had driven Mollie to their room just before the accident. Balancing the pasta dish in his one good hand, he approached the table while forcing an appalling smile on his misshapen face designed to give Sarah Brandt the chills. His voice charming, much like the actor Vincent Price might use to lure his unsuspecting victim into the House of Usher with an air of jocosity. "My dear, Ms. Brandt, please don't fret over Mollie, she will be fine. It must have cost you a fortune to have this delicious pasta dish delivered all the way from Mill Valley. How thoughtful of you. I do insist that you try just a wee spoonful of Mollie's lasagna. It will be quite a surprise."

Sarah looked as if she was about to scoot her chair back as her cruel setup of Mollie was turning on her.

Chewing their pasta, while pretending to be disinterested camels, the tenants watched with a blossoming glee as Michael took the next step forward.

"Please be careful, Ms. Brandt, my Mollie has been quite busy. The wax on the floor shines to a perfection, but it is slippery." With that he reached out with his broken wrist to catch himself as he feigned to slip. As he seemed about to fall the pasta dish rose striking the sputtering fat woman atop the front of her head, ruining her spring bonnet with the dried yellow flowers, before sliding down onto her ample bosom. Before the woman could say anything as she blotted the lasagna away from her eyes Michael added: "Once again your generosity amazes me. If you had not been there to break my fall I might have hurt my wrist again."

A cheer went up from the table as Michael bowed, his back to Sarah, and returned to the kitchen where Mollie had to cover her mouth with her hand to force back the laughter she did not want Sarah Brandt to hear.

Betty did not try to hide hers, even though she knew that Sarah's revenge would be forthcoming.

That night the kitchen welcomed the unfamiliar feeling of family as Harvey and Oswaldo volunteered to help with the dishes. After, a bottle of red wine was opened, Oswaldo brought his *rondador*. This was an attention getter, no one having seen or heard one before. It is a panpipe that produces two tones simultaneously through pieces of cane placed side by side in order by size with one end closed. Oswaldo's was handmade with sixteen pieces of cane. No two panpipes sound the same because each piece of cane produces a different sound. They soon learned why the rondador is considered the national instrument of Ecuador. It produces a gay, dance-worthy sound; beautiful.

Once Oswaldo began to play Betty remembered that she had heard it being played somewhere down on the wharf. They spent the evening sharing the wine, music, and song. This was the first time since leaving the Honeysuckle Rose that Michael felt accepted for who he was rather than what he looked like. Their music and laughter carried out through the open windows as neighbors in the small Sausalito neighborhood enjoyed a different type of night music.

Later, as they prepared for bed, Michael picked up his saxophone, wanting to step out into the cool of the evening to play his heart music. *In time*, he thought, as he sat it back in the corner where the broken instrument waited to be repaired, *tonight there is something else that I must do.* He turned to his wife, aroused instead of anxious, confident with feelings that for too long had been confused and daunted. She was just slipping into her nightgown made of light purple silk, thin, not quite transparent, the rise of her nipples guiding his eyes to the firm soft mounds of her breasts as he took her in his arms.

"Music has always been my life." The timorous uncertainty of a scared little boy she had heard in their bedroom so many times before, now gone, as the man she wanted reached out for her. "Man created music to appease ancient gods, to stir feelings that a man was more than flesh and blood. Drums and horns prepared men for war, to hunt the great beasts of the land, a man and a woman to mate. Then, one day, a man saw a woman differently – he saw her as more beautiful than a sunrise, or all the flowers in a field, more than the butterflies and the birds in the sky. A reason to make war no more. He made love to her first by telling her through his music what he saw, felt, and desired."

He knew that he had gone on too long, speaking one's heart was something he had never done before. His hand gently cupped her left breast as the nightgown floated breathlessly to her feet. Returning each other's kiss, they drew closer, his muscle, her softness meeting. Her fingers gently teased his penis, which came alive as she felt her husband tremble, his electricity charging his member as it hardened like a mighty oak. Aroused, he picked her up, placing her gently on the bed, his fingers exploring her warmth, her wetness. As he slipped into her he found her music, more powerful than he could have imagined.

He had no idea of the beauty she saw as she looked in his eyes, their bodies raced towards a crescendo of passion experienced for the first time together.

"Oh Mollie, my dear Mollie, how I do cherish you."

Chapter Eight

After ten days in the hospital Michelangelo
Palazzeschi was a changed man. He was weaker from his
injuries, the surgeries required, medications, and bedrest.
When they wheeled him out of the hospital he avoided
eye contact, and hadn't much to say unless asked, then he
would answer with as few words necessary. He had lost
that marvelous twinkle in his eye.

His fellow clergymen could see that he wrestled with
daunting questions regarding his faith. These issues had
been coming on long before the accident – his fall only
bringing his damaged soul into full view. He did not know
why he now doubted his faith, there did not seem to be one
cause, but rather a creeping sense of self-awareness that he
did not want to be a pastor, and perhaps never had.

With the Sausalito Church closed he had been offered
a room at the Archdiocese in which to recover. There he
would find nuns well practiced in the painful, often slow,
healing of the flesh, and pious advisors to help him with
his spiritual challenges. The Archbishop did not insist that

Michelangelo come to the Archdiocese to sort out his issues with God. Michelangelo's outright refusal had reluctantly given the Archbishop the impression that it would not be long before the troubled priest would ask to be absolved from his obligations to Christ, and to the Mother Church.

* * * * *

Michelangelo was born the third of five sons to a good Catholic family in Grass Valley, California, a small farming community north of Sacramento. For three generations in America, twelve generations in Italy, likely more, a son of the Palazzeschi family had entered the priesthood. The one known exception had been back in 1348 when the bubonic plague took all the sons leaving one lone girl child. In time God gave them one last son, being the only one, giving the church a priest had to wait a generation. Growing up, Michelangelo was quiet and introspective, with a golden alto voice a gift for the choir. What drew him towards his promised future was the church itself – its history. There was never a moment where he heard a voice, or felt a spark, that ignited his faith. He played baseball, an alert second baseman. Otherwise he did not standout and was simply known as one of the Palazzeschi brothers. He was tall, dark haired, with a natural olive tan, with blues eyes that drew the girls in.

He was a good boy.

He never spoke about his future as a priest. He just thought of that as something that would happen when he grew up. It wasn't until his senior prom that he told Christina, his high school sweetheart, that he had been accepted to Loyola University in Los Angeles where he would study Divinity. "What the Hell!" Those were not the exact words Christina used as she stared at him on the dance floor. More mad than disappointed she gave him a resounding slap that stopped others on the dance floor. Her plans for Michelangelo had just fallen like a gut-shot love bird. She had even planned on giving him her virginity that night, thinking that they would marry a few months after graduation. The idea had not occurred to Michelangelo who had his sights on his future with the church, going to college, and finally stretching his wings beyond tiny Grass Valley. From that day forward, he was content to begin his studies at Loyola where he would study ethics, communication, and church history.

Michelangelo was a good student, graduating with a bachelor's degree in Philosophy, a minor in history. Through the process of discernment, he entered the seminary where he completed his four years of graduate work. With his parents and two of his brothers present he received his sacrament of holy orders - to his mother's disappointment. She had wanted him to become a parish priest.

Michelangelo had been too good a student, the church preferring that he should become a teacher at a small but promising catholic boarding school in Salisbury, Connecticut. It was a small school, with a small student body, and a faculty that suffered from their lack of numbers. He was to teach both history and philosophy, be the baseball coach if they could muster enough of the students to field a team, and to live on campus as the Resident

Senior and Junior Dorm Master.

The year was 1942, the world was at war, and the United States was not faring well against the Nazis and the Japanese Empire. The Salisbury School's student body was shrinking through lean financial times and the war as patriotic young men graduated early to serve their country. No sooner than Michelangelo unpacked his bags the school's headmaster died suddenly. The church began to question the viability of the Salisbury School continuing – at least until the war ended.

Michelangelo's older brother Robert lost his life at Pearl Harbor – not by combat - a jeep accident after a late party on December 5, 1941. Robert's death, followed by his younger brother Stephan signing up with the marines, hit Michelangelo hard. He soon left the Salisbury School to become an Officer and a Chaplain in the United States Army.

June 6, 1944, on the bloody sands of Omaha Beach, Father Michelangelo Palazzeschi's heart was ripped from his soul. He was in the second wave of landing crafts, V Corps, 1st Infantry Division, rushing pell-mell to unload their cargoes of terrified human beings into the maelstrom of war. No sooner had Michelangelo slipped over the side of his landing craft into waist-deep, teeth-chattering cold water, then he was surrounded by dead bodies and mangled limbs in the blood red surf. Bullets ripped through the air, killing men around him. Terrifying explosions shook the earth, billowing plumes of sand and body parts rose high, before raining down on them. A decapitated human head with half of its skull missing, it's one good eye staring with a 'why me' gaze, bobbed in the surf, rolled into him as he tried to give last rites to a dying Jewish sailor who had driven the landing craft Michelangelo's company had come in on. The sickening absurdity of the death and maiming of his fellow human beings on Omaha Beach brought grave questions: *Can one break a contract with God if he knows that God is wrong? If the violence and cruelty of war is proof that there is no God, then any promises of forgiveness or an afterlife I might make to a dying man as a priest is all hooey. Where was God, when these men needed him most? Not on Omaha Beach, here was Satan who owned the day. If there is no God, then there is no Satan. If there is no Satan, then we are doing this to ourselves; if this is true, how can one live with the guilt?*

Here, Michelangelo's faith had forever been frayed.

After Omaha Beach, Father Michelangelo Palazzeschi doubted that God was a loving God. After the Battle of the Bulge and countless last rites, his faith slipped further away.

America fielded over ten million soldiers in WWII. A few, chosen by an unusual twist of fate, were called upon to liberate the Nazi's Death and Concentration Camps; an unforgettable experience. Michelangelo did not enter one of these hell holes. However, in April 1945,his unit followed the forced death march of some 22,000 prisoners from the Flossenburg Concentration Camp to Dachau, one of the most notorious of the German death Camps. Along the way S.S. guards shot any inmate too weak or sick to keep up. Most of the 7,000 victims were already dead as Father Michelangelo Palazzeschi's jeep slowly passed by, the eyes of the dead silently following his passing. The harshest memory he would never be able to let go was of one nameless victim who lay in the mud on the side of the road. His hand raised, one finger pointing to heaven, his body crushed to an unrecognizable pulp by the tread of a German tank. No one would ever know who he had been. From that moment on he knew there was no God. How could there be?

Afraid that Father Palazzeschi was so devastated that he might take his own life – suicide an unforgivable sin - Michelangelo was reassigned to duty serving as an army chaplain on the RMS Queen Mary steaming from Southampton with a record number of mostly wounded and sick men: 2,332 passengers. For these men, including Michelangelo, the war was over, and they were all heading home to a nation grateful for their service. Michelangelo spent time with men anxious and happy to be alive and going home. He helped some write and read letters that had long needed attention. He ate well, slept some, read, and prayed not at all. On board he found a book about Italy in the 14th Century and silently resolved that even if there was not a God, the Church had a living history that fascinated him.

He and the army parted ways in June 1945. He returned to the Archdiocese of San Francisco where he read, paced in the garden, and talked with his fellow clergymen. It was decided that what Father Michelangelo Palazzeschi needed was a small parish where he could mend his faith as he tended a small flock – where he could do no harm.

＊ ＊ ＊ ＊ ＊

Betty had kept Michelangelo's room, and there he returned, with both legs in casts, no way to pay his fare, and for the moment few thoughts for his future.

While Mollie did not fare well in the kitchen, she did seem to work miracles with the wounded Padre, his desire to just become a simple man no longer burdened by his priestly collar growing with each conversation he had with this beautiful young woman, who listened well and made him laugh.

Doyle was more angry than frustrated. His failure to put to death the old Chinaman had left him edgy, short tempered, with tremors to his hands, and a developing nervous tick to the left side of his face. The pain in his stomach, the dysentery, stayed with him, leaving him lethargic and withdrawn. He had run out of heroin, his boys unable to locate his dealer. Sausalito was not a haven for heroin addicts. Doyle's focus was on his immediate need for a fix, one kind or another.

With his addiction to violence, Scotty found it unusual that Doyle could not remember if he had pushed the Priest and that ugly mother out the window. "I was close enough to that son-of-a-bitch to have done it. If I had, why would I have left Mollie-girl as a witness?" Scotty did not think that Doyle did it. He did not have enough time to do the deed and make it to the bathroom on time. On the other hand, it was something Doyle would do, and brag about it later. Scotty kept telling him that he had done it to brighten his day. The only answer he got was a sneer, and the occasional passing of a most unbearable stench.

Afraid that Doyle might suffer a violent breakdown, Scotty took a walk to a pay phone down on the wharf. It was time to get the boys together. Doyle needed to take a road trip in search of a heroin fix, more importantly to find Doyle a sacrificial man – his blood lust as powerful as a werewolf at full moon. This time Scotty would go armed, one should never trust a werewolf.

Michelangelo remained in his room, his injured legs as good as an excuse as any for his isolation. He read, mostly a collection of books on the history of the Catholic Church. Mollie brought, and read to him, a copy of *Farmer in the Sky* by Robert Heinlein. This he enjoyed, admitting that he had not read any science fiction since he had been a boy. That had been *From the Earth to the Moon* by Jules Verne. Because his room was on the first floor Betty sometimes joined them - the three of them discussing the books they read. He never read the newspaper, not wanting to hear about the Korean War, or the crimes men committed against each other which newspapers faithfully reported with a certain zeal. There were times he just wanted to be left alone and watch the clouds or the birds as they darted back and forth from a feeder that Oswaldo had hung on a branch of a small willow tree just outside. After dinner, he would listen from his wheelchair as Michael, Mollie, Betty, and Oswaldo chattered in the kitchen, and played songs that made him smile. Harvey often joined them, though he could not sing a note, nor play an instrument, and usually mixed up the punch line ruining what might have been a funny story.

Michelangelo participated from a distance, never read the bible, prayed, talked about the war, nor asked about the small church property up for sale five blocks away. There were times that he lit up, when there were one on one conversations with those that he knew would not ask questions he would not answer. Those were personal questions about family, anything to do with the past, his future, things that touched emotions in a way that might cause self-reflection. Then he would fall silent and close his eyes, or simply watch the birds at the feeder. If asked if he as okay, he had one word to fit all: "Fine."

"Are you feeling alright?"

"Fine"

"Would you like some coffee?"

"Fine."

"Something stronger, perhaps?"

"Fine."

"Would you like to talk about it?"

"Fine." But there were no words to follow.

"Would you like some fresh strawberry pie?"

"Fine." He was allergic to strawberries. There was never any anger in his words, he was never dismissive, nor apologetic. He was a kind man, who just wanted to be left alone, and could not say no or be rude to a friend who cared. He knew they cared, but could not say "Thank you, Mollie, I'm fine." Saying more than '*Fine*' left him vulnerable to say more.

Two weeks after Michelangelo's return to the Bayview House Archbishop Peter Sutton shared a glass of port and cigars with Archdeacon Alistair Dawtry. Discussions between them were almost always kept between themselves; the Archdeacon's chief responsibility to keep the dirt that exists in the real world off the Archbishop's desk, to keep his hands clean, to keep inquiring eyes – and tabloids – from learning anything about the imperfections. A secretly married priest, theft, the occasional exorcism, homosexuality, child abuse, a priest whose politics is straying from the approved message of the church, rumors whether true or false. Within the Archdiocese of San Francisco, a visit by the Deacon, was rarely announced, fear of the man often enough to resolve the problem.

The next day over tea the Deacon asked Sister Mary Benedict to act in his stead. "The Archbishop, and I, are concerned about the health, and well-being of Father Palazzeschi recently of the Sausalito Parish. The Parish has struggled through some difficult financial times and has been closed. We know that Father Palazzeschi has taken this hard. He has just been released from the hospital having suffered two broken legs. We're told it was an accident, we're not sure of that." He sipped his tea watching the nun for any expressions as he continued. "Michelangelo – Father Palazzeschi served as a combat chaplain in the European Theater of War. His experiences have now led him to a crisis of faith. A visit by the Archbishop, or myself, might tip Michelangelo in the direction we pray he does not go."

They spent some time discussing the priest's background, known strengths and weaknesses, and what was known about his war experiences. It was agreed that Sister Mary would approach Michelangelo with a soft and caring heart, test his heart just enough to see if he was salvageable.

As far as the Archbishop was concerned, Father Palazzeschi was not doing very well. Millions of soldiers had gone to war, among them many Chaplains. He knew that many had been tested by the horrors of what they had seen and done. Many had nightmares that would haunt them for years to come. He had checked, the Vatican reporting back that Father Palazzeschi was not the only Catholic Chaplain that had come back with his faith shaken. Most, who had faced similar or more harrowing circumstances, as had Palazzeschi, had returned with a stronger, if not renewed relationship, with their Lord and Savior Jesus Christ. The church teaches you that you are a priest forever. It is true, that a priest can resign from the priesthood and seek dispensation from his clerical obligations, yet the church will always regard him as a '*laicized priest*'

At Loyola Michelangelo showed himself to be gifted, if not brilliant. His studies in philosophy worthy of his finding an academic path, where the church, the world, could benefit from his mind. Maybe he was too smart, questioning things too much, too deeply. A position had opened in the Vatican Library in the study and preservation of ancient manuscripts. Sister Mary Benedict had been instructed to only quietly mention this opportunity if she thought Michelangelo might genuinely be interested; if not, to say nothing.

Michelangelo was doing fine, enjoying a stimulating game of chess with Michael, when Betty announced that he had a guest. She was hesitant, because while he was beginning to open-up, uninvited guests were not welcome in his chosen sheltered world. A nun? Up until that moment he had been enjoying the match; Michael had him three moves away from *check*. Michelangelo had been teaching him the game and this was the first time his opponent had the better of him and knew it.

Michelangelo saw the warm, caring, crafty blue eyes of the Sister without taking his eyes away from the board. He could also see that the good Sister was almost as taken aback by Michael's face as he had been – almost. While he did not expect her to jump out the window, Michael took a little of the starch out of her coif; a white headdress worn beneath a veil. "Saved by the bells of St. Mary's," he said in a soft voice. "Shall we finish later?"

Michael excused himself. He would win the game, but his moment of victory had been disappointedly postponed. He did note that this was the first time Michelangelo had said anything that even came close to religious since they had met.

"Please come in Sister. I was actually expecting the

Archbishop."

Renata had visited the larger parish that had gobbled
up hers and found it wanting. She needed to talk with
Father Palazzeschi – knowing in her heart that he no longer
considered himself a priest, she still considered him as hers.
Praying to the Holy Mother to protect her from the evil that
was a living entity at The Bayview House she prepared
herself for her confrontation with Father Palazzeschi, and
to ask Betty for forgiveness in deserting her in her hour of
need. Loneliness is part of life's struggle, being alone was
aging her, and at her age that was not a good thing.

"The Archbishop sends his blessings. He asked that I
might come in his stead, being that I carry no authority
to your challenges of faith. How are you doing, Father
Palazzeschi?" Sister Mary shared her best smile.

"Fine."

"She looked with tenderness at his casts. "Your legs are
healing?"

"Fine."

Michelangelo reviewed his chess moves in his mind
as he smiled and answered the Sister's questions. *Fine*
did not fit as an answer to several the Sister's queries as
to his health and mental well-being. He was not rude, nor
apologetic for his limited responses. *Fine* he was, and *fine*
was all the response he was willing to give. He knew why
she had come and was not ready to tell anyone that he

had reached the point where he was willing to give up his priestly collar. Close. He had asked Jesus some questions, not in a prayer, but as a simple humble man to God, and had not received an answer yet. The Holy silence was telling.

"When your legs have healed, and you are feeling up to it, the Archbishop would like to talk with you about your next posting . . . he thought something academic might be to your liking. Perhaps, a posting at the Vatican library." Her eyes lit up thinking that this would help lift him out of his lethargy.

He did not answer.

Mollie peeked in the room. "How about some nice herbal tea." She asked.

"Fine."

"No thank you, dear, I really must be going. I'll tell the Archbishop that you are . . ."

"Fine. And please thank the Deacon for sending you in his stead. God and I . . . He still owes me a conversation. Please tell the Deacon that I am still waiting, though my patience has limits."

Once he heard Betty bid farewell to Sister Mary Benedict, Michelangelo called out. "Michael, shall we finish our game?"

Michael, who had been waiting in the kitchen, answered as he remembered his game winning move. "Fine . . . and dandy," he responded.

Michelangelo smiled, appreciating more than ever how quick he had been to judge his new friend a monster before they had ever met.

Chapter Nine

The calendar pushed June out of the way allowing for the cold fog bound days of July to put a winter's chill over Sausalito. True winter brings wind and rain, July a chill that grips one right down the marrow of their bones. The bank of thick fog that engulfs San Francisco Bay allows its cold grip to ruin your summer day. All one has to do is look across the bay to the mainland where it's ninety degrees and ask the question: *Why the hell am I here?"*

It's July 1952, and around the good planet earth brotherly love seems as cold as a San Francisco fog bank. The Korean war continues to escalate. Model bomb shelters, set up and sold in Washington Square, brought on a mini-building boom across the bay. In San Francisco, where only a few weeks before, the city had become alarmed by a rumor that Russia would drop an atomic bomb into the ocean creating a 100-foot radioactive title wave that would devastate the city, the bomb shelters offering no safety. No one bought or built a bomb shelter in sleepy-town Sausalito. If a radioactive tidal wave were to pass through the Golden Gate, there was nothing the good folks of Sausalito could do about it.

The Bayview House, while still a slow boiling cauldron of pretense and mistrust, was beginning to stitch together as a family. Things first began to change with the arrival of Michael and Mollie, but it was the return of Renata that stirred the good juices in the stew.

Renata stood silently in the kitchen doorway as Mollie played patty-cake with a meatloaf that would never live up to the name. Betty was on the phone, her back towards the doorway.

"Yes, Mr. Fisher, we'll do what we can. But, I must tell you that rents are going down in Sausalito. Yes, I see . . . but . . . it's the fog season and no one in their right mind would want to move here now." Betty put the phone on her lap allowing the voice of the attorney to ramble on in its self-importance to the pile of garden fresh haricots verts nesting in her apron where she had been trimming them.

"It says here," Michelangelo reported as he wheeled himself into the kitchen, his two legs in casts stretched out annoyingly in front of him as he constantly bumped into everything in his path. The good news was that the good Father was at least getting out of his room. The bad news, that he was constantly bumping into most everything – though it was humorous to listen to him try to find an appropriate substitute for a swear word when a sharp ding to one of his legs caused him to want to utter a few damns until the pain went away. "It says here," he held up a copy of the Oakland Tribune, ruffling its pages, "that Dashiell Hammett the mystery writer I have been enjoying has been sentenced to six months in prison for refusing to tell where the Communist Party gets its bail money. I was just about to order a copy of *The Thin Man* – you don't suppose they'll put that on the black list, do you?"

Betty hung up the phone, turning her attention to Michelangelo. Renata pushed open the screen door and marched into the kitchen as if she owned it, which she had for more years than anyone there could measure. She plopped her carpet bag on the floor. "I've come to see about the room. The ad did not say if it came with the bay view." There had been no ad for a room to rent. It was the old woman's way of saying that she needed her job back in exchange for lodging.

If it came down to a choice of making meatloaf or giving Renata her job back, Mollie was prepared to take off her flour and tomato sauce stained apron then and there.

The two women hugged as Betty broke into happy tears. She had dearly missed the older Italian woman, especially her biting, sarcastic humor. Renata saying that she had come about the room meant that she was coming home. After clutching Betty's hand in her own, with two quick pecks on each cheek, Renata turned towards her favorite Padre. "Are you still sucking in the sympathy while everyone else is doing the work around here? Get out of that chair and go dust off the cobwebs catching dust all over your parish."

"I never thought of the cobwebs as mine." Michelangelo said as he swatted his newspaper teasingly in her direction. He knew that this endearing old devoted Catholic would always be on his case for giving up his calling. She knew it. He knew it, he just hadn't announced it to anyone yet. Once he was up on his feet again he would pay a call on Deacon Dawtry; until then, it was no one's business but his own. The truth was that he was quite comfortable with his decision, neither fearing eternal damnation or the wrath of an unforgiving church. The timing just wasn't right.

Renata always had a little place of her own, never asking for room or board, just a small amount of money for her help in the kitchen. That she needed a room concerned Betty; however, for the time being, she would not embarrass her old friend by asking. The lawyer had just ordered her- unfortunately - to increase the rents. Renata's cooking was more valuable than gold and she wasn't about to charge her rent. She would be able to build in Renata's room and a little pocket money in the process, without hurting Mollie, who would continue with the general housekeeping. The improved menu would delight everyone.

"Renata, my old grand-mama, you've come home? Yes?" Hearing the commotion, Oswaldo burst into the kitchen like a bull moose charging into the kitchen, embraced the petite older woman in a big hug.

"Put me down you big lummox, unless you want me to bite your nose."

Renata's welcome, followed by a bottle of red wine, allowed Betty to sort out all the pieces. "Mollie, go find Michael and bring him here. I have an idea."

Betty wasted no time once Michael joined them. "First, Renata, of course you can have a room. Mollie, give Renata your apron before she changes her mind. That bastard lawyer Jacob Fisher has just told me that I have to raise all the rents – except Sarah Brandt's." It had not occurred to her until that moment that perhaps Sarah was behind the rent increase – spiteful revenge sometimes sneaks in the door like a sinful serpent.

Renata pretended to spit on the floor at the mention of Sarah's name.

"So, you are both now on the payroll, with rent included. I also have been told to rent out the spare rooms. This . . ." she held up a finger for emphasis. "This gives me an idea. Molly and Michael, please follow me. Everyone, except Michelangelo, followed her out the kitchen door where the swirling mid-day fog was bracing. When they were all far enough out on the driveway to be able to look back on the house, she turned and pointed. "When the house was built there was a guest room up there in the attic." She pointed towards the peaked roof, her hand trembling from the raw chill. The room was closed off long before I got here, so I have not seen it. I've been told that it is fully furnished, complete with its own bathroom including a free-standing bath tub. The roof was redone five years ago so I see no reason why it shouldn't be perfectly habitable, though a bit dusty, I suspect. Unfortunately, the only access is the fire escape which is why it has never been available for rent." She had had enough of the cold and turned back towards the kitchen, Oswaldo pushing her wheelchair up the ramp. "If it's livable – and I can see no reason why it wouldn't be – I'd like you and Michael," she said to Molly, "to have it. That way I can rent your current room and keep the skinflint lawyer happy." She stopped just at the kitchen door turning back to Molly. "You can't see it from here, but beneath the pitched eve, the roof is flat where Michael can play his horn."

"It sounds lovely." Mollie answered, her hand brushing Michaels wrist that had just the day before been freed from its cast. The idea of her husband climbing up and down an upright ladder attached to the side of the house concerned her – was he up to it?

"You two, go up, and have a look at it. Oswaldo, would you please go along. Michael is going to need some handyman help. I know that your carpentry skills will be useful."

Michael was all in. He loved playing on the roof, and they just about had enough money saved to get his horn repaired.

Once everyone was back in the kitchen Betty continued with a list of the improvements needed, and who would move where, rolling off her tongue. "Oswaldo, there is a spare door down in the basement. You can bring that up to replace the window nearest the fire-escape with the door. You will need to put in some handrails of course. No one uses the little table and chairs on the patio, they're always in the shade. Bring them up so you and Michael can have a place to sit and play your music."

"I wonder how your flute would sound if I were to teach you a little jazz." Michael teased as they cheerfully headed towards the stairs on their way to explore the mysterious apartment above.

"Michael, wait until I get our coats," Mollie implored.

Michelangelo, while happy for Michael and Mollie, was

saddened by not being able to contribute. He wanted to take a set of big kitchen shears to free his legs, but alas, he had several more months - if not longer- of his legs to be encased in their itchy plaster casts.

Renata took Betty's apron and the verts, placing them with authority on Michelangelo's lap. "Here, Father, make yourself useful." She picked up her bag to take it to her room saying as she disappeared into the hallway, "Father wash your hands. Tap water will have to do, we don't have any holy water."

Betty had another thought, calling loudly to Oswaldo: "And put in a sitting area underneath the eve where you and Michael can play your music." She was being a bit scatter-brained, but no one mentioned it. "For your help, I give you room eleven on the second floor, right by the door you will put in. The room is bigger, closer to the bathroom, and closer to Michael and Mollie's They'll make good neighbors, you'll see."

Oswaldo agreed, he and Michel set off to see what the project would look like. Michael had little experience as a carpenter. Mollie followed, wanting to see what their new home would look like.

"Renata, you will have room one just across from the kitchen. I'm sorry that your neighbor is Sarah Brandt. If you can find a way to change that, you have my full support. Michelangelo, you will remain where you are. Scotty, we'll move next to Doyle on the second floor. Harvey across from Oswaldo in room seven. That will leave rooms five, six, to rent out." She did not mention room ten which had been Mary Griffith's. Mary's belongings were still there, and until the police told her that Mary would not be coming back, Betty wanted to keep the room just as she left it.

Chapter Ten

"Vera, my beloved wife, would have loved the soup tonight," Anton Lapin thanked Jiang Hua the restaurant's owner. "The dumplings, as always, were perfection. I, myself, could never eat soup as hot as Vera demanded that it should be – a boiling cauldron."

"She was here, just once before her death. I remember her very well. Never before have I heard a voice as lovely as hers." Hua replied with grave courtesy. His wife, an overbearing prima donna, had demanded that the chef and all the kitchen staff come out, so she could thank them for the dumpling soup. She than sang something from a Russian opera, addressing the rest of the patrons in the restaurant in French when she was done. She died of a bad heart a week later.

Now Anton Lapin came into the restaurant every Wednesday night at a quarter to eight and ordered the dumpling soup. Always the same, a boiling cauldron, just the way his wife liked it. Having finished his ritual soup Anton stepped outside the restaurant and lit a cigar as he prepared to walk over to the California Street cable car for his ride home to his lonely apartment. Three months his wife had been dead, and every moment of his daily routine seemed fixed on her memory. As he passed the darkened alley behind the restaurant he heard a sound. A feral cat he thought, as he looked up at the moon, wondering if his wife Vera could see the same from her place in heaven.

Stars . . . The sudden blur of stars dissolved the glow of the moon, as the club forever silenced the memories of an old man who had spent his life a refugee to die a solitary death in Chinatown – San Francisco, America.

Fearing for its own life, the alley cat hissed loudly, as it jumped from one trash can to another, a lid clanging against a dumpster causing the perpetrators to flee into the night.

Four brutal blows had rearranged his skull – his face so badly beaten that Jiang Hua, when he opened the alley door to see what the ruckus was, could not recognize Anton Lapin except for his suit, which was something a gentleman of means might have worn back in the 1920's.

After several months of investigation Homicide Detective Ralph Schmidt had come up with no new leads that might connect the attempted murder of Edsel Wo with the murder of Sam Lim besides the obvious fact that both were Chinese, elderly, and family patriarchs. Neither knew each other, nor had any known business connections. They lived in different parts of town, did not frequent the same restaurants. Wo liked to gamble, and never borrowed to do so. Lim did not gamble. Both headed large families, neither family connected with a Tong Gang, or any known family rivalries. Both wore glasses and shared the same optometrist. This was not unusual because Chinese optometrists were few for the entire Chinese population. Neither had an appointment within the same month, within the last few years. There were no witnesses to the murder of Lim. The attempted murder of Wong involved a small gang – possibly white. They might as well have been green – the witnesses recalling little. Schmidt hoped to be taken off the case finding it frustrating and pointless.

"Captain?" Schmidt gave an invisible knock on Captain Sancy's open door, the gateway to Dante's Infernal.

"I see by your latest report that you have accomplished nothing – zip – a big fat zero." Captain Francis Sancy was rarely in a good mood, having to be in the same room with Schmidt really pissed him off. "I am tempted to take you off the case, close it. There is a freezer somewhere in the basement full of Chinese cold cases. One more won't change diddly-squat. How e...v...e...r, there has been a new murder that might – might – be connected. Sometime last night a Russian immigrant, one Anton Lapin, was found behind the Tarpon Noodle Parlor in Ross Alley. Cause of death, he was beaten to death by some sort of club. Witnesses, none. The Noodle Parlor is frequented by Chinese and Russian immigrants from China, many of whom had lived in Tarpon, Manchuria, the last stop on the Trans-Siberian Railway."

Shit, Schmidt swore to himself. Then he said it aloud. "Shit, Captain, I don't speak Chinese, Russian, Jap, or any other foreign language. What the hell do you expect me to do with this?"

"Meet Officer Leland Tse, your new partner. Until this morning he was a patrolman in Chinatown. Let's just think of this as an experiment, having a Chinese cop in Chinatown. It is also an experiment having a Chinese officer working on loan to the Detective Division. This comes down all the way from the top, they're interested in seeing if a Chinese Officer can accomplish anything with their own. When in Chinatown, Officer Tse is in charge." He gave Schmidt a hard look.

Schmidt looked at Tse and saw that he was unarmed. Leland Tse's shoulder emblem showed that he was one of the San Francisco Police Department's best and brightest traffic cops. Schmidt's fingers clinched at the humiliation. He knew that the captain wanted to kick him off the Detective Squad. Rumor had it that the Captain had even tried to lose him in a poker game to the Southside Division; Schmidt knew it wasn't a rumor. Schmidt was within one sucking breath of pulling his badge and gun – but then everyone would know that he had been placed under a chink traffic cop. He sucked in the grief the Captain dished out at him as he waited to be dismissed. He would have to have a talk with his new partner about their arrangement.

"I will try not to abuse my authority," Leland said as they checked out a patrol car. He pulled out a chain that he wore around his neck. "If I get in trouble, I'll whistle." He smiled, waiting a moment for Schmidt to do the same.

Schmidt did not have a whistle.

Doyle and Scotty had not operated in San Francisco since the night they had screwed up the attempted killing of the old chink. Doyle, who blamed the boys on making too much noise, now mulled over the idea with Scotty about finding a new crew. Mostly Doyle was out of sorts because of his drug addiction and a troublesome bowel condition that gave him no relief.

"Hell, Doyle, the boys have always come through, when busted for petty crimes of their own making they have never brought any of the dirt back to your doorstep. What you need, boss," Scotty suggested, "is a change of scenery. Someplace where the food is good, the women hot and cheap, and their John's wallets thick and ripe for picking." They decided on Fisherman's Wharf in Monterey, threw some overnight bags in Hector's *Woodie*, and took Smokestack along as the driver. Smokestack was a braggart, loudmouth and a buffoon. None-the-less, he was the best pickpocket they had ever seen; if only he could keep his mouth shut. This would be a test, if Smokestack screwed up they would fire the three of them. Hector and Smitty were left behind.

Schmidt looked at the menu. "No burgers?" He complained. "No beer! Tse, how can you eat this crap?"

"Please call me Lee, that way you don't spit my name."

"Try one of the noodle dishes, the Mongolian beef is good."

Schmidt had never eaten Chinese food and wasn't feeling very adventurous. He looked around the restaurant at the various steaming plates and bowls. "Let's come back later, we can eat in Little Italy. There they know how to do pasta – besides, the owner looks busy."

Ignoring the detective's tantrum, Lee waved at the owner that they were ready.

Jiang Hua came to their table with a small pad and a broad smile. "You are ready." The restaurant's patrons were all Chinese, curious, but uncomfortable with two policemen dining in their midst. Lee was in uniform; Schmidt, dressed in a cheap brown suit, looked like the kind of cop who harassed the Chinese just because they were Chinese. Knowing that Hua was the owner and not a mere waiter, Lee bowed slightly in respect. "Yes, we will have the Sizzling Rice Soup, and an order of the Shrimp Dumplings." He smiled at Schmidt. "Rice, pasta, and shrimp, how could we go wrong." He knew that Schmidt would not let him down regarding complaints about the food. "We are here about the unfortunate murder last night."

"Please excuse me one moment." Hua delivered their order to the kitchen returning shortly with a pot of hot green tea. "As I told the officers last night, Mr. Lapin has been a favored customer for some months now. He and his wife Vera immigrated from Shanghai, China, after the Communists kicked all foreigners out. Mr. Lapin grew up in Tarpon, same as I, which is why he chose to visit my humble restaurant. Sadly, Mrs. Lapin passed on a few weeks after their first visit here." He wondered if he should tell the officers about the Russian woman's annoying opera skills. "Since then Mr. Lapin has returned every Wednesday night, always the same table, always the same soup. He then smokes cigar and walks to the cable car to go home. Where, I do not know. That is all I can tell you. Mr. Lapin was a very nice man, lonely, he missed his wife very much."

Schmidt looked on disapprovingly as Lee poured some of the tea into small cup and set it in front of him. He grits his teeth as he made several allergic nasal twangs as officer Tse and the restaurant owner bantered back and forth in Cantonese. He watched as the patrons scattered about the restaurant talked among themselves, few if any speaking English. Five minutes passed, and the owner excused himself, returning shortly with their meal.

Schmidt had to admit that he liked the soup. The rice sizzled when dumped in the broth, and he had to admit that it was tasty. He picked apart the shrimp dumpling, tasting part of a shrimp before pushing it aside.

Outside they walked back to the alley where yellow police tape still marked the alley as a crime scene. There were chalk marks where the body had been, though there was no missing it due to the large pool of dried blood. Two chalk marks identified where the victim's scalp and beard had been found next to the body. There had been no robbery, and no witness except for Jiang Hua who had opened the alley door scaring the culprits away, unable to identify them because of poor light. Tse suspected that they were Chinese, because the homicide had taken place in China Town.

"Not much to add to what we already know," Lee said as they got back into their patrol car. "The victim's wife died from a heart attack shortly after arriving in the city. Did she, or was it something else? There were three young Chinese men at the table to your left – did you see them?"

Schmidt said that he had. He lied; he had not, did not want the traffic cop to know that he was doing some decent detective work.

"They seemed more intent on listening to what Mr. Hua and I had to say than having any conversation between themselves. Most young men I know talk incessantly about sports, girls, and not having enough money. Mr. Hoa said that they are new to the neighborhood. They had only been in once before that he knew of. That time they had been loud, offensive in their language, and had argued with the waiter about the bill. I asked the owner to call me the next time they come in."

So, the traffic cop wants to trade his whistle in for a detective's shield, Schmidt thought.

The three Chinese youths watched through the window as the patrol car pulled away.

Chapter Eleven

Mollie scampered up the fire-escape like a kid discovering a new playground. The last ladder, parallel with the house, was a little more strenuous on Michael's wrist, which gave him some concern about how often he could go up and down the damn thing until his wrist was fully healed.

Oswaldo, who was last up, noted the challenge. "In bad weather, you had best be staying home, this ladder will become slippery." It was slippery now.

Both Michael and Oswaldo had to duck beneath the pitched roof; as promised the floor beneath was a flat deck. Between several tall evergreen trees whose branches shaded the roof, the deck itself would remain mostly dry and out of the wind. Michael could easily see himself playing his sax there for hours on end.

Mollie stayed back from the edge of the roof. She had never been one for heights and the three-story drop was dizzying. "First things first," she said to Oswaldo firmly, "we're going to need a railing – a sturdy one." She went to the window which was badly in need of cleaning, and peered in. She could see another window on the far side of the room but not much between. "Strange there is no door." She pushed against the window.

Oswaldo pulled a large fishing knife out of his pocket using the blade to free the window which had become stuck over time.

"Oh golly," Mollie marveled as soon as she stood inside their new attic apartment. All they had ever had, including their room back at *The Rose* had been small, designed for one person without much in the way of personal stuff. A double bed, if lucky, dresser, end table and a chair – that was it. This was a palace by comparison. The bed was in a loft - what's one more ladder to climb - which left the main room feeling spacious and open. The room was fully furnished with a small couch, two overstuffed sitting chairs, a dresser, small table with two wooden chairs, and a circular floor rug in front of a small wood burning stove. The water closet had a sink and toilet, the biggest surprise beneath the loft was a freestanding claw-foot bathtub. The kitchen wasn't much to speak of, a counter with some open shelving – no sink, that was in the water closet. No stove or refrigerator, but a pot of coffee or a small pot of soup could be heated over the wood burning stove.

Mollie peeked into the closet which was no deeper than a standard coat hanger. A closet was a luxury they had not had since they were married. Next stop was the loft where once she reached it she looked down from the loft with an animated smile: "Oh Michael, a real goose feather bed."

Michael wondered if they could stay where they were until his wrist fully healed. He was about to climb up to Mollie when Oswaldo called him over to where he had opened two tall bay windows that faced the back of the house. They were almost as big as doors, starting from just a foot off the floor, reaching six feet up. Unfortunately, they let in little sun as perpetual shade from a shadowy steep hillside and a cluster of tall evergreen trees whose layers of branches let in little light and warmth from the sun. "This here answers a lot, "Oswaldo said as he leaned out the windows looking first up, then down. A moment later he gripped a rope which operated a block and tackle disturbing a sleepy squirrel who chittered in protest. Looking down from the loft Mollie watched as the pully slowly raised a sturdy metal basket. "We had one just like that back on my folk's farm. Pop used it to put hay up in the loft. That is how we can get the firewood up for the stove."

"And a lot more," Oswaldo said as he tested the pully for strength. "The ropes will need replacing, the gears and wheel some grease, and it might be strong enough to act as a lift." Looking down he spotted an ancient pile of firewood and a tree-debris covered gravel path that led most likely back towards the kitchen driveway.

Molly scampered down from the loft, checking the water closet next. She tried the sink which burbled and belched for a moment before flowing with nice clean water. Hot water took a little longer, but it worked. The toilet had water in the basin which flushed as if it had been used just yesterday. She was delighted to see that neither the sink nor the toilet had water stains – if they had it would have taken her hours to scour them out.

For an apartment that had not been used in years it was remarkably clean and ready to occupy. The bedding of course needed to be washed and hung out in the fresh air for a while.

Mollie leaned out the window and shouted to her husband, "Golly, isn't this wonderful." Neither of the men had noticed the narrow wooden walkway, with a handrailing secured to the side of the house, that led from the bay windows to the side of the house where the fire escape was.

"Where do we start," Michael asked?

"The pully system," Oswaldo answered. He saw Michael rubbing his tired wrist. "Maybe it will be strong enough to haul your scrawny-ass up here."

Oswaldo scratched his hairy chin. "For not having been used in a couple of years it's in remarkable shape." He was looking at the front of the house at the fire escape below. "I think we can attach a flight of steps from here down to the second-floor deck . . . narrow and steep like you'll find on a ship. With a solid railing and some support beams, it will be easy to build. I say we put it together on the second deck and then hoist it up as a single piece."

"Can we get the hoist working today," Mollie gave the ladder a foreboding look.

Oswaldo turned back to the attic apartment to take another look at the hoist.

Michael looked towards the far side of the house where

the other window looked over a sloped roof, no access or a flat roof to balance things out.

Chapter Twelve

Michelangelo sat in the kitchen with Betty and Renata. "One does not have to do the math to see that the increased rents are not going to keep the landlord happy. Renata, Michael and Molly, and I are here, at least for the time being, with little or no rent to be paid. You said that Sarah Brandt's rent is not to be increased?" He raised his eyebrows as if the sin of usury was sneaking up from the basement.

Betty paused to think about that. *Sarah not paying rent wasn't usury – unless she had something on the lawyer, but still -*

Michelangelo continued. "Sadly, Mary Griffin is most likely no longer of this world, yet you hold her room as if her return is expected at any moment. I trust that Scotty and Doyle's rents are paid up, but would you agree that trust is not part of their contracts? Oswaldo, bless his heart, has a hard time keeping a job, and now you are allowing him a discount for needed handyman work around the house. That leaves Harvey?"

Betty bit her lip. "Two weeks late," she said as if it were his usual state-of-affairs.

"And you?"

"I get your point, Father. I have three rooms to let, with no prospects knocking at the door. Most everyone else is a freeloader, including yours truly. If a banker wanted to know what we might have to offer as credit I would have to say . . ." She looked around the room for an answer that might be fluttering around like a moth. "The only thing I might have to offer is Renata's cooking."

He humorously directed Betty to tell Renata, whom he knew would always call him Father, "Please remind the dear woman not to refer to me by my prior profession. My name is Michelangelo."

"His Holiness, Father Michelangelo, asks that you not refer to him any longer as Father." Betty said, offering the best curtsy she could muster from her wheelchair.

Knowing he would not win in that one, he poured himself a glass of wine as he finished the spring peas, placing the finished bowl on the counter.

Betty noted the early hour for the wine, saying nothing more.

"What was the vocal tone of the lawyer?" He asked Betty.

"Seriously, I'm worried about my job."

"Do you suppose the reason why he wants a quick increase in the rents might be because he's planning on putting the Bayview House up for sale?"

"Oh, dear. Do you think?"

"I do," answered Michelangelo. "This place has been hemorrhaging money for some time now. While I have not resigned from the church yet, I am in no hurry to take up residency at the archdiocese."

"Don't worry," inserted Renata. "It will never sell, no one in their right mind would buy a house with a curse as a regular tenant."

"Sarah Brandt has been awfully quiet since Michael shared Mollie's lasagna. It's not in her nature to not seek revenge when she thinks it's due. You don't think that she would . . ."

"Sell her home to spite everyone else?" Michelangelo followed through on the thought.

"She doesn't own . . . ?" Renata asked.

"God forbid, but she has influence." Betty answered.

Mollie burst into the room. "Oh Betty, you should see it, it's simply marvelous. Why it even has a claw-footed tub. There is a bed in a loft, and a wood-burning stove. I'm going to go up and pack things right away. That is," her face took on an innocent demure look, "if I can put off some of the chores until later? I promise I will be all caught up before the sun goes down tonight."

Betty waved her on.

"It sounds like the little apartment we had in Modena when I first married Aldo, my first husband. I remember the aroma of the fresh breads rising from the bakery below. It was a nice apartment. Aldo, he was a bum." She gestured by bringing her fingers to her chin. "That was a long time ago, him, I don't give a damn. Mi scusi, Padre, ma ere solo un uomo viscido."

Michelangelo laughed, he did not know a lot of Italian, but she had just told him: "You should excuse me, Father, but he was a slime-ball." He poured himself another glass of wine as he thought that Renata was reason enough to fight for the old house. He hadn't had a home where he was this happy since he had left Grass Valley. He had no intention of ever going back to his childhood home town, too many folks would be let down by his giving up the priesthood. So, he might as well plant his feet here and put up a good fight. He looked at his two legs in their ugly heavy casts and had to laugh – *yes sir, plant my feet here.*

"What's exciting your chuckle muscle, Father?" Renata asked.

Michelangelo found his pipe, tapped a little of his favorite Burley tobacco into it, lit it, drawing on it until the tobacco took to flame. "Renata, if I were your father, why I'd be so old God must have forgotten me. Come to think of it, He has."

"A little bite to your humor this morning," Betty said with an understanding smile. *I've been feeling somewhat the same way lately; forgotten.*

"Tell me of Oswaldo," Renata asked. "He is such a nice, gentle man. A little frightening by his size perhaps, but a

nice man. No wife? No children? He never speaks of himself. Sometime ago, you mentioned that he was a political
refugee. Is this true?"

"Once, he shared a little," Betty answered, "not enough
to know his whole unfortunate story, but enough to know
what broke his heart. Why he cannot go home, I'll tell you,
but you must promise to keep it to yourselves." Betty's
eyes glistened as she began to share Oswaldo's story.

* * * * *

*"**Jorge is missing again.**"Oswaldo's mother had told
him shortly after supper. Jorge was the black sheep of the
family. He had been different since he had been a small
child, preferring to play with the girls or by himself. He
had soft features, and never gained a man's voice. He was a
reader of fantasy, living in a world all his own – his mother
thought that someday he would become a famous writer, a
poet, or an artist that would make the family proud.*

*Ecuador had harsh laws against homosexual behavior.
The shame caused by Jorge affected the family in social
circles forcing his father to raise his hands in exasperation
and anger. "No son of mine is a pansy."*

*Life was not that simple for Jorge, who did not see
himself as a pansy. He just saw things differently than
his brothers. At home, he found nothing but threat and
ridicule. Finding his identity was easier on the streets.
From the age of fourteen Oswaldo's brother Jorge was*

perpetually missing. Banned from his home by his father he disappeared into the shanties and the ghettoes in the underside of the city. However, when his father was fishing, his mother, Hermelinda, welcomed her third son home with an open wounded heart. Brothers Sabastian and Ricardo would soon send him bruised and bleeding back out onto the streets. Matilda, a well-known drag queen brought him home after finding him brutally beaten and raped in a back alley a few blocks from the 'bathhouse' in the neighborhood frequented by many gays. In 1949, in Ecuador it was a crime to engage in same sex unions and being caught often led to imprisonment, and sometimes worse. What Jorge suffered was not that uncommon for young men who looked and acted the part.

Under Matilda's tutorage, Jorge full-heartedly adopted the role, and found himself welcomed in a community he had been seeking. Jorge became Bianca, an eighteen-year-old drag queen, known for her lascivious laugh and the frequency, and multiple partners at the bath houses.

Drugs were part of her scene, to the point that Matilda had to tell her to leave. By the age of twenty Bianca had tried to commit suicide twice, been beaten and raped too many times to count.

No one in her family cared anymore when news reached them that Jorge was in trouble again. Except for Oswaldo's mother, whose heart ached for her son that she could no longer see, but never stopped loving. "Oswaldo, your brother Jorge is missing again."

To Oswaldo, Jorge was family and despite all his sins he was just that, and someone had to look out for him.

Oswaldo would give his mother an understanding look and quietly go out to find out if his little brother was alive. Each time he did this he knew that the day would come when Jorge would have disappeared from the streets and bathhouses to never be seen again.

Oswaldo, who worked in the lumber industry swinging an ax, was big enough, and mean enough looking, to go into the underworld of the city without feeling threatened. This time it was different and would be the last time he saw his home. Matilda told him that she had heard that Jorge was living in a shanty where drugs and prostitution had brought him to the lowest dregs of the city. Oswaldo found his little cousin as he was being brutally kicked and beaten by a policeman. Yelling for him to stop, Oswaldo grabbed the policeman from behind, pulling him off his brother. Stronger than he thought, the policeman freed himself from Oswaldo's grip. In the short wrestling match that followed, the policeman pulled and dropped his gun. While reaching for it, Oswaldo was struck in the right temple by the policeman's baton causing him to momentarily pass-out. Disoriented, the policeman forgot about his gun just long enough for Jorge to find it and fire two bullets at point blank range, killing the policeman.

*Oswaldo woke to find the dead policeman and his little brother holding the gun. Without thinking Oswaldo took the gun from his dying brother's hands. Jorge's last words were: "I had no choice, they will think that it was you."
A witness said that it had been a big gay guy defending his lover that had killed the policeman. Oswaldo fled his home, and country, with a murder wrap for killing a cop, while in a homosexual rage. The penalty for either being a*

firing squad under Ecuadorian Law. He was to be married to Pricilla, a woman he loved dearly, and never had the chance to say good-by.

Sausalito is a good place for Oswaldo to hide. He earns a few dollars as a handy-man, and on occasion working as a fisherman on small seasonal crafts. The one thing he cannot do is take a job where someone might ask questions -if arrested, he will be extradited back to Ecuador.

Betty finished telling what she knew about Oswaldo. Sometimes he pays the rent, sometimes not. I don't worry about it. For me, he's family, and like most of us in this house he will be sorely challenged should the Bay House close its doors."

Renata crossed herself.

Michelangelo's heart bled for Oswaldo's suffering. He eyed the wine bottle, to ease his own.

Betty saw what he wanted, doing, or saying nothing as he filled his glass.

"Have the police come up with anything regarding the disappearance of Mary Griffin?" Michelangelo asked. "Mollie told me that you were pushed. Was it the same person? Do you have any ideas on who it might have been?" Sarah Brandt is the obvious candidate he was thinking of, but she was too big and slow to have been the one who had pushed him and Michael out the window. He had not dwelled on the question, but the conversation had brought them to the point where perhaps now the time was to bring it up.

"Pushed?" She had lost many night's sleep remembering that terrible day. Time after time she saw herself tumbling, over and over, feeling again and again, the moment when her spine snapped. The pain! Now the pain was gone, but not what she felt as she sat, forever a prisoner in a wheel-chair which she loathed more with each day she was bound to it. "Pushed? It all happened so fast, I can't say. I don't remember enough to say whether I was pushed or not. But deep down, I believe I was." She looked at Michelangelo, her eyes haunted for that moment with the memory.

Michelangelo rolled forward and poured Betty a small glass of the wine. A tear formed in each of her eyes as she searched his for a clue – had they both been pushed? She knew that he was about to answer her, and his answer was going to frighten her. She drank the wine down in one gulp. He poured her a second glass, pouring the last into his own.

Renata stopped what she was doing taking Betty's hands into her own. She too feared what Michelangelo had to say. He had never spoken of the curse that haunted Bay View House. She took the glass from Betty's hand and drank part of it herself.

"I was pushed." His voice was determined, as if answer-ing the question in a court of law. "I was not only pushed, I was shoved. As I sit here in this chair I can remember clearly the pressure of two human hands press firmly into my back with enough force to cause me to fall forward into Michael. My fear was not who had attacked me from behind, but where I was going. I did not know Michael at that time. I did not know that his unfortunate condition was an accident of birth. I saw his face at that moment as a gargoyle, a spawn of Satan sent to challenge my faith. That Satan himself had shoved me forward."

Renata crossed herself as she saw in her own mind Satan laughing as Father Palazzeschi tumbled through the window taking Michael with him. She felt Mollie's presence, having seen only the accident, not the cause, as her husband dropped from view.

"Renata, my dear," Michelangelo said with deep kindness, "it was not the Devil who was there that day. "I was pushed by human hands."

Chapter Thirteen

"Jager Schnitzel?"

A thickset man, perhaps fifty-five, dressed in a natty double-breasted charcoal suit with matching vest, a button down white shirt, finished with a pinstriped dark blue bowtie, a Rotary International Pin in the right lapel, had just knocked on the restaurant window in front of where Harvey Freed sat.

A lone fly waved back.

Unless one knows someone, knocking on a window would be considered rude. Harvey hadn't really understood what the man had said, as much as he was able to put together what he thought the man had said, and the fact that he was pointing at the steaming plate the waiter had just delivered. The man did not seem to be a beggar, he was too well dressed, even the cut of his curly silver-fox gray hair suggested wealthy gentry. The Rotary Pin suggested pedigree. The one thing missing, which most men and women within eyesight wore, was a proper hat. Without a hat, his dress, his first impression, was as noticeably incomplete as a snowman without a nose.

Harvey knew hats. Well, he didn't know hats; he was too new to the business. However, his business card said that he was an expert, whose knowledge of hats was to be respected. He was now the regional salesman for the *Dobbs Hat Company of America*, purveyors of the finest in classic straw and felt hats. The card did not complete the truth, that his newly found expertise was merely two days old.

The stranger moved on without tapping on the window a second time. The fly buzzed contentedly on the sun warmed window. Harvey returned to his Jager Schnitzel.

A moment later the man entered Schroeder's, the famous German Restaurant, an icon in San Francisco, and approached his table. "I apologize for interrupting your meal, sir. I can assure you that being rude is not a habit of mine. I saw your . . ."

"Schnitzel," finished Harvey as he cut and stuffed a large bite in his mouth, fearing that this copious stranger might suddenly seize his plate and run laughing down the street.

A waiter came over to see if Harvey was being disturbed.

"Your sales case." A large black sales case proudly stamped with *Dobbs Hat Company of* America was perched on a chair immediately next to where Harvey sat within full view of the window. "I'm sorry, I have failed to introduce myself, Caesar Augustus Pinfield, recently of Exeter, New Hampshire."

"Sir," the waiter, with dark grave eyes, interrupted, "shall I show the gentleman out?" By this time, many eyes in the restaurant were turned, curious regarding this unusual event. Schroeder's was a fine dining establishment, frequented by regulars, almost exclusively men, especially in the front bar. The offending party who had knocked on the window was obviously a man of means – this being the one the waiter was threatening to remove from the bar. The gentleman seated was unknown and dressed like a lower-class salesman. Harvey, who had taken off his coat, wore purple suspenders, a black tie, and a wrinkled white long sleeve shirt with yellow stains marking the underarm area. A gentleman would have worn the coat. Flustered, the waiter wasn't quite sure who should be removed and why.

The fly, having been born and fed at Schroeder's with its own pedigree, moved on to buzz a more inviting patron.

The gentleman wants to buy a hat, Harvey thought as he extended his hand. "Harvey Freed," he answered back, a dab of gravy on his upper lip. "That will be all right, waiter, I'm buying Mr. Pinfield a stein of your finest pilsner. I'll have the same." The schnitzel had been the blue plate special, he hadn't ordered a beer because he could barely afford the schnitzel. Two days on the job and he had not sold a single hat. The hats in his case were samples which he wasn't supposed to sell, although he had paid a full salesman's discount for each, the difference between salesman's discount and wholesale was marginal. But, the gentleman needed a hat, and Harvey needed to close a sale, and he would be damned grateful for the money.

"The schnitzel looks exquisite."

"You are not from here," Harvey said, having forgotten that his guest had said where he was from.

"No, my fiancé and I had a parting of the ways, and I decided to take a sabbatical and head west. As the late Samuel Clemens once said. *"So here I find myself in the great windy city without a hat."* He chuckled mirthfully, "My hat took a flier at the top of the hill on your Powell Street cable car. As you can see I am not in good enough shape to have chased it down your crookedest street..." His explanation hung in the air as he could not remember the street's name.

"Lombard," Harvey helped him out.

The waiter delivered two frosty pilsners. "Chicago," he corrected."

"No, I believe I would prefer the wiener schnitzel, the *Holstein* anchovies sound interesting." Pinfield, looked up with a perplexed expression to his face. "Oh, yes, I see. You are absolutely, right, my good man. Chicago is the windy city. Yes, the wiener schnitzel will be just fine, and please bring an order of the spätzle dumplings with that."

Over lunch, Harvey became mesmerized with Pinfield's rich baritone voice. He spoke with a deep timbre, aged with a lifetime of rich red wines and well-aged brandies, choosing each word decisively, fully pronouncing each, adding just the right touch to emphasize emotions and visions of grandeur things. He was a storyteller of the highest caliber, and unbeknownst to this inexperienced hat salesman a conman without peer.

They finished their lunches and an additional beer. "May

I call you Caesar?" Harvey asked thinking that it was time to get down to business.

"Good friends and family call me Augustus, and I would be honored if you would do the same."

Harvey opened his sample case.

"Oh, I do like that one," Augustus practically purred. It was a two-tone white straw fedora, and with luck it fit perfectly. There were several others he liked, but they were not in his size. Finally, he selected the two-tone white fedora, along with a summer wavy striped orangish brown fedora that he said matched one of his favorite bowties. Harvey added two dollars each above the salesman's discount, elated with his success.

"What is it that you do, Augustus?"

"I, kind sir, am an orator. I travel here and there, between various schools and institutions, and educate the young and curious about the American Presidents, along with a few of our heroes whose deeds have made this country great. And, if time allows, a song or two." *And a game of poker when the stakes are high enough,* he did not add.

"You sing?"

"Oh yes, many years ago I was asked to do a Carnegie, which sad to say I had to pass up due to the untimely passing of my father." With that the self-proclaimed scholar rose and began to sing:

Oh, mein Papa war eine wunderbare Clown.

Oh, mein Papa war eine große Kinstler.

Hoch auf die Seil, wie war er herrlich anzuschau'n!

Oh, mein Papa war eine schöne Mann.

And then in English:

Oh, my pa-pa, to me he was so wonderful

Oh, my pa-pa, to me he was so wonderful

No one could be, so gentle, and so lovable

Oh, my pa-pa, he always understood . . ."

Singing again in German, he quickly educated
Schroeder's clientele with the German language refrain.
The German song and the American song varied greatly.
When finished, he tipped his hat towards the bar and the
applause adding: "Thank you, I am most humbled by your
appreciation."

"Waiter, the check please," Augustus called out to
the waiter. "Well son, it's time to go our separate ways.
Another day in the city, then Santa Barbara, I think. I am
a simple man with simple tastes. Alas, the big city is too
noisy for me, the never-ending traffic, sirens in the middle
of the night, can't sleep a wink.

"Have I got just the place for you, a nice quiet boarding
house called The Bayview House in Sausalito. I have a
room there myself."

"Do you now?"

Caesar Augustus Pinfield promised that he would pay
a visit to the Bayview the next day. The checks arrived.
Augustus feigned reaching for his wallet. Harvey was faster

on the draw saying that he would not have a good customer like him paying for his own beers.

The two said good-by. When the waiter brought back the change Harvey found that the two lunches and four beers had just cost him $1.35 more than he had charged Augustus for the two hats.

Augustus eyed the street for an available cab humming as he did so:

Oh, my pa-pa, he drove my mother mad

Oh, my pa-pa he stole everything I had,

Oh, my pa-pa, he beat me unmercifully

Oh, my pa-pa, may he rot in hell,

There was no mirth in his eyes as he spoke the last words aloud, "as he rots in Hell!"

"Taxi!" He dropped the extra hat, scooping it up as he ducked into the cab.

Harvey had planned on sleeping in his car that night, but for some reason he just couldn't sleep. He realized too late that he had not charged the recommended retail price, stupid for him, good deal for Augustus. He had never met a man quite like Caesar Augustus Pinfield, and already admired him greatly. He wondered if the great man would keep his promise to ask about a room at The Bayview House. As a child, Harvey had worshipped his father's every move – just wanting a little recognition – and love he never got. Augustus's voice and the song played on in his troubled dreams as wisps of fog stole what heat remained in his car.

Chapter Fourteen

Scotty and Doyle were having a grand day. Smokestack had picked five pockets giving them enough cash to dine and drink like kings without a worry in the world. Compared to Sausalito, Monterey was a breath of fresh air. Why they were wasting time running a small-time protection racket protecting down and out businesses was a question they were clearly asking themselves.

Patrick Doyle had to admit that Monterey was a more interesting place than Sausalito. It was a bustling fishing port that had been taken over by the 7th Infantry Division, U.S. Army, Fort Ord. Just over the hill the towns of Pacific Grove, Carmel, and Pebble Beach, land of millionaires and movie stars. Neither Scotty, Doyle, nor Smokestack had ever played a game of golf, let alone chased a little white ball around acres of well-maintained grass and mansions that modestly spoke of true wealth. They quit after six holes on the golf course at Del Monte Lodge, quite aware of the fact that they had made fools of themselves while holding back experienced golfers who had waited almost an hour for the two stooges to give it up. The third stooge – Smokestack - cased the men's locker-room and several guest suites while following the maid service in quest of an easy buck.

Doyle returned to the lodge in a murderous rage where he threatened the head-waiter at the clubhouse after being refused service because they were not dressed appropriately. They took a seat in the bar where afternoon dress was more relaxed. Doyle's grin took a vacation, replaced by a dark somber expression as he smoked five cigarettes mixed with two scotches straight up. Scotty smoked one cigarette while he waited for his boss to explode. What he did not know was that Doyle was thinking.

Smokestack returned, begging to tell his boss of his triumph. Instead he sat on the far side of the bar drinking a beer while waiting for Doyle to smile again. When he did, Smokestack caught Scotty's nod and went to get the car.

They returned an hour and a half later having been liberated of some three hundred eighty-five dollars they had spent at the Viennese, an upper-class men's clothier, located in the swanky Seven Arts Building in Carmel. This time the headwaiter kowtowed and strutted his stuff when he saw what they were wearing.

"You done good Smokestack, you done good." Doyle praised as their orders of steak Oscar and champagne arrived. The young thief had stolen several thousand dollars. The police had been called, but the three well-healed hoods were not considered suspects.

After lunch they wandered through the lodge enjoying

the show as police tried to calm all the *Daddy Warbucks* who had just been robbed. "An ocean of money flows through this place, Scotty, an ocean of money," Doyle said, sated from their rich lunch, while sticking a match to an El Rey Del Mundo cigar, chosen by Doyle because it was what the power brokers around them puffed and sucked away on.

They stopped to look at a schedule of events posted near the concierge desk. Most of the events were centered around the Second Annual Concours de Elegance to be held there at the Del Monte Lodge. The event, sponsored by the Sports Car Club of America, exulted that some of the most distinguished sports cars in America, will compete Sunday afternoon, August 11, in the Second Annual Pebble Beach Road Race. The cars would be available for viewing Saturday and Sunday at the practice tee and driving range near The Club House adjacent to the main lodge. Pictures of the prior year's race winner, a *1950 Jaguar XXX120*, along with the winner of the Best of Show, *a Stub Edwards R-26 Special Sports Roadster*, custom made and named after the owner, were framed and posted nearby, as well as numerous photos of sports cars, and celebrities abounding.

Doyle let out a long appreciative whistle. "Yes, Sir, an ocean of money flows through this place." He looked at Scotty. "Are you ready for the biggest hit of your screwed-up life?"

Scotty looked confused but knew to agree with his boss no matter how cockeyed his scheme might sound. "Scotty, call Hector and Smitty. I want them here as soon as Smokestack can drive back and get them. The moment they're here I want them to be fitted for these great monkey suits we just paid for. No, that's the wrong picture. Stop off in San Francisco and find a place that offers some of those Ivy League sweaters and sports jackets – I hear that Stanford is big around here." He motioned for Scotty to take a seat at a small table near the putting green. Smokestack; to wait by the *Woodie*. We're going to need two cars, look around this place and see what people are driving, then swipe one in Frisco. Change license plates in Santa Cruz. Drive through Stanford University, its somewhere near Frisco, and swipe what a young and upcoming rich kid drives; that's for the boys, everyone's got to fit in. Switch the license plates somewhere in Monterey. Stash the Woodie somewhere in Santa Cruz where we can retrieve it later. Meanwhile, I'm going to book us a couple of rooms."

Scotty spotted a phone booth. "I'll call the boys and give them a heads-up. Boss, can I ask?"

"I don't have it all worked out yet, but we're going to rob the casino."

"Boss, there's no casino here, maybe a card game somewhere, but no casino."

"The crowd that is going to be here this weekend will have their checkbooks out needing plenty of cash for everything this place has to offer. There is no bank, that makes the front desk the place where all the heavies will be looking for rolls of bills to mark their self-importance. There is a casino, all right. While you and I take the front desk, the boys will pick some of the deepest pockets you have ever seen. Oh, I almost forgot, when you get hold of Smitty and Hector tell them to come packing."

"Guns? You're kidding, right?" Scotty knew that Doyle traditionally stayed away from guns. He wasn't afraid of guns, preferring knives or his faithful baseball bat - no qualms about murder, it was just a thing he had after the war.

"The guns are for you and me. You don't think we're going to take down the front desk with a martini glass in your hand, do yeah?" He slapped Scotty reassuringly on the back. "Make the call, then meet me at the concierge desk."

He reached into his pants pocket, and pulled out a roll of bills, peeling off a dozen hundred-dollar bills. "Come to think of it, you had better go with Smokestack, we can't afford for any of the boys to screw things up."

Chapter Fifteen

"I'd like a pot of tea, please." Sarah Brandt asked, "with a spot of cream, if it's not too much trouble." Sarah had appeared in the doorway between the kitchen and the dining room. She had taken her meals in her room since her clash with Michael and Mollie and had not been seen otherwise. Everyone expected her next appearance to be an ambush of retribution for her humiliation in a personality war of her own creation.

Sarah now wore a pleasant, rose colored evening dress, topped with a flower bonnet indicating that she might be going out for the evening – which she never did – which made her dress, along with her unusual politeness more unnerving.

"What kind?" Renata asked, her tone of voice none too polite."

"Earl Gray would be lovely. With two cups, sugar, and cream on the side. I'll be taking it in the parlor – the dining room, I mean." She smiled and started to turn, and then turned back as if she had forgotten something. "Has anyone seen Mr. Freed around?"

"Harvey started a new job last Monday. Some sort of sales job, men's hats I believe." Michelangelo answered. "I suspect that he will be doing a great deal of traveling"

"Oh, I see." Her smile did not quite cover the look of scorn that crossed her face. "I'll be in the dining room."

All three were relieved that neither Michael or Mollie had come into the room while Sarah had been there. There was still a great deal of anger in the house, and it would be a long time before the storm blew over.

Renata eyed the box of rat poison on an upper shelf as she set the kettle on the stove. Michelangelo waved a finger uttering a humorous tsk-tsk. You wouldn't want to offend the rats, now would you?"

"A gentleman caller?" Betty pondered. "Not in this life time."

"I've got to admit, I'm as curious as a cat at a mouse hole.

"We have no mice, no rats either," Betty protested. She would have put down her foot if she could have reached the floor.

"There's one large rat in the dining room." Renata said as she mischievously reached for the box of rat poison. She couldn't reach it without a step stool. The intent was enough to bring a chuckle to Michelangelo as he struck a match to the bowl of his pipe.

There was a knock on the door.

Renata answered.

A dour little man, wearing a dark gray coat, white shirt with a dull red tie, tipped his hat, exposing his mostly bald head, offered his card as Renata answered.

"I'm looking for a Ms. Sarah Brandt, I believe she is expecting me."

Renata took the card. "She is in the parlor, Mr. Bixby. Right this way." The gentleman offered his hat. Renata did not take it. After showing him to the dining room, pulling the door shut behind her, she returned to the kitchen reading the card aloud for all to hear: "Quinton U. Bixby, Funeral Director, Specializing in fine caskets and Plots worthy of Eternity."

The tea kettle whistled. Renata's eyebrows rose while a smile crossed her lips. "There is always hope."

Sarah Brandt conducted her business behind closed doors, their voices bordering on conspiratorial whispers. Bixby understood that if he broke their contract, their secret prematurely by anyone, regardless of circumstances, he would forfeit her business, and perhaps face some legal actions brought on by her lawyer, J.Fisher, Esquire.

Bixby did not like Ms. Brandt, but business being what it was in Sausalito, left him little choice but to sign the papers which to his surprise had already been prepared by her attorney.

Chapter Fifteen

Friday morning, Augustus checked out of his hotel and waved down a cab for a short exploratory trip to Sausalito. He had thought about it and the idea of renting a room for a few weeks across from the city while he wormed his way into a few plush card games appealed to him.

That was until he saw the headlines in the morning Chronicle where all the gossip was about the up-coming sports car race in Pebble Beach. As a card player and an amateur magician, lifting an occasional wallet often came in handy when he needed a stake for a high-roller card game. With a glint to his eyes, he rented a car and located Pebble Beach on the map. That many golf courses, he determined, always attracted foolish men with fat wallets and little awareness to their vulnerabilities. Better yet, foolish widows. While he had never been to Pebble Beach before he knew that in this paradise even the seagulls were monied.

He hummed as he drove. This would need to be a quick

hit and run. There would be no time to get to *know the right people.* Most likely there would be no hotel rooms from which to operate out of. He would have Friday night and Saturday night to work the cards. That would mean no limit, high risk. Because of the race, auctions, etcetera, the players would come and go, few if any dusk to dawn players. Under those conditions players are more likely to fold after losing a couple of large hands. He would have to do the same without drawing suspicion. Ideally, if he could find three good games he could bounce back and forth. The first thing he needed to do once he reached the resort is find out where the caddies hung out, they always knew where the games were. No, the first thing he need to do is mingle, while allocating a few thick wallets for a stake. He suspected that ten thousand dollars would be needed for a seat at the table. Pretty rich stakes, but oh, what a payday

Chapter Sixteen

Michelangelo had little money.

What he did have were plenty of friends, and former parishioners, who would do almost anything in the world for him. He had thought about how he could help his new family who had been more than kind to him - of course there were those who never raised a finger to help another. While Oswaldo, Mollie and Michael were busy with the move, he made a phone call: "Jacob, Michelangelo here."

"Father Palazzeschi, I heard that you had left town when the Parish closed. What can I do for you?"

"It just plain Michelangelo these days," he said. "I'm not calling on behalf of the church. I have a friend who needs a favor and for this favor I thought of you."

"Sure, sure, Father, for you anything."

Jacob Ritter had faithfully kept the parish organ in perfect tune for years. Retired, he often supplemented his meager income by going to schools, theaters, and music halls fixing and tuning various musical instruments for whatever they were willing to pay him. He had a magic touch in turning old horns and such away from the junk yard and back into things of beauty.

He lived in Sausalito not that far away and agreed to come by that afternoon to see what could be done to fix Michael's saxophone. "So, his is the music I have heard for so many nights from my bedroom window. Your friend is very good. I will do what I can, no charge, except for one thing. . . he must continue to play his wonderful night music."

That afternoon, just after supper, there was a knock on the kitchen door. Betty answered, expecting Jacob Ritter. With Sarah no longer taking her meals in the dining room, Scotty, Doyle, and Harvey often absent, meals were served in the kitchen. Mollie hurried with the dishes anxious to return to their new attic apartment to help Michael. With Michael's recent discoveries with the joy of sex, she was planning on an early evening – with the entry to their new apartment so daunting, privacy was almost a given. Oswaldo was trimming some rope at the small kitchen table. Michelangelo puffed on his pipe as he waited patiently for Jacob's return.

Everyone's eyes immediately darted to Mollie at the first knock. Everyone but Mollie knew of the gift that Jacob brought. Jacob took off his hat as he stepped in the door-way. In his hands was a bright, shiny copper colored tenor saxophone, looking as good as new.

"No? It can't be." Then, come to think of it she hadn't seen nor thought about it during their move. "Is that

Michael's?"

"Yes," Michelangelo said. "Jacob, here, had some spare time so he offered to look at Michael's saxophone. Mollie, this is my good friend Jacob Ritter."

"Mollie, so nice to meet you. Here, your husband's saxophone had suffered a dent or two, and was missing a valve, which I fortunately had a spare. Mostly it needed a good cleaning. It should sound as if it were new. He will know when he plays it. Where is this wonderful musician of yours?" He glanced around the room when no one stepped forward. "Neighbors have asked why the music has stopped. It started so mysteriously, no one knew where it was coming from. Soon we were all sitting on our porches or by opened windows listening . . . and then it stopped. The whole neighborhood, we all are anxious for it to return."

He held it out to Mollie.

Tears flowed down Mollie's cheeks as she took the saxophone and gave Jacob such a thank you kiss it made him blush. "Michael," she started to call, then remembered that he most likely could not hear her from the attic.

Oswaldo spoke: "You go to Michael. I will put this in the basket. Tell Michael that there is a blanket in the basket to keep you warm tonight." Oswaldo took the rope, a blanket, and the saxophone towards the back of the house where the pully-system waited.

Mollie turned towards Jacob threatening him with another kiss. "Right now, I only have a little change, but I can pay you over . . ."

"You will pay me nothing, dear lady. It is Michael who will pay." His smile was large, and honest, showing the gap where one front tooth was missing. "As I walk home I would very much like to hear his music. I like it very much."

Mollie grabbed her skirt, practically flying up the stairs.

Michelangelo smiled, holding out both hands as he sat in his chair. His legs itched beneath their casts, and his buns hurt from sitting, and sitting, and sitting. "Thank you, Mr. Ritter, you have done a wonderful thing. Can you stay, share a glass of wine with us, please?"

"Jacob, please."

Renata already had the glasses out.

Ritter took a small glass of red wine, as he pointed a finger up. "When I hear his music, then it will be time to go, our neighbors will be gathering to listen." His slight laugh showed a touch of embarrassment. "I can't keep a secret."

Under Oswaldo's tutelage Michael was finding out that he had a natural talent for carpentry. He enjoyed working with his hands and was already thinking that in time it might become a means to earn a living. When Mollie came in through the window, his attention was fully on the floor to the closet where he was carefully sawing out the floor as Oswaldo had marked it. Their plan was to insert a narrow, somewhat steep set of stairs that could be raised or lowered on two rope pullies. With his head in the small enclosure and the rasp of the saw the loudest sound, he did not hear her come in. On tip-toes she went to the windows at the back of the room and quietly raised the basket with the creak of the pully sounding dreadfully loud as she kept her eyes on Michael, the rasp of the saw louder than the pully.

Michael's saxophone in hand, she snuck back out onto their small patio and sat in Michael's chair. She had tried to play the saxophone once before only to produce a sound that was a cross between a horn on a sputtering Model-T Ford and an angry goose the old car was chasing. Embarrassed and mortified she had sworn at the time that her lips would never touch his horn again.

She broke the promise.

Michael almost pushed through the partially sawed floor, the saw still vibrating where it had been left in the saw line as he crawled back out of the closet. In the closet he had not recognized the horrendous noise.

Then, she did it again.

"What? Mollie?" He turned towards the window quite at a loss as to why his wife was attempting to play his damaged saxophone. At first sight he saw that his horn was no longer damaged, appearing almost new.

Grateful that she would not have to attempt another breath into the squawking goose, she held the magical horn up to her wide-eyed husband. "Please, play something for me." As he took the horn from her, she rose from the chair whispering with passionate joy, "and for Sausalito."

Hands in his pockets, eyes smiling, Jacob sauntered

home where neighbors were already gathering to listen.

Sarah, sitting alone in her room, poured herself a second bourbon over ice as she pondered her decision. There were moments when she had second thoughts, the most recent when she went to the kitchen to fill her small ice bucket. She couldn't remember when she had started to shut herself out, to want to be alone – when she had stopped liking people. She had a son who she had pushed away as a child sending him to boarding schools, including summers, rarely visiting him, or allowing him to come home for the holidays. As his mother, she had signed the permission papers for him to join the Navy underage. Then there had been embarrassing visits by the shore patrol wanting to know if she had seen or heard from him. Marty had deserted, and in time of war that carried a terrible penalty. They watched her at the shipyard where she worked, asking questions of her neighbors. She was embarrassed and angry. With the neighbors knowing that she was the mother of a coward and a deserter, she had moved to the Bayview House where all she wanted to be was left alone; there was another reason she dared not speak of.

One day she received a letter that her son Marty Brandt was missing in action and considered to be deceased. She did not make any inquiries regarding the truth. When asked she told people that he had been killed in a jeep accident a few days before Pearl Harbor. In time she began to believe it herself.

Over the last few weeks, things had changed at the Bayview House. Instead of a house full of tenants just passing through there seemed to be a sense of community. People gathered to just chat; there was laughter, and there was music. The thought that it had all started when Michael and Mollie arrived she hadn't clicked on, especially since they were her primary focus for revenge. To not be included only made her more resentful.

Michael started with *Sweet Lorraine*, moving emotionally to *A Kiss to Build a Dream On, Tennessee Waltz, Kisses Sweeter Than Wine,* and on and on until the listeners around Sausalito surrendered one by one to a good night's sleep aided by Michael's night music.

Mollie fell asleep in the window sill until her husband played the last note, then, feeling some pressure in his healing wrist, he carried her somewhat awkwardly up to their loft's feather bed.

Chapter Seventeen

The concierge was quick to confirm that there were
no rooms to be had at the Del Monte Lodge or any other
reputable hotel on the greater Monterey Peninsula. A line
had built behind Doyle, expecting that the mere mention
of their name and pedigree would secure for them that
room that did not exist. He stood aside pretending to
thumb through a notebook as he discreetly listened for an
opportunity. The front desk was likewise busy; those with
the means to not have to check-in, only had to go to the
concierge for their key, who quickly snapped his fingers to
notify a bell-hop that a premiere guest had just arrived.

Liam, the concierge, said to the couple waiting patiently
behind Doyle "Mr. and Mrs. Eichendorff, a pleasure to see
you as always." His Irish brogue, well-rehearsed, melted
every woman's heart, while confirming to the husband that
all was right with the world – *"Tis ah wonderful world. tis
it not?"* The last time he had checked in Mr. Eichendorff,
less than two weeks prior, the young woman with him had
not been his wife. He briefly covered his mouth feigning a

slight cough. "I'm afraid that our Spyglass II Guest House is not available. There is a problem with the water heater which unfortunately cannot be fixed until the first of next week. We always keep one suite here in the lodge available for just this kind of emergency; otherwise, the weekend being what it is, all our accommodations are full."

"Oh dear," whined his wife, "I don't mind moving to a smaller room, but we are planning a fairly large gathering for cocktails Saturday evening. Whatever are we to do?"

The concierge smiled. The couple were frequent quests and known for their gatherings. "Yes ma'am, we have anticipated that you might have numerous friends among our guests and we have set aside our Twin Pines Room for your use. How many do you anticipate attending, Sir?"

Relieved, the wife answered, looking at her husband for confirmation. "Twenty-five, thirty perhaps."

"Very good. I'll have Sid, our bellhop, show you to your room. Miss. Janet Smith, our Guest Hospitality Manager, will be calling you shorty regarding your specific needs for Saturday."He snapped his finger at Sidney, a handsome nineteen-year-old with feathery blond hair who was already handling their bags.

Without any change in facial expression the concierge accepted the generous tip the now placated guest slipped into his palm. "Sid, on the way back please attach a note to the door on Spyglass II that the guest house is closed until next week."

Collecting a small overnight bag, that he had entrusted to the front desk, Doyle asked a waiter in the patio bar which direction their Spyglass 1 guest house would be. He guessed that the second guest house would be nearby. He ordered a Guinness and waited until he saw Sidney the bellhop return.

While waiting he felt his nervous tic start to return, along with some familiar stomach distress. He had to tell himself that he needed to be calm. He had never had an opportunity like this to score big enough to change everything. He watched the fat-cats around him - so secure, so complacent with their way of life. Closing his right fist tight enough for a fingernail to draw blood, he let the pain draw his fear away. After a moment he wiped the blood on a napkin, folded it so the stain would not draw any attention. Finishing his beer, he smiled. *Time to check out my accommodations.*

The guest house, one of four located off the sixteenth green, was easy to find. It was Mediterranean in style, pink – not a color Doyle was partial to, but nevertheless pleasing to the eye. The front patio, large and accommodating, decorated with new outdoor furniture, was open, allowing for an extensive view of the sixteenth hole and the seventeenth tee. A neat, hand-written note hung on the front door stating that the house was closed for remodeling. Interior lights had been left on. On a quick trip around the house, he discovered that there was no driveway – this would be a problem. The path he had come on allowed for access either by foot or service cart. Well-maintained hedges mixed with a line of cypress trees insured privacy between the guest houses. The one to the right had the same Mediterranean look, but was painted white, the one to the left Cypress III, yellow. The fourth unit he assumed was around a bend in the path.

His biggest concern would be foot traffic - only the concierge, Sidney and the maintenance crew knew that the guest house was not supposed to be occupied. The downside, no hot water.

"There's my four-leaf clover," he chuckled as the sliding glass door in the rear slid open; it had been left unlocked. The house had four bedrooms, with three and a half baths. With the curtains drawn no one on the outside would know if someone was there. Taking a moment to refresh himself and shave, he made a mental note that he needed to buy a nice golf shirt or two at the golf shop. Leaving the notice on the front door; he left it unlocked, then walked back towards the lodge with a self-confident stride that suggested that he was monied and where he belonged. Stopping to ask for a light, and short conversation about the sports cars, he lifted the gentleman's wallet, adding $437.00 to his bankroll. He had not noticed that the nervous tick in his left cheek had almost disappeared. While he still had a slight limp, he hadn't felt this fit in some time.

After a brief viewing of some of the sports cars parked on the practice green he visited the golf shop purchasing two sport shirts. He wore the bright coral-rose colored one, as he continued to explore the property.

Another four-leaf clover.

He whistled to himself as he approached a building set off the parking lot. A sign said that it was their voluntary firehouse, which was small, with room for one pumper truck if parked out front. The pumper truck was being hand washed by two volunteer firemen. "Gentlemen, beautiful day isn't it?" The discovery of the firehouse couldn't have met his needs better. He spent the next few minutes asking harmless questions, gathering valuable information, each answer putting together an easy jigsaw puzzle.

Chapter Eighteen

Harvey swore as he watched his gas tank waver on empty, the car in front of him idling patiently for someone to vacate a rare parking space. There were seven shops in Carmel that sold men's hats and other apparel; dismayingly there appeared to be a dozen expensive cars for every parking space. He punched his horn impatiently, only for the driver to politely wave him around. *Sorry pal, this parking space is mine.* Then, after a quick view in the mirror came the snub: *I didn't think they allowed junk-heaps like that in Carmel.* One thing that Harvey noticed in his forty minutes in search of parking was that he had not seen a gas station.

A City of Carmel, *Proudly We Serve* marked police car slowed to a stop directly across in the opposite traffic lane. The officer gave him a look, like a cat ogling a fear-shaken mouse, that impounding his car for vagrancy would make his day, while the car in front proudly seized the prized parking space.

"Olly olly oxen free, there is no safe place for me." Harvey watched his safe spot the highly prized parking space vanish with a last gasp of exhaust in his face. As a cat will raise its rear and flip its tail a second before it strikes, he could almost imagine the cop wagging his butt as he reached for his ticket book. *Do I have enough gas to get back to Monterey?* Harvey thought, looking guilty as hell at the gas gauge. His car sputtered its answer as it struggled with what few drops of fuel remained, falling obscenely silent. The policeman turned on his overhead lights as their two cars blocked both directions of traffic on Carmel's busiest street on one of the busiest weekends of the summer season.

The officer leaned in towards where Harvey sat impotently behind the steering wheel. "License and registration?" A bad day just got worse as the officer practically licked his lips as he looked at Harvey's driver's license; it was expired.

J. Thomas. That was the name on the officer's badge. *Damn you to hell, J. Thomas, if you had any humanity, any pity, you would have taken out your gun and shot me.* Harvey stood on the street corner and watched as the tow truck impounded his car for vagrancy. It might as well of been the junk yard - it wasn't going to bail itself out. All he had was three bucks in his pocket. He checked his pants pocket. "Crap!" Everyone on the street stared at him as he vent his anger – helplessly.

J. Thomas did not look amused.

Harvey had put his money, mostly change, in an empty coffee cup when he slept in the car last night, so it wouldn't slip from his pocket into the crack between the seats.

"One more outburst like that and I'll be handing you more than a ticket." The ticket for the expired driver's license, seven dollars and fifty cents; might as well of been a hundred. He wouldn't be able to get it renewed until the DMV opened on Monday, which wouldn't do him much good because he lived in Sausalito and had no other form of identification. Without a proper driver's license, and twenty dollars a day, plus towing, and don't forget the gas, he wouldn't be able to bail his car out of impound.

He was stranded.

All he had was his suitcase full of hats. Without thought as to where he was going he followed the crowd down the hill towards the beach. At the bottom of the hill the road split; one into a parking lot that was full, the other towards a security gate where there was a guard's shack and a sign, 'Welcome to Pebble Beach.' A double-decker tourist bus idled by a second sign: *17 Mile Drive.*

He just stood there, suitcase in hand, and stared at the bus.

"Yes, ma'am, the shuttle will take you to the lodge. If you have a reservation, no charge, otherwise the fare will be 25 cents. The last returning shuttle will leave the lodge at nine this evening. The parking lot at the lodge is full. I'm sorry to say that this is your only option." That's all Harvey needed to hear. He did not have the 25 cents, hell, he didn't have a car. He walked towards the gate where a uniformed guard stepped in his way. "Sorry, no pedestrians allowed. You'll have to take the shuttle."

Harvey did not say a word, which one could he choose?

He did not know why he needed to get to the lodge, he had never heard of it before. He had been handed a big *Not Welcome* card in Carmel and felt like a blind man with his hat on the sidewalk with no pencils to sell. Everyone was someone in Carmel accept him, and these rich *somebodies* were all headed towards this no-name lodge. Maybe destiny was going to play a dirty joke on him. Maybe not, but at this lowest point in his life he had to find out. He walked towards the parking lot, then down onto the beach. In the distance he could see a golf course and an expensive looking lodge sitting on a grassy knoll facing the sparkling surf of Carmel Bay. *It's not that far,* he told himself, though the sand made each step harder. *I've got to sell these hats. I'm homeless and don't have a person I can call for help.* The wind picked up like a bully kicking sand in his face.

Parking at Carmel Beach was open and free to the public, except for special events, then it was first come – first served for the shuttle to the Del Monte Lodge. There was no parking anywhere on the 17 Mile Drive nor sightseeing on Saturday. Parking at the lodge was strictly valet for premier and celebrity guests Friday through Monday until five o'clock in the afternoon.

Augustus' luck was running like a star quarterback when a stretch limousine was booted from the beach parking because of its size. There had been a car in front of him, but when the limo backed out it was forced to the side where it crowded a row of parked cars by a fraction of an inch. Determined not to lose the soon-to-be-opened spot, Augustus willingly risked a small dent to the rear passenger door to his rental car. It took exercised diplomacy to keep the losing driver from doing more than nick the door. Having won the prize, Augustus managed to avoid eye contact with his competitor. With a small overnight bag in hand he boarded the shuttle.

Neither Augustus nor Harvey had seen the other.

Chapter Nineteen

Sergeant Ralph Schmidt held his Cheshire Cat grin as patrolman Tse entered the office with a small steaming paper bowl of Chinese dumplings in his hand. The cat left the room as soon as Schmidt smelled the fragrant pastas. "God, no wonder you people are yellow eating crap like that." Tse pulled a second set of chopsticks from a pocket offering them, his own grin present.

Schmidt took his pistol from its shoulder holster, held it thoughtfully for a second, then placed it within easy reach on his desk.

Two detectives observed from across the room. "Mexican stand-off," one commented. "You think," the other replied.

Schmidt offered them a middle finger.

"Getting a bit cocky these days." One of the detectives responded with a polite nod to Schmidt. "Me, I've got my money on the chink." The other replied.

Quickly chewing and swallowing a dumpling, Tse placed the remaining dumplings on a shelf out of Schmidt's way.

"You've got something?" Tse asked hopefully.

"A witness in an all-night laundromat half a block away identified a late 1930's Ford Woody Station Wagon as being near the alley when the old Russian guy was killed. Whoever killed the old man might have run to the station wagon when Hua opened the alley door. No make on the driver or any suspects."

"That's not much to go on."

"Vehicle records show that there are eight possible make and model Woody Station Wagons in San Francisco. Four in Berkeley, and one in Sausalito."

"And anyone just driving through. At least it's something. Anything on the license number?" Tse asked.

"No, only that the Woody had some paneling missing, a fixer-upper."

"That's a start." Tse picked up the dumplings, quickly popping one into his mouth.

Schmidt patted his pistol as if it were a sleeping cat.

"Schmidt get in here". Captain Stancy bellowed.

Chapter Twenty

Augustus' first point of business was at the front
desk. But not before he went out of his way to pass a room
service cart where he dropped off a woman's billfold he
had discreetly acquired on the shuttle, her purse conveniently open. Women loved to shop on excursions like this,
preferring not to bother their husbands with the details of
what they spent – thus Augustus preferred an open purse to
seed his own needs.

The front desk was busy, mostly people cashing checks,
but not as busy as the concierge desk where Liam –
Augustus made a mental note of his name from his name
tag – was happily accepting healthy gratuities to deliver the
same news to all. "It's a sad day, but I regret to inform you
that the lodge has been booked out for months, and there
is wee chance of finding anything in Carmel. I'll be glad to
make a few calls to see what I might find, but I wouldn't
be counting on anything." The unspoken truth was that he
was too busy to make any calls, and by the time anyone
checked back he would be off duty, leaving the regrets and

apologies to Richard, the night concierge.

Augustus knew exactly what to do when his turn came up at the front desk.

"Yes, Sir, how can I be of service." The night manager's name tag read *Gregory*.

"Yes, busy place, what fun." Augustus mopped his brow with a handkerchief feigning that he had already had a long and taxing day. "Admiral Stanton Hemphill, Her Majesty's Royal Navy, recently retired. I have a reservation, seven nights I believe." He used Admiral Hemphill as an alias because no one wanted to embarrass a high ranking foreign officer; a most regrettable foreign incident. If there was a problem, it usually went to someone in upper management bypassing concierges and middle management types who had no real authority. He looked around as if expecting nothing short of the best service and to be shown to his accommodation immediately.

Gregory thumbed through the register, quickly developing a painful 'oh dear' look on his face as he picked up the phone. The Admiral noted the immediate ring on the phone at the concierge's desk. There were now two faces for the worry.

The Admiral did not have a reservation. How could he, he didn't exist. That was all part of the con.

"I'm sorry, Admiral Hemphill," Gregory looked again in the registry confirming that he wasn't mistaken, I have no reservation for you."

"Bloody hell, this won't do, not at all," he said, taking

on an indignant posture. "See here now, I've just flown in from Whitehall, my reservation was made by – let's see, I have it here somewhere," he said, taking out a notebook. "The reservation was made from the Admiralty. I just retired and have flown all this way to see my daughter." He raised his eyebrows. "She married a Yank, but that's our little secret," he twittered, the humor forcing the Night Manager to de-escalate the situation.

The concierge quickly stepped to the front desk and pulled the Night Manager into a quick whispering embrace. A moment later Gregory turned back to their troubled guest. "Admiral Hemphill, this is our busiest weekend of year. I don't know what has happened to your reservation. There is one thing we can do. We have a guest house, which is currently down for maintenance. No hot water, you see. If you can manage the water situation until Monday, we will be able to move you to accommodations a man of your stature should have; of course, your temporary accommodation will be on the house."

"Over my many years at sea I have managed many a shower that shall we say, were briskly refreshing."

"Wonderful: Gregory beamed. "I'll have housekeeping check on the Spyglass II Guest House to see if it is guest ready. The bellhop will tend to your luggage. Please let us know if we can do anything to make your stay more pleasant. We could perhaps provide you with a cart and driver for the race tomorrow?"

"My luggage is somewhere between your Monterey Airfield, and Toronto, I'm afraid. I'm told that they will deliver it here sometime this evening. My car is stranded in your Carmel beachside parking. Your gatekeeper could not find my reservation, so I was forced to take the shuttle. I'll get back to you on the cart, thank you."

"If you will please have a seat in our Garden Bar, I'll have someone find you soon as housekeeping is done. If I might have your car keys, I'll have someone fetch your vehicle immediately."

Liam, putting on his best brogue, offered to fetch the vehicle. "I'm due to get off soon, Sidney can drive me over in a service cart. As for parking, there isn't any at your guest house, and most everything else is reserved."

Gregory interrupted. "Park it at the firehouse, I sincerely doubt that there will be any fires tonight."

The Admiral handed Liam the car keys, followed by a knowing wink. "I'd work on your accent, Liam. You might fool the Yanks, but not an officer in Her Majesties service.

Liam swallowed back his pride. "This way to the bar, Sir."This time he did not sound even remotely like an Irishman.

Doyle held court over a four-top table with a full view of the restaurant and garden bar. It had a limited view of the greens, which was fine by him. An evening breeze was drawing in what might prove to be a classic August fog bank. He was sure that there were numerous private parties throughout the popular lodge complex. He was looking to meet, share a few drinks at his table, and eventually to be invited to one of the private parties. Inclusion within

a group of wealthy patrons at the car race tomorrow was
the alibi he needed. Tonight, he might still pick a pocket
or two, but not at the risk of missing the opportunity to be
included with a group of regulars; no longer viewed as that
odd-man out, a more likely suspect for the robbery he was
still hatching in his mind.

He looked at his watch.

Right now, he was waiting for a call from Scotty. It
was paramount that Scotty and the boys got here sometime tonight, regardless of how late it was. There were
challenges, some risky. The car had to be brought to the
lodge despite the security guard at the entry-gate from
Carmel. He had studied a map of the golf course and found
a service gate near the guard shack. It was a paved service
path, designed to accommodate a service cart, a small
delivery truck, or an emergency vehicle, and weaved its
way to the back of the lodge. Unfortunately, it went right
by the driving range where the luxury sports cars were on
display. There would be security there throughout the night.
There was no parking left in the lodge's parking lot. Scotty
needed to park the car as close to the front entrance to the
lodge as possible – which it was not. That was where the
volunteer fire department building came in. There were five
reserved spots which required a posted permit. Doyle had
pocketed one when he had chatted with the fireman.

Scotty had been told to call him in the Garden Bar.
There was no other contact point. Their original plan was
for Scotty to get the car and the boys to the lodge sometime
tomorrow morning. Things had changed, now it had to be
tonight. The hit on the front desk would have to take place

in the middle of the car race – most everyone would be cheering on their favorite entry out on the 17 Mile Drive. He sipped his drink as he looked at his watch for the umpteenth time. It was time for Scotty to call.

Alfred, the headwaiter, was quickly informed that the Admiral was a First Level VIP guest and everything he needed was on the house.

The Admiral brandished the stance of the cultured class thanked Adolphus as he might excuse a servant who shouldn't idle too long in his presence. "A gin martini – Bombay Sapphire - two olives. I trust your bartender knows how to make a proper martini. I'll just take in the view while they bring my car around. That will be all, thank you." The turn of his head towards the view of the golf course dismissed him. He did not like playing pompous, but he did not want the headwaiter to become too familiar.

"Mr. Doyle, telephone." He saw a waiter bring a phone to a table on the far side of the bar.

The Admiral detected that Alfred's accent appeared to be authentic. The headwaiter he would have to be careful with. He was a professional used to working with people of influence and character. One mistake and he might start asking questions; that would just not do.

Light laughter floated across the bar, perhaps Milton Berle or Danny Kaye had entered the room. It wasn't difficult to determine the cause as the laughter spread like a wave across the bar. A young man had just run across the 18th Fairway with a large suitcase in tow, ruining what might have been a bragworthy shot for the golfer who had just teed off. "Look out you, ignorant fool. Four! Four!"

The ball missed the Harvey by a few inches causing him to throw himself comically to the ground, his suitcase flying up, then crashing down. The lid popped open, releasing an assortment of hats which immediately caught in the wind, riding the playful breezes back towards the edge of the course and Carmel Bay where the ignorant fool had come from.

Augustus – Admiral Hemphill – couldn't help but laugh. Sadly, sometimes life's follies are laughable even when they bring unbearable pain to the one who has suffered it. In this case the 'fool' was the unfortunate hat salesman he had shared lunch with at Schroeder's in San Francisco. He felt guilty for having conned him out of their lunch fare. Grass stains now marked his knees and elbows as he ran, limping, towards the clubhouse.

Trying to remember his name, Augustus waved him over, cautioning himself to be careful, remembering that the salesman had a nasty habit of talking incessantly, often saying something no matter how idiotic, just to fill the blessed sounds of silence. Dare he risk letting him in on the con?"Here, here, lad, you have suffered a most unfortunate turn of events." As Harvey meekly approached the table, grateful for the save, so did the headwaiter. "I'll explain later, for the moment just go along with whatever I say." He urgently whispered as he pointed towards a chair.

While the laughter had mostly stopped, the room was quiet as everyone waited for the show where the headwaiter dealt with the riff-raff who had made a run across the fairway, leaving his broken luggage behind, along with multiple hats, fleeing like rabbits as the golfer rightfully claimed another shot.

"You there," Alfred waved his fingers menacingly at Harvey to rise from the table. He waved another hand towards the driving range where a security guard watching over the exclusive sports cars now hurried in their direction. One of the bartenders stepped out from behind the bar rapping a miniature bat in the palm of his hand as he moved to block the intruder's flight.

"Caution, lad. Sometimes, Daddy Warbucks', have mean-streaks hidden behind the olive in their fourth martini. They have no heart for fools and their second cousins." Wide-eyed, and quite confused, Harvey looked at Augustus for protection, and would have crawled up on his lap like a beaten puppy for sheltering if he could have.

"Admiral Hemphill, I do apologize for this most unfortunate incident. We will have this *person"* – the word *person* was long and drawn-out spoken in such a way as to indicate that no one really thought of him as being human, "removed and will see that you are not bothered again."

Those nearby heard the title Admiral, and hearing his accent, became more than curious. *A British Admiral, what delightful war stories he must have. All that daring do.* Heroes are always sought after in the best of social circles.

Augustus, giving Harvey a cautionary wink, fell immediately into his chosen Thespian role. "Tut tut, gentlemen. I have been expecting this young man. Though Harvey, I think your entrance was a wee bit dramatic. Gentlemen, this is Harvey Freed, son of one Walter Freed, an American war hero I had the privilege of meeting during the historic Dunkirk evacuations. Though only a boy, Harvey here assisted his papa on four trips back to that damned beach to rescue our lads. On the fourth run a Messerschmitt shot the hell out of their boat, killing two of our brave lads, while mortally wounding his father. Sadly, I was only there for the last few moments of Walter Freed's life as they tied-up one last time on British soil. I promised to see that the boy got back to the States to his mama." He reached over and gave Harvey at pat on his hand. "I sent him a telegraph that I would be here."

"Very good, Sir." The headwaiter and the waiter with the bat backed off.

The Admiral could see that they were still uncomfortable with Harvey's wardrobe. "You must have quite the story as to how you came to be here by foot, and those clothes - we'll have to do something about those. What time does your golf shop close?"

Alfred looked at his watch. "right about now, Sir."

"No, it isn't. Please call the shop and let them know that Harvey here is on his way, fit him out with something a proper Yank would wear, and put it on my account." He looked around the bar spotting a nicely dressed man in his early thirties wearing a men's cashmere sweater. "Something like that," he pointed out. "Run along now, and we'll sort all this out when your properly dressed."

The headwaiter motioned for Harvey to follow him.

"Waiter, two orders of your fish and chips for myself

and the lad when he returns." The well-rehearsed Admiral Hemphill finished. His eyes quickly searched the crowd, many of whom were now interested in meeting him. *Thank you, Harvey,* he thought, *you have done the old man a great service. Now if only you can play your role without ruining the whole play. In other words, keep your damned mouth shut.*

Doyle's four - leaf clovers kept in play as he finished his call with Scotty. They were still in San Francisco where they had just bought the appropriate attire at a men's store near the St. Francis Hotel. Hector had been quick on his feet taking the keys to a mint condition 1948 Bentley Mark VI Countryman, green aluminum body covered with ash trim and mahogany veneer on alloy panels. The car, rare, was on its way to Carmel. The owner, knowing of the crowded conditions at Pebble Beach, and late hour, opted for a night in Frisco with an early start in the morning. Dressed smartly, Smitty took their luggage into the hotel while Hector promised to park the prized Bentley where no scratches or harm would come to it. The owner tipped Hector two dollars for the privilege of stealing his prestige car.

They parked the W*oodie* behind an old Mausoleum in Colma – the City of the Silent, a small town whose sole business was cemeteries, where the living is outnumbered by at least one thousand to one.

Scotty thought that they could make Carmel by three in the morning. Doyle opted to meet them in Carmel at the service gate to the golf course. The service road would be hard to see in the dark. They were to turn off the car lights when they got near where he told them the entrance would be so as not to risk the attention of the night guard at the gatehouse to the 17 Mile Drive. It was going to be a long night, he just found one more four-leaf clover, now if only they would be on time. It looked like it would be foggy overnight.

Harvey was pleasantly surprised and slightly over-whelmed by the attention and personal service he had received at the golf shop. Not ten minutes before he had been both homeless and humiliated. He still did not have a dime in his pocket, nor any hats to sell for bus fare. He had paid for the hats, and would have to pay for new hats, for which he had no money, so he was also unemployed.

Now he had a benefactor - well sort of - if buying a stranger, a new set of expensive clothes defines one as a benefactor. Stranger would be the correct term here. While he had lunch a few days earlier with the man, he now had no idea who the man was. He had been told one thing at Schroeder's, but here all these high and mighty titans of industry were calling him Admiral. *Well,* he thought as he headed back to the Garden Bar, *I'm going to go with whatever the Admiral says until told differently. I'll stick close, if he'll allow me, and keep my mouth shut. Yea, right . . . me keep my mouth shut.*

The headwaiter failed to recognize Harvey, who no longer looked like an impoverished reprobate as he passed the reception desk. Normally, seats at the bar were open, but with business being as brisk as it was, seating was limited even at the bar. The headwaiter was there for a reason, and one did not get service without first greasing his palm. "Excuse me, Sir, there are others in front of you," Alfred instructed the line breaker.

The Admiral rose from his seat just enough to be seen. "That's quite all right, waiter, he's with me. Would you please see to our fish and chips? I'm feeling ravished." Referring to Alfred as a mere waiter was a subtle insult that several in the crowded bar noted. It wasn't that the head-waiter was rude or overbearing, with most he was quite charming – however, all had paid the piper for their seats at the bar. A slap on the wrist now and then reminds the servants that they are, after all, servants – even the highly compensated ones.

"Well done, lad," the artificial Admiral beamed as he welcomed him to the table. He quickly observed that his penniless dining companion had spared no expense in his selection of a Midnight Blue Herringbone Harris Tweed Jacket, with leather elbow patches, over an egg-shell white, subtle burgundy pin-stripe shirt, with gray trousers that were a bit large, but purchased right off the rack, would do.

"Now if you will follow my cue for the rest of the evening we shall both have a few dollars in our pockets when the sun rises tomorrow." One thing he did not know about Harvey was his character. *The young man was somewhat innocent. Did his mama and papa teach him to always tell the truth? Had he ever stolen a penny candy from the Five & Dime? Could he keep a straight face in a con, or would he be more of a hindrance? Put him to work tonight or buy him dinner and a bus ticket?*

It was obvious that Harvey needed to vent. He had had a tough day and was quite insecure regarding his current circumstances. Harvey told his woeful tale of the cop with no heart, the loss of his car, including what little pocket money he had, until his final humiliation on the 18th Hole and his memorable hat trick. Looking out over the golf course, there was not one hat to remind him of his brief and unsuccessful career.

"Your fish and chips, gentlemen, served English style." While served on a plate, the fish and chips were tucked into a folded newspaper doused with plenty of salt and vinegar, with a side dish of minty green peas mash. Putting the vinegar on the fish was presumptive – for which the Admiral cooed with delight. It wasn't good English vinegar, but the American version had a more powerful bite.

Harvey grimaced at his first bite of fish, the vinegar not to his liking. Neither was the Guinness the waiter brought at the Admiral's request. Beggars should not be choosy, and he was starved having not eaten anything since Schroeder's.

"Will there be anything else, gentlemen?" The Admiral smiled *no*, the waiter turning back towards the kitchen, giving the headwaiter a carefully concealed thumbs-up regarding the Admiral's care.

I've had Hollywood prima donnas easier to please than this bastard, Alfred thought as he turned towards an eager patron waiting to be seated. The handsome, yet rotund man with a gorgeous brunette twenty-years his age in tow, tucked a two-dollar bill into his palm. Pocketing the bill Alfred looked at his list, sighing Mr. . . ."

"Burrell, Mr. and Mrs. Thaddeus Burrell."

"Mr. Burrell," he wrote the name down. "It appears that there is still at least a thirty-minute wait."

"Nothing sooner?"

"Are there any seats at the bar while we wait?

"I'm afraid not Sir. I'll have a waiter find you and Mr. Burrell in the waiting area.

Burrell reached in to his pocket finding a five dollar bill this time.

"That won't be necessary, Sir. We are doing the best we can."

Those waiting gave the Burrell's a weak smile. The main dining room had been reserved for weeks. The Garden Bar was their only option with patience their appetizer.

Augustus took in everything Harvey had said. Indeed, he had had one miserable rotten day. He was stranded in an almost hopeless situation. If he did not get some help he would be reduced to begging, and it would take a lot of begging to get all the way back to Sausalito. It was doubtful that his rent was paid, so there might not be a reason for him to go home, if that is what he called it. In his day, during hard times there had been hobo camps – fewer and far between these days. The army? Jail? He doubted that the skinny, fair-skinned, incompetent young man would survive either. What he needed was a benefactor.

The easiest thing to do would be to feed him, give him a grub-stake and send him on his way. But . . . but, if he could teach him a few tricks of the trade, he might prove to be useful. *Well, so be it, I think I am developing a soft spot, fool that I am. Time to see what this young man is made of.*

Augustus spoke in *a careful low voice, his British accent all but gone.* "Look at me, son. I'm the same man you shared lunch with, who bought two hats from you yesterday. I am not who I said I was yesterday, or who I might present myself at the present. For the duration of our stay here you are to think of me as being the Admiral, and the cover story I told about you is as true as the sun will rise tomorrow. Much of which you hear and see this weekend will not be true. I am an artist, a con artist, and I might be willing to teach you a few tricks of the trade if you are a willing student. Anything less than an A+ is the same as an F. If you have scruples leave them with guest services. What I can teach you will put a few dollars in your pocket, and if you learn them well you will never be in the penny piss poor position as you are today." He raised an eyebrow in question. "You can pack it up now or stay for the ride."

It took a moment for Harvey to answer. If he answered yes, he would be crossing a line that would forever change his life. As a boy he had never cheated on an exam, stolen an apple, or stolen a quarter from his mom's purse. He had been a boy scout – with few merit badges. His mother had loved him, his father saw him as a loser. He had desperately tried to win his father's approval. The harder he had tried the more his father had pushed him away. Where had honesty gotten him; nowhere. He was a loser, always had been, and was fed up with being one. He was being offered an opportunity and nodded yes.

"I will give you one more chance to walk away." He slid a twenty-dollar bill across the table. "This will get you home. If you stay, there is a chance you might be arrested. Wealthy people who have been made fools of can be very unforgiving, in which case jail would be preferable to what they might bestow upon you. If things turn ugly, and we are separated, disappear – and perhaps one day we will meet again at Schroeder's." He carefully watched Harvey's facial expression, his eyes, Adam's apple, anything to show a nervous reaction. He still held the money he had been given tucked into his hand. If he said anything about it, or tried to return it, that would be it, they would part their ways. A nod was not enough, he had to say it.

Harvey pocketed the money. "I'm staying. I don't want to know who you really are – best I don't. If it is okay with you, between you and me, you are Professor Flimflammer." He tasted a chip, which like the fish, had too much vinegar on it.

Professor Flimflammer laughed aloud.

Harvey started to push the fish away.

"Do not." The two words were quick, crisp, and authoritative. "Do not put down your fork for any reason until I say so. Continue to eat, or at least pretend to."In the civilized world one does not interrupt a stranger's meal and obvious conversation. You wait until either the conversation is over, which is difficult to judge, or the meal is finished. If one is eating a steak, the plate mostly full, and the knife and fork are set down, the meal is not done. If only a few trimmings are left of the steak and the knife and fork are put down the meal is finished." He smiled. "There is quite a curious crowd lusting to meet our Admiral. As soon as either one of us puts down a fork they will assume that they have permission to occupy the Admiral's time. In a con there is a time and a place for each action and reaction, that is part of the con." He raised his eyebrows while tasting his Guinness. "Our food and drink, your new clothes, the expensive guest house given to me are all part of the con. Neither of us belong here. Charles Crocker, one of California's big railroad barons, established the resort in 1880, the first true resort complex in the United States. Since the first day it opened it became popular with guests like Theodore Roosevelt and Ernest Hemingway. In 1919, Samuel Finley Morse, cousin to Samuel Morse inventor of the Morse Code, bought the unincorporated township of Pebble Beach, all the surrounding coast and forest lands, the lodge and its properties, and then some. The rich get richer, as the rich and famous pay homage with their wallets. Most of the ladies and gentlemen, our peers, staying here are members of a very elite club – they are superbly wealthy. Our con is to fit in, the slightly eccentric admiral to become well-loved and adored, to be sought after, as we skillfully pick their pockets. Next week, when they prepare what should be a sizable bill, we will be long gone with no forwarding address."

The waiter was working his way in their direction.

As if by magic Augustus disappeared replaced by Admiral Hemphill, in voice, bearing, complete with the infamous British stiff upper lip. "With luck we will find one or two card games, high stakes, of which I plan to take home a bundle. Along the way I will pick a pocket or two. When I do I will either return the wallet – now empty of cash – or pass it on for you to discreetly place in a nearby planter, trash can, or perhaps a woman's open purse. Never place it on top, let it drop to the bottom, or don't do it at all. If I touch the left side of my nose near my eye you are to say something, make a distraction, make it brief, then be silent. It's okay to be annoying, you are annoying. If I ask you about your room in Carmel, then you are to leave, never to be seen together again." He whispered one word: "Schroeder's." The admiral's plate was nearly clean. "Any questions?"

Harvey shook his head.

The Admiral noted that he had barely touched his food.

"Good. Are you ready? Put down your fork. When the waiter comes order an American cheeseburger to go."

They waiter arrived. "Will there be anything else, gentlemen? May I interest you in our selection of deserts?

The Admiral needed to retain his table longer.

"A cheeseburger with fries . . . to go." Harvey ordered.

"What do you suggest?" The admiral quarried.

Thinking of what a British Admiral might like he suggested: "We have a very nice fruit and cheese plate, with a delectable Stilton; perhaps with some cognac. Our cherries jubilee would also be an excellent choice."

"The Cherries Jubilee, for two, along with your best cognac."

No sooner had the waiter left than a woman, 30ish, strawberry blond, quite proud of her breasts, her evening gown proof, flirtatiously interrupted the Admiral's well placed pregnant pause. "Did I hear that you are a British Admiral, Sir?"

The admiral cleared his throat, stood extending his right hand. "Yes, Admiral Sir Stanton Hemphill, Her Majesty's' Royal Navy. If anyone tells you that is of any importance than they are a few sandwiches short of a picnic." Having added the *Sir*, he had just knighted himself King of the Del Monte Garden Bar and Grill for the evening. A small crowd soon gathered around the Admiral, others seeking the empty seats at the bar, causing a moment of alarm for the headwaiter.

There was just enough chaotic chatter to allow the Admiral to give his new apprentice a quick whisper. *"Harvey, become as invisible as you can. Some of these good people will be joining our table. When your burger arrives – to go – give up your seat and enjoy your burger somewhere nearby. Watch for my signal."*

Harvey had wondered why the burger had been ordered to go. Now he got the hint. The crowd around the table was large enough for the admiral to deftly pick a woman's billfold out of her purse, passing it to Harvey, without the cash, beneath the table.

When the Cherries Jubilee arrived, the crowd had to shift to accommodate the waiter as he brought it to flame. There were now six chairs crowding the table. Harvey took leave, allowing room at the table for a third couple, in the process dropping the woman's billfold back into her purse.

He glanced back wistfully, not sure how far to go, he had never tasted a Cherries Jubilee before.

Chapter Twenty-One

Doyle did not want to risk going back to the guest house and take a nap. He needed a nap; if he overslept Scotty's arrival it would be an unforgivable mistake on his part. He had plenty to do but it was a long stretch until three in the morning. He inquired about a men's room, and left his coat at his table before edging his way through the crowded bar. While working his way around the bar he spotted a woman's purse conveniently hanging on the back of a barstool. By the time he reached the other side of the bar he had pocketed the cash.

His way being blocked by a throng of merrymakers he opted to take a short cut through the garden, but before doing so he took advantage of the distraction caused by the whoosh of a flaming dessert dish to drop the pilfered billfold in a woman's purse who was seated at the over-crowded table.

For a moment he thought he recognized someone –*the guy from back at the boarding house –Harvey, what the hell*? That put up a big red flag. He had only caught a glimpse of the guy's face for a fraction of a second. *If it had been Harvey, that would throw a big clog in his plans.* He stepped back into a shadow not wanting to be seen. The guy disappeared around a corner. Doyle counted to five then slowly followed. Whoever it was, he had melted into the crowd. After thinking about it for a moment he concluded that it could not have been Harvey, Harvey was a poor slob that couldn't keep a job. This guy was wearing an expensive wardrobe. Still…?

Harvey found a quiet spot behind a mature magnolia to lean up against a wall and enjoy his burger –cold, but delicious. From his cover he could clearly see the Admiral, a quick glance from the boss told him the astute older man knew exactly where he was.

Doyle took a few minutes to scout the front desk. There were three on duty behind the reception counter, with an open door to a small windowless room immediately behind them. Inside, stood a small walk-in safe. His best guess was that if the front desk was open so was the safe – there was too much demand for access to the money. He stepped up to the desk asking for change of a fifty. His eyes followed the desk clerk into the safe where the clerk reached onto a shelf stacked with money for the change requested.

There were double doors on each side of the reception desk leading to the parking lot. To the left the reception desk, followed by a house phone, a cubby hole for the bellhop's luggage chart, a flight of stairs, finished by a hall-way leading to guest rooms. To the right were two doors, marked Men's and Women's accordingly, and the entry-way to the formal dining room. Here there was another headwaiter, another set of watchful eyes, not counting multiple guests. That put a minimum of five eyes on the reception area. They would have to be taken care of.

Outside, he stopped and lit a cigarette. It had been awhile, and he drew in the smoke slow and deeply. The parking lot was full. Tomorrow it would be the same, except during the race when everyone would be out on the 17 Mile Drive. His eyes caught on the volunteer fire house where there were several reserved parking spots, with one taken.

The front of the lodge was nicely decorated with a well-maintained flower garden, some rhododendrons, four stately Eucalyptus trees that towered above the two-story lodge. Doyle stared through the glow of his cigarette at the bark of the trees – their bark and sap were explosive in a fire. A moment before he had decided that robbing the safe was almost impossible without guns. There were too many people, too many witnesses. Now he knew exactly how to pull it off.

After a quick visit to the men's room he returned to his table in the Garden Bar, lit another cigarette as he worked over the details in his mind.

One of the three couples that had intruded on the Admiral's table were called for their reservation in the formal dining room. Jack and Annie Smith, who were invited to the cocktail event of the evening in the Twin Pines Room, insisted that Hans and Liz Eichendorff - Dear friends of ours - would be most disappointed to have missed meeting Admiral Sir Stanton Hemphill. And of course, Lyle and Ruth Cohen, the remaining couple who had been fortunate enough to join the gathering, were invited. The Cohen's knew no one of importance at the lodge, but Ruth, the strawberry blond with the gorgeous boobs, was quick to make friends.

The Admiral had the last of the Cherries Jubilee put into a to-go package for Harvey and put the last round of drinks on his account as they agreed to meet at the entrance to the Twin Pines Room in thirty minutes.

Hands in his pants pockets, the Admiral took a casual stroll, looking here and there, using a toothpick to scrape the dinner barnacles, aware that people were watching his every step. When Harvey caught up with him, he gave him the Cherries Jubilee along with a silver dessert spoon. "The ice cream is mostly melted, but it still tastes as sweet as a Savannah sunset."

"Have you ever been to Savanna," Harvey asked?

"Nope, never been there." *Here is a grown man who is as curious as a twelve-year-old, I'm not sure if he is going to be annoying, or perhaps a little fun – time will tell.* He took a bar napkin from a coat pocket. "Don't wear your Jubilee like that; some girl might want to kiss you. You ever been kissed properly?"

"No Sir, I had me a girlfriend once, but she was Catholic."

"What's that got to do with anything?"

"She said that because I wasn't Catholic like her, we

couldn't marry. She wouldn't have anything to do with it. She just liked to spend my money, only I didn't have none. I wouldn't have known how to get around her braces anyway."

The Admiral laughed aloud, tutoring Harvey might be more fun than he had had in years. "Harvey, we are about to go to a cocktail party where everyone is rich, full of themselves, and about to go gaga-eyed over a Knighted British Admiral. Once in, you are to stick close while becoming invisible. After your story is told, no one will give a damn anymore and ignore you." He showed Harvey how to carry a napkin in such a way that a wallet could be passed to him and tucked inside without anyone seeing. Put the money in your coat, then pocket than get rid of the wallet – carefully. A likely place would be under a table with a floor length tablecloth. Second best is an open woman's purse – make sure the wallet slips to the bottom. When we have enough, I will step outside to have a cigar. There, you will give me the money, and I will give you the room key. Go and get a good night's rest, we have a busy day tomorrow. If I can find a poker game, I won't be in until close to sunrise."

After tipping a waiter, Doyle found out that there was a card game scheduled to start in a back room of the golf shop at eleven o'clock. The buy-in was five hundred dollars, so he doubted the true heavy hitters would be there, but there would still be plenty of money on the table. He played a decent game, bluffed better than most, but when it came down to betting a large sum he didn't have the guts. The players here were better than him and Doyle knew it, but he wanted to sit down with these titans of money and success, stare across the table as if they were peers, thinking that his hand was good enough to take that damned thousand-dollar pot. He did not want to admit to himself that when the stakes got that high his hands would begin to shake, sweat would build on his brow, and God forbid his nervous twitch would become the last horse in line breaking into a full cantor. Sure, it was someone else's money, but it was big money, the kind he rarely saw, let alone touch. He looked at his watch, counted his money, deciding that he had time to build up his playing stakes.

There appeared to be a party going on in the Twin Pines Suite. Through the open door he could see tables piled with food, with plenty of champagne for all. He entered, planning on making a five-minute sweep. Looking as if he belonged, he wandered to each side of the room, studying his mark before craftily moving in for the take. To his surprise, he found himself unsteady on his feet, mildly nauseous, suddenly aching from head to toe.

He needed a fix.

His hands shook as he tried to light a cigarette. The match burned down to his finger-tip without allowing the cigarette to take. Hands shaking, he lit the cigarette on the third match. He took two martinis from a passing waiter before quickly stepping outside, quaffing the first martini which only brought a burning pain to his gut. The second martini steadied his hands enough to be passable. Several people gave him an odd look as he sucked in the nicotine as if it were life's air. He could not pick a pocket with hands shaking like this. Even with the acrid Camel tobacco smoke, he could smell that sour sweat that came with the nightmares, when he killed for the sake of killing, and when he thought that he could manage the small amount of heroin he used and couldn't. He needed a fix and wasn't going to get it. He ought to try to sleep it off but couldn't risk it. Staggering just enough to cause whispers, he found his way to the guest cottage and was grateful for the cold water only to be found in the shower.

As the cold water poured down on Doyle, a martini-endowed entourage escorted their guest of honor, the Admiral entered the Twin Pines; the party immediately elevated by his noble presence. The Admiral was introduced to the hosts, and they, in turn introducing the Admiral to all. After a brief humorous war story, the Admiral introduced Harvey, retelling the story of his father's daring-do at Dunkirk, as if it had happened. As if on script, those nearest Harvey made polite condolences regarding his heroic father, then moved in to be closer to the Admiral, leaving Harvey invisible to all but Professor Flimflam's skilled hands and eyes.

Chapter Twenty-Two

"It's late, I'm old, and I have had too much wine. Time for this ancient bag of bones to go to bed," Renata reminisced.

"Renata, please stay just a little longer. All of you, please." Michelangelo said with a wishful voice. "I have something I want to share with – need to share with you." He held up his almost empty glass, practically demanding it to be filled.

Betty looked at Renata.

Renata looked at her empty glass, at her favorite Catholic priest, then at Betty. Michael's night music still haunted the night. "Sure, on two conditions. If I fall asleep standing up, you won't allow me to fall. Second, that Betty opens that last bottle of vino." She whispered to Betty. "I live just across the hall now, if need be one of these hand-some men can escort me home."

The wine was opened and shared. Renata, stopping her pour at half. Oswaldo took a full measure. "What are we drinking to?"

He asked.

Michelangelo raised his glass: "Salute." The toast returned, "Salute."

"Well, padre, what is this big news you have?" Renata asked.

"Tomorrow morning, they will take off these casts once and for all." A cheer went up. "And immediately after that, I will surrender my Holy Orders, without regret or any misgivings for a new joy refreshing my heart."

Renata looked stunned, with all the kidding she never thought that he would do it. *A priest is a priest forever, you just don't on a whim walk away.*

Michelangelo knew what the next question would be. "Am I sure? Positive. I've had some time to think about it. I even left room for God to knock on my door – 'Michelangelo, my boy, you have doubts. Let's talk about it. You bend my ear, I'll bend yours, and we'll see if we can come up with something.' He never knocked, not even a singing telegram from the holy angels above. I thought about that and realized that one must have a shred of faith to have a conversation with God. Faith for faith's sake, is what brings life to the myth. For as long as man has looked at the stars in the heavens and wondered, our species has sought evidence of what made all those stars in the first place. The ancient ones, from the cliff dwellers, Peloponnesians, Egyptians, Greeks, all created myths that concocted beings who were magical, wiser, and more powerful than mortal men. They investigated the depth of the heavens, and the hot coals of their fires and created gods in their image, focused around all their shortcomings, that brought them suffering, poverty, love, jealousy, hate, war, and even the wish for immortality. All the while, the overseers of these myths - the priests - gained power and wealth, while the faithful who struggled to survive continued to look to heaven for a place that was more forgiving and kinder for their broken-down bodies and souls."

"Father, please don't say it."

"Renata, you have lived a very long life, and all those years you have kept faith with your church. But a church is not God. An institution that requires more and more to sustain itself is fool's gold with all its glitter and no real substance. Without faith there is no God, whether it be Christian, Jewish, Muslim, or the Emperor of Japan. The Christian faith teaches that Christ died for mankind's sins. If true, then everyone is going to heaven, Catholics, Jews, Protestants, Hedonists, even Nazis."

"That's pushing the envelope," Betty said, shocked by his addition of Nazis to his narrative.

"Christ died on the cross before there was a church. If one wanted to worship God in a way other than demanded by the doctrine of the Holy Mother Church, then the Church called that heresy and burned alive those who strayed. We do not have a noble history. For centuries European nations, depending on whether their people were Catholic or Protestant, killed, looted, and raped the other in God's name because the other worshipped the same God in a different way."

"I saw the evidence in Hitler's concentration camps, the horror of violent death on the battle fields. How can there be a God of mercy when there has been slavery, the great plague, brother killing brother in many civil war, the starvation of millions in the Ukraine, the mustard gas at Ypres, the missing at Flanders Field, what is happening in Korea at this moment. It's all madness, and to maintain one's sanity against it all, we are told to have faith that there is something greater, and kinder, that if we are faithful we will someday be sitting by our Lord's side in heaven."

His voice softened. "I have managed to keep my sanity by finding a restless peace in understanding that there is wickedness and good in all of us."

"There are no Gods." He repeated.

"If you cause harm to someone, don't ask for forgiveness from a priest hiding behind a window or a curtain in a box. Go to that person you harmed - if you can – and ask how you can make up for that harm. One honest *"I'm sorry,"* is worth a hundred *"Hail Mary's."* Asking in your last breath for forgiveness for a lifetime of selfish, often harmful behavior, is not going to suddenly grant you a posh life in a heavenly kingdom. Nice try - but those were just your last words. Better yet to know, at the moment of your death, that you have had a life, compared against all the trials and tribulations, well lived."

Michelangelo stopped, he had said enough. In the eyes of The Church he was now a heretic. In his heart, he was at ease for finally being able to be honest with himself. His throat had become dry and he drank his wine.

Renata wanted to cry but couldn't. Her voice and face, that of a very old woman, whose faith showed in every wrinkle and age spot she wore as her badges of honor. Her question was as innocent as a four-year old child, the pain rising from her heart as her lips formed the words: 'There is no God?"

Michelangelo's answer was both honest and compassionate. "Keep your faith, old woman, because it warms your heart. I have tasted and tested that same faith, and my faith is born anew that there are no gods on earth or in heaven. If your faith helps you, then you continue to believe. None of us are going to heaven as the Bible tells us so. But oh, those stars from down here on our only home sure are pretty to look at up there."

There was a moment of silence, then Betty rolled her wheelchair to the open kitchen door. The night was clear, a thick cotton candy fog bank overwhelming the Golden Gate Bridge would soon change that. Michael's last note for the evening said goodnight as it trailed away. Looking up she began to sing.

"Twinkle, twinkle, little star,

How I wonder what you are!

Up above the world so high,

Like a diamond in the sky."

Tears rolled down from Michelangelo's eyes.

When the blazing sun is gone,

When he nothing shines upon,

Then you show your little light,

Twinkle, twinkle, through the night.

Then the traveler in the dark

Thank you for your tiny spark;

He could not see where to go,

If you did not twinkle so."

Michelangelo brought his wheelchair next to hers. While he did not sing aloud, she could hear him.

"In the dark blue sky, you keep,

And often through my curtains peep,

For you never shut your eye

Till the sun is in the sky.

As your bright and tiny spark

Lights the traveler in the dark,

Though I know not what you are,"

Betty's voice faded, the last words finished in rich Spanish by Oswaldo. Renata drank her last drop of wine and went to bed. As she left the kitchen Oswaldo spoke softly. "Old woman hold onto your faith."

Renata remained shaken.

"Michael, are you asleep?" Mollie whispered from the soft dark of their bed as she snuggled in to hold him nearer.

"Yes."

"Oh, never mind, my love."

"What is it?" Michael asked.

"I'm afraid," she whispered. I love this place."

"I do too."

"I'm afraid that we are going to lose it, that whoever owns it is going to sell it, leaving us all without a home."

"I've been thinking the same thing."

"What can we do?" She trusted that her husband would have an answer. His answer was a soft snore. For some strange reason she thought of the song *Twinkle Twinkle Little Star* as she too drifted into sleep.

Chapter Twenty-Three

The Admiral was an unabashed storyteller, instantly becoming the center of attention, especially with the ladies. He tucked just enough bravado into his tale-spinners to draw in the most experienced veteran. Because of the average age evident in the gathering, it was easy for him to determine that few had seen active combat in the last war. There might have been a Full-Bull Colonel or even an active Reserve General in the room who would have served as high ranking desk jockeys, none willing to challenge the authenticity of his enriched fabrications. Now if there was someone in the crowd who had served on General Eisenhower's staff, or in direct support of all Allied Forces, their curiosity would certainly be raised when the name of a high ranking British Admiral floated across the room that wasn't recognized.

Word was out that a famous British Admiral was in attendance which put Augustus, aka the Professor, in his best con ever – the problem being that he was so popular it became almost impossible to lift a wallet. Harvey hung in close, watching carefully for signals from his boss, only there were none.

Augustus realized he was at risk of blowing his cover because of over saturation. Everyone wanted a piece of the Admiral's attention, and the more he gave the more likely he would make a mistake and it would be discovered that the Admiral was a fraud. He was much better working one on one, or small groups. Everyone had gathered around their celebrity, all eyes and ears focused too closely on his every move.

Harvey saw the same thing.

While the spotlight of attention was on the Admiral, no one paid any attention to Harvey, which freed him up to quietly work the room. Harvey was no finger-smith, far from it, he had never picked a pocket in his life. That did not mean that there wasn't opportunity right in front of his nose. Many of the women's purses were open, some with their billfolds practically falling out. He caught the Admiral's attention, directing his eyes to a rose-colored billfold sticking out of a woman's sequined evening purse. The billfold was small, as was her evening purse. The thin green edges of four or five bills just visible beneath the snap did not promise much in the way of pickings. The Admiral cleared his throat, raising his voice to get every-one's attention for a humorous story he once heard that was just naughty enough to even please the ladies. He then lowered his voice, as if it might be too risqué, everyone leaning in closer to hear.

The rose billfold found a new home hidden in a large dinner napkin. As did a matching fur evening bag that rested trustingly on a trim mink jacket that a woman had left at a table before being lured closer to hear one of the Admiral's stories. While pretending to ogle a plate of assorted cheeses and delicate meats, his hands hidden by the linen table cloth, he removed all the cash as well as a room key. The rose billfold emptied, he placed it in the fur bag, and returning it no one the wiser.

Quietly leaving the room through a side door he counted the cash. The rose billfold had held only forty-three dollars. The fur lived up to its pedigree, four hundred dollars in fifties. Harvey beamed with pride. Though scared almost witless he had done it. Now he held four hundred and forty-three dollars in his hands, more money than he had had in a long time. He was tempted to try his luck a second time but remembered the story of the gambler who threw the dice one too many times; same old cautionary tale, the house always wins.

The key was for room 212, just upstairs. Making as little noise as possible he dashed up the stairs and inserted the key without knocking. He could have slapped himself right there. What if someone had been in the room? Luckily, the only occupants were down at the party. After a quick search of their luggage and the dresser he found a tied-up roll of silk cloth, inside a stunning diamond necklace with matching earrings. They looked as if they were worth a fortune. He rolled the cloth back up, pocketing it. That was it, no more stealing tonight, he had been gloriously successful and more than excited to show Professor Flimflam how good a student he really was. And how guilty his conscience was as he flip-flopped between his values.

Chapter Twenty-Four

Doyle felt better, marginally. Naked, still wet from the shower, dripping on the tile floor, he lit a cigarette, then padded about the guest house. He envied the luxury, especially the ability to wonder around ala natural – not that it was something he did. Back at the boarding house he had a shared bathroom – but the freedom to do it because he could . . . that was something. The only lights on were back in the bathroom and the neighboring bedroom. He opened the living room curtains and stood there looking out onto the golf course envying the luxury. Twenty-four hours from now he would have the money, the wealth, to get himself his own place, to live in the manner he now lusted after.

He did not know how much money was in the vault – a vast fortune or a little one. He knew it had to be somewhere north of half a million bucks. After splitting it with the boys – now he was thinking - *if he split it with the boys, after this he was going to get out of the business once and for all. The boys were a liability, they knew too much, and could not be counted on to keep their stupid mouths shut.*

*Smokestack he liked, it was Hector and Smitty that would
have to be taken care of. Would Smokestack rat him out for
taking out his two pals? No, he'd always be looking over
his shoulder to see what I'm going to do next. Well, that's it
then, once we're out of here the boys will be silenced.*

*Scotty, he's a pal come hell or high water, if asked, he
will even help me get rid of Hector, Smitty, and Smokstack.*
He planned to ask just in case Scotty had other ideas.

He dressed, hoping to get back to the Garden Bar before
it closed. He needed some soup to ease his stomach, then a
card game to hold him until three a.m. when he was to meet
Scotty.

On his way back to the bar he figured out where and
how he would eliminate the boys. It needed to look like
an accident. He and Scotty would get them drunk on the
way back to Colma where the Woodie was parked. At the
cemetery he and Scotty would knock them out, leave them
in the stolen car, then drive it to a place called Devil's Slide
just outside of Pacifica. Devil's Slide was a treacherous
twisty road perched high on a promontory that frequently
eroded into the ocean, sixty to one hundred or more feet
below. Three drunk car thieves drive off Devil's Slide –
case closed.

He would keep the Woodie, at least for a while. He had
won it in a card game, the registration still in the name of
Bart Swanson, who got thirty to life for homicide, a job
Doyle had done. Bart, the patsy, had met with an unfortunate accident with a license plate stamp and died in year
two of his stay at San Quinton. Bart was never good at
making friends. The car was as much a ghost as the guy

who once owned it.

The Admiral saw Harvey do the deed with the two women's purses without discovery. *Nicely done, but where had he gone?* Harvey was a rookie, rookies made mistakes, and that sometimes comes back to bite the master – thus Augustus needed to know where his aggressive pupil had gone.

Harvey was standing just outside on a garden path looking as innocent as a caddy mapping out the hazards on a golf course. The Admiral excused himself to find the men's room, which he carefully bypassed to be followed at a respectable pace by Harvey where they met by the rental car which was parked just beside the voluntary fire department building. In the shadows they were free to speak.

"Well done, lad, well done." Augustus had been using his British accent for so long he forgot to change back. "How much did we get?"

"Four hundred and forty-three dollars." Harvey answered handing over all the cash to his boss.

Augustus quickly counted out two hundred forty-three dollars, pocketing the rest. "Here's some well-earned pocket money." He was proud of his younger apprentice, patting him on the back. "I think for tonight, we should leave the rest of the pickings until tomorrow." Augustus saw the smile on Harvey's face, the cat who had caught the canary who still had the feathers in his mouth. "You got a third one? Where?"

Harvey glanced around to make sure they could not be overheard or seen, then pulled out the tied silk package.

"What's this now?" Taking the package, he carefully opened it, his eyes widened with surprise as the necklace and earrings came into view. A long drawn out whistle followed, which could have been heard across the parking lot had there been anyone there. "These must be worth a fortune." In other circumstance, Augustus might have thought them to be copies – valuable but nothing like the real thing – and here in Pebble Beach, the odds of them being real were as spectacular as the jewels themselves.

Harvey had no idea what jewelry like these might be worth. "Fortune?"

"Yes, lad, a bloody fortune, perhaps twenty or thirty thousand."

Harvey's eyes practically popped out of his head.

Augustus knew that they couldn't keep the jewels on them. He was quite comfortable that the Admiral was beyond suspicion but with a theft like this one could not be too careful. Popping the trunk to the rental car, he partially pulled out the spare inserted the jewels into the tire along with a piece of newspaper to keep it from rattling around.

"Well done . . . well done. I think we'll call it a night, no more fun and games, there will be plenty of opportunity tomorrow. We'll get a good night's rest and start the day tomorrow with a nice plate of smoked Kippers with eggs and black pudding."

"Black pudding sounds awful. Kippers?

The Admiral laughed.

Doyle had a cup of seafood chowder and a gin martini, neither of which did much good for his stomach. If anything, the combination made him sleepy. Afterwards, he wandered over to look at some of the sports cars. For a moment, he regretted that he had scheduled the robbery for the same time as the race - he would have liked to see it.

A tip to one of the security guards, not too bright nor armed, told him that there was a card game about to start in a back room of the golf shop. Fortunately, there were still two seats available. He did not plan on playing aggressively; neither his brain or his cash position was in his favor. He would have plenty of cash tomorrow.

Chapter Twenty-Five

It was the third all-night café that Leland Tse was about to check for Sergeant Schmidt. Schmidt was lazy, usually hanging out in a couple of neighboring greasy spoons to pass the time rather than chase down any clues. Until now, all they had was thin to practically non-existent clues into the murder of the old Russian.

Sitting at the end of the counter with a cup of coffee and a half-eaten day-old donut, oblivious to the patrol car that had just pulled up, lights on, Schmidt was in his 'I don't give a damn zone.'

Tse tweaked the siren just long enough to get his Sergeant's attention. The Sergeant almost moved, his slight motion could have been caused by gravity and a gas bubble. Now Tse would have to go in and drag his ass off the barstool.

"What the hell do you want?" The Sergeant was his usual chipper, anti-Asiatic self.

"We've got something," Tse said, taking the last of his

donut. "Next time order the chocolate, the speckled French twists suck.

The Sergeant eyed his fork as a potential weapon.

"I've been working some of the leads on the Woodie." Tse said. "The one in Sausalito is registered to a Bart Swanson. Swanson died two years ago doing a thirty to life stretch in San Quinton. Swanson registered the Woodie last year to an address in Sausalito, only that address turns out to be a broken-down pier, barely above water, near the old shipyard. The registration gives us a California license number that matches one that has just been reported as abandoned in Colma."

"Abandoned, no such luck. You said this Swanson guy is dead, and Colma is nothing but one big cemetery. The guy just took it home."

Tse did not laugh, the Sergeant was rarely funny.

"Ten to one, whoever left it there is planning on coming back for it. Colma is not a place you tend to leave a car unless you want it towed. I say we go and sit on it for a while and see who pops up."

Sergeant Schmidt hated to admit it, but his Chinese sidekick might be on to something. "Shelly," he called out to the waitress, "pack up the rest of those donuts and two coffees to go."

"Tea," Tse winked at the waitress. Shelly, who did not like Chinks, gave him coffee.

"Hey, you gotta pay!" she yelled as the officers left.

"For what," Tse answered as he left the bitter motor-oil coffee on a table near the door.

Chapter Twenty-Six

The card game broke up a little before two thirty in the morning. There had been no big winners or losers, boredom holding the pot. Doyle yawned, stretched, and cashed in his chips – down three hundred and change - easy come, easy go. His mind had not been on the cards, he might have been looking at a Jack high diamond flush, but thinking about the big money, every movement, everything that needed planning to the second, paying little attention to the cards in his hands. The men with the money to match their playing skills must have thought him the fool for sitting down at the table - he had played badly from the time the first card hit the table.

He was relieved when it became time to hike over to the service gate to let Scotty and the boys in. A cold thick fog had blown in making it hard to figure out where the gate was. The lights from the lodge quickly faded, leaving him with a dark dream-like space to wander through, much like his war dreams only without the screams, explosions, and flashes of light. He could see no more than two feet in any direction and even then, the darkness swirled, his vision blurred, as it did when salty tears failed to wash the grit away. It was the sound of the surf to his right that guided him. He followed that sound, afraid with each step that if he miscalculated his next step would be off the cliff to the jagged rocks below. He did not know that the beach was only about ten feet below, a sloped rocky incline, easily overcome in daylight when the tide is low.

A foghorn somewhere off in the distance moaned for all the dead that ate at his soul, bringing them closer with each step. Scotty had told him that he might have an ulcer, with each step he was becoming a believer. Finally, the darkness trapped within the fog lessened just enough for him to feel that he was getting closer. He stopped, stared ahead as he tried to figure out if the light was there at all. A couple of steps further and the light penetrated the dark but not the cold pea soup fog – he thought he had heard someone call out once and now he believed it. Were they calling for someone else? Not at this hour. Two narrow yellow beams of light turned on and off, then on and off again. "Doyle, that you?" A man stood not ten feet in front of him between the two beams of light. "Doyle?"

Doyle quick stepped towards where Scotty stood and punched him hard in the belly.

"UMPTHH."

"I told you before, no goddamned noise," he hissed barely loud enough to be heard. It was at that moment that Doyle changed his mind. He had already made up his mind about the boys and up until now still thinking Scotty to be a friend worth keeping. In the fog and the early hour of the morning the Judas had shown that he was nothing more than a fool. He had told Scotty to steal a car that would fit in with the Pebble Beach crowd. He smacked his lips as he touched the still warm headlights. He had seen it briefly - even with its lights off it was a beauty – a 1948 Bentley Mark VI Courtyard 5201. There had been one shown at the inaugural race last year. It had been polished apple red with mahogany paneling, and there had been only 1000 of the special-order cars made. In the early post WWII years there was a steel shortage across Europe. The Bentley was the first luxury car to come out of England as the British struggled to rebuild after their nation's brutal war years. He laughed, this baby really did fit in, with the last flash of light he had seen that it was a polished Irish Green. *Please daddy, can I keep it, can I . . . can I.* He answered his own question. *No son, this one is promised to the devil. You always were a bastard dad, nice to know you still can be counted on.*

Doyle left the gate closed but unlocked. He stopped for a moment before getting into the car, his stomach hurting, a deeper, burning pain. Riding herd on these incompetents would give him an ulcer if he didn't already have one. *One of these shitholes could make a mistake that could blow* everything *out of the water*, he thought as he belched a bile promising burp. Earlier he had spit up some blood, which meant that he was either dying, or needed to kill the old Jap that haunted him. He wasn't dying, he was too mean to do that, but his killing moon would soon be full phase.

He crawled into the front passenger seat of the Bentley, with Scotty driving, and Hector, Smitty, and Smokestack jammed into the back. The interior smelled of cigarette smoke, stale sweat, garlic, and pepperoni from a pizza they had picked up along the way - so much for the new clothes. The empty beer bottles rolling around the rear floor space told him that the boys were not going to be on their toes. "Great," he muttered to Scotty as the car accelerated on the gravel path, the beer bottles clinking restlessly.

"Sorry boss, I sent them in for a pizza and they came back with a couple of six packs extra."

If Doyle could pull off the robbery by himself, or just with Scotty,he would get rid of the boys now - the fog good cover, and the ocean would take their bodies to where they wouldn't be discovered until he was long gone. "You got the guns?"

Scotty slid a paper bag across the seat.

"Good, we'll deal with the beer issue when everything is all said and done."

Scotty glanced at him without saying a word. He hadn't realized until that moment that this would be the boys last trip. *Shame about Smokestack, he was finally starting to grow in the job.* If the boss had made up his mind, there would be no arguing the point, not without putting himself at risk. They turned off the path cutting across the 17th Fairway to pick up a second service path behind several of the guest houses until finally reaching the parking lot.

There were lights around the lodge, like low stars only without any luster. The fog absorbing much of the engine noise, Doyle broke the silence that almost brooded around them. "From here on out, no one says word one unless asked a question by me. Anything you need to say will be in a whisper. Anything else, and I will rip your tongue out. Got that?"

The idiots in the back tested his patience.

Doyle quietly took a handgun out of the bag, checked to see that it was loaded, making sure the bullets were slid into the cylinder. "Over there," he said heeding his own words, "is their volunteer fire department. There is a parking space on the far side. Park there." He turned towards the back seat. Once parked, you will sit there until I get the fire station's door open. When I motion for you to come, you will do so without making a sound." He almost said: *Got it?* This time he pointed the gun at them, his finger on the trigger: "Not a fucking sound."

Smokestack had told Hector and Smitty of what he had seen, the thick wallets, the riches that were just waiting for the picking. Now the boss had some grand scheme, and this time it was beginning to scare him. He looked at his two partners in crime and could see that they were beginning to get that same feeling.

Earlier in the day Doyle had unlatched a window to the fire station. He tried to slide in, the pain in his belly and a whoosh of gas causing him to change his mind. On his second try he coughed and spat blood. Catching his breath, he slowly turned, expecting to see the old Okinawan. Not yet, but soon. He waved a finger at Smitty, because he was the closest, to climb through the window.

Once all were inside and the door was shut, their only light a single bulb hanging in the back as a security light, Doyle put his finger to his lips to remind them to remain

silent. He looked them over. Their new clothes looked good
- they would fit in for the short period of time they might
have exposure. Hector had some pizza sauce on his white
sweater, all smelled of cigarette smoke, beer, and their
confinement in the car. He would have to add a little time
in their schedule for some cold showers back at the suite to
make them more presentable.

"Okay, here is how it's going to go down. There will
be no changes or alterations to the plan. If done right, we
should have no problems with the cops, security, or eye
witnesses. Sometime after eleven tomorrow morning most
of the guests in this swanky place will be heading out by
foot to the main road - the 17 Mile Drive – where one of
the hottest sports car races in the entire country will take
place at one o'clock in the afternoon."

He pulled on the string to turn off the security light.
"Take a look out that window," he directed with a finger.
"That is the main entrance to the lodge, just inside to the
left is the reception desk. There is a second entrance, used
mostly by room service, on the other side of it. Normally
there are three people behind the reception desk, a concierge at a small desk on the other side of the far doors, and
one or two bell-hops. There may be a few old ladies left
who would prefer an extended lunch than to watch the race,
both in the dining room and the garden bar.

"Concierge?" Smitty asked. While he spoke with an
indoor voice, it was not a whisper.

The smack of Doyle's slap across Smitty's face was
louder than his voice had been. His whole body shook from
the sudden shock of the blow, rage, and fear." If Smitty

had any thought of revenge it passed with one glance into Doyle's eyes. His killing moon was nigh.

Scotty knew that if something wasn't done to tamper down Doyle's paranoia he was going to explode. Scotty raised both hands to placate the tension, then reached into a pocket and pulled out a small package containing a small spoon, shoelace, candle, match, and just enough heroin to help dial back the boss's killer moon. Doyle nodded, took the magic elixir and sat down at a neighboring counter.

Doyle just needed to be left alone for a few minutes.

Scotty knew the layout. "Behind the reception desk is a large walk-in vault full of money . . . lots and lots of money; and we are going to take every dime of it." He could tell the boys were chomping at the bit with questions. "When the race starts, what security they have will either be out on the 18th Green where the fancy sports cars will be parked or out by the entrance to the parking lot where the finishing line is. Pebble Beach is a small private community for the rich and famous; nice people, very trusting. They don't have their own police department, hospital, or fire department." He waved his hand around the room. "They're all volunteer. There are two ways into town. When the race starts the main road is closed, so if someone calls the cops, they can't get here until the race is over."

He looked back to where Doyle sat, his eyes closed. "Boss, you okay now?"

Doyle nodded.

Three minutes passed until Doyle opened his eyes. He was pale, his eyes glassy, the pupils infinitely small.

He rose, catching hold of the chair to steady himself as he made his way back to the window. Speech slurred, he returned as their commander and chief: "Over there, in front of the hotel there's a line of trees, four just outside the main entrance. Those are eucalyptus trees and they burn like there is no tomorrow." The 'O's' rolled like dry marbles in his mouth. "Tonight, we will soak the base of those son's-of- bitches with gasoline. We'll pour some in the parking lot, so it looks like one of the cars had a leak in case anyone wonders about the smell. You three will dress up in those fire uniforms hanging over there. It will take about five minutes for you to roll out the hoses and pretend to put the fires out, while Scotty and I hit the vault, take the cash, and put it in the trunk of the car which we will park close enough to have the trunk open and ready."

He turned, coughing up blood.

Scotty quietly left the fire station, found a beer in the car, returning a moment later, giving it to Doyle.

It was warm, the gassy bubbles helping to clear his throat. The alcohol hurt as soon as it reached his stomach. He handed it back to Scotty and continued: "The entry way on the left will be on fire. Smokestack, you will hose down the entryway, creating as much smoke and panic inside as possible. Put that high-pressure stream of water right through the front door, blocking any view of the reception area. If anyone tries to come out of the main dining room hit them hard, knock their summer bonnets off. Scotty, you and I will coach everyone near the desk to evacuate out towards the garden bar. When those trees catch they're going to go up like giant roman candles; no one is going to want to be anywhere near the fire. The vault has a cart which we will use to haul out the greenbacks. It should take two loads, like I said guys . . . lots and lots of money. When the car is loaded and ready to go, put out the fire burning in the door entry and fill the lobby with smoke and water. You two hit the burning trees with as much water as you can; anyone looking our way will fall back as those trees hiss and crackle."

"Anyone parked near the lodge will be doing their best to get their expensive cars out of there. The only way out is straight across the 18th Fairway, and that's just what we are going to do. You boys put on the show for another minute or two, then drop the hoses, and fall back to the firehouse. Dump the uniforms, join the panicked onlookers, and head out towards the 16th or 17th Fairway. We'll pick you up in Carmel, about three blocks up Ocean Avenue."

He took the gun out of his coat pocket. With his heroin pin-point pupils, the devil would be scared. "Now, any questions?" None. "Good, you will each be assigned a role; I will go over your roles once. We will then put the gas on the trees and entryway. After that we will go to the suite I have managed to acquire and shower. I don't want any of you smelling like gasoline or looking like you have had too much to drink. If you are all good boys and girls, we'll have a nice breakfast at the café until it's time for us to get into costume.

Everything went well until they realized that the plan wouldn't work. "Pack it up, everyone back," Doyle whispered to Scotty, who in turn whispered to the boys. The boys were busy applying gasoline via wet mops to the eucalyptus trees when Doyle waved them off.

Back in the fire station Scotty was ready to protect the boys. He knew what Doyle had in mind for them at the end of the day, but they had not screwed up here, in fact they had done a better job, silent and with precision, than he expected.

The boys were skittish, they had tried their best and thought they were doing a great job. When Doyle called it off he had said that everything was screwed up. Had they screwed up, if so, how? They knew the boss to be a very unforgiving task master and had promised them hell handed to them in a basket, which was good enough reason to scare them now.

"Relax, it's not your fault, I'm the dummy here." He said as he continued to glance back and forth through the station window to make sure they had not been seen. "By the time the race starts tomorrow most of the gasoline will have evaporated, the trees might catch, but *might* isn't good enough to get the party started. We've got to hit them with the gas just before lighting them off."

"There are going to be too many people around," Scotty cautioned. "Trying to light off the trees in broad daylight is as stupid as jumping out of an airplane without parachutes."

Scotty's right, Doyle thought, *we can't just walk in and start splashing gasoline around. Anyone got a match? We can still pick up a bundle picking pockets, but nothing like the money in that vault. I'll never get a chance like this again.* If anyone else sounded as defeatist as he felt now he would put a bullet through their head.

"Armed robbery," Scotty continued, "that's a long hitch no matter how you look at it. Armed robbery and arson you can kiss your ass goodbye – add in potential manslaughter, none of us will ever see the light of day again. The original idea made the risk worthwhile, but now maybe we had better pick a few pockets and call it a day." Scotty could see that Doyle was not liking where he was going with this. Doyle wouldn't rest until he had evened a score with a traitor. *Damned no matter what I do, best thing for me to do is shut up.*

Hector and Smitty heard the doubt in Scotty's words. Doyle's pin-point eyes made them fear the devil in the details.

"There is a way."

It was Smokestack who spoke. He had been there in the light of day, picked a few pockets, seen and studied the layout of the place. People thought he was as stupid as Smitty and Hector; he wasn't. If he was right, he just might bump Scotty out for being the doubter, becoming the boss's number two. It would give him a bigger share of the pot. He was tired of being treated as being dumber than a block of Limburger cheese.

Doyle knew the screwup had been his. His so-called pal had just suggested that they close shop and go home with their tails between their legs. He wanted to reach out and strike someone, big time. He did not have time to listen to idiots like Smokestack play Pin a Stupid Idea on a Donkey.

Smokestack grabbed his chance. "They . . . the lodge,

have a couple of gas powered service carts the are used by the bellhops and room service. So, we borrow one of the carts. When it's time, we stage an accident. The rental car clips the cart just in front of the front door, causing it to crash into the euca – whatever trees. In the back of the cart we've got a couple of buckets of gas which spills all over the place. One cigarette butt – whoosh - the fire is bigger than we had originally planned. In come the firemen . . ."

Doyle lit up, forgetting for a moment the whisper rule. "That's exactly what we want, the firemen happily polishing their shinny fire engine, the water pump full, hoses rolled and tucked where they're supposed to be, everything looking normal."

Smokestack continued as if he had permission to speak, that he was now close to the boss. "We steal the cart and hide it here in the fire station after we've tried up and gagged the fire crew. By staging the accident, we have a reason for the car to be exactly where we want it to be. I'll drive the cart, Doyle and Scotty will be in the car. As soon as the cart explodes, I run back to the station and switch into the firemen's gear." He looked at Hector and Smitty. "The three of us drive the fire truck over and block the view from the main road, so the trunk can be popped. We hook up two hoses." Smokestack looked just like Sylvester the cat who had just chowed down on that damned Tweety-bird.

Scotty was relieved, but he also knew that the boss now saw him through different eyes.

Doyle, who was beginning to come down from his high, took a curious look at Smokestack."You chase everyone out of the lobby with the high-pressure hose, and plenty of smoke."

Smokestack interrupted. "There's one thing . . ."

WHACK. Doyle backhanded him hard enough to knock him to the ground, blood pouring from a split lip.

All glory is fleeting, son. You just lost whatever favor you thought you had gained, Scotty quietly gloated. He looked at Doyle, raising an eyebrow that said he wanted to speak. "The boss should be the only one in the car. I'll be inside the Men's Room. Look, people are going to rush towards the sound of the accident, that puts too many people near the reception desk. Smokestack, you throw a bucket of gasoline on the far entry doors before you run back to the station. Boss, you hit the spilled gas in the cart with a hot cigarette. Me, I'm going to be coming from behind driving everyone out of the way with a fire extinguisher. Most importantly, I'm going to get behind the registration desk to make sure no one closes the vault." He patted his pocket indicating that he had a gun.

"Big problem, too many people will get a good hard look at you," Doyle said. Even with the heroin, his mind was filling in all the pieces.

"Tomorrow morning I'll go the gift shop and buy a pair of nylons for a mask, a 17 Mile Drive shirt like a hundred other people will be wearing around here, and a cane. The only thing I can't hide is my size."

"Cane?" Doyle did not connect.

"Yeah, soon as we make good our escape I dump the

disguise. If stopped, I'm a big guy who needs a cane, I've got a war injury, can't straighten out my leg for noth'in."

Smokestack rose to his feet, taking shelter behind Hector and Smitty. At this moment, if he had a gun he would not hesitate to kill his boss. Doyle didn't even give him a second look. When everything was done, all Doyle's boys would be taking a thrill ride off Devil's Slide.

"That's it, let's head back to the guest house and clean up. We've got only a couple of hours before the sun comes up. "Smokestack," he gave the kid a look that was almost forgiving, "take a quiet look around and see if you can find one of the service carts. If you can steal one without drawing any attention, park it behind the fire house. Bring back the key." He tossed Smokestack a handkerchief for his split lip and gave him directions to the guest house.

Chapter Twenty-Seven

Harvey couldn't sleep. He dozed off a few minutes here and there, but there were too many thoughts racing around in his head. The glorious twinkle radiating from the diamond necklace danced like fireflies as he thought about how rich he was going to be - and what a terrible thing he had done. He was proud and grateful for Professor Flimflam having taken him in, and ashamed of becoming a thief. But, he couldn't walk away; he was more ashamed of having been an incompetent penniless fool. This was his first real chance to become somebody.

He heard the front door open followed by a voice: "No lights. Use the first bath down the hall on the left, leave everything else alone. Scotty. You first."

Scotty? Holly crap, what gives here? Harvey was now wide wake.

Doyle took a seat at the kitchen table. The only light were the matches as each of the boys lit up waiting in silence for their turn in the shower.

Doyle closed his eyes as he went over each step he and the boys had completed without error. Without error? "Smitty, take your smoke outside and keep an eye out, at this hour in the morning there should be no one besides Smokestack coming our way. Hector will replace you after he's cleaned up."

Augustus, having taken off his shirt, shoes and socks, slept on top of the bed. Awakened by Harvey's hand over his mouth he sat up abruptly. "Shhhh, someone's here. Four men. I think I recognize one of them." Augustus pulled his clothes on. Outside of his undershirt and shorts, Harvey's clothes were back in his room, he'd been in too much a hurry. "Who?" Augustus whispered.

Harvey swallowed hard as he became more certain who their invaders were. "Doyle, Patrick Doyle, he has a room at the same boarding house as me back in Sausalito. He hangs out with a guy named Scotty. Both are mean, Doyle is dangerous. I've heard that Doyle is a murderer. I don't know who the others are."

They heard the shower water go on.

Whatever they're here for, they're too casual. They just walked in like they owned the place. This place was conned for the Admiral. In a split second it dawned on him. They don't know we're here. "Quiet as you can be, get your clothes and go out the back door. I'll meet you at the lodge - don't go in until I get there. There should be a night clerk on duty at the reception desk, and some security guards over by the driving range where the cars are parked. If I'm not there within ten minutes, the Admiral needs help."

He thought for a moment as he realized that suddenly everything was in flux. They needed to be flexible, cautious, and willing to give up the con instantly without regret or pull together a con that just might ride the winds. "Harvey, here are the car keys. Get the jewels out of the trunk. If we need to get out of here, there is no guarantee we will use the car." He thought for a second. "I'll stash them in my hat."

When Harvey was clear, Augustus slid open a window for his own escape, then stayed to listen from his closed door, opening it a crack to hear better. The shower went off, the light in the bathroom giving Augustus a quick view of Hector as he dressed. There were two cigarette glows near the kitchen. The man left the bathroom, tapping one of the smokers on the shoulder that it was his turn, before sitting down next to a man who appeared to be asleep. The one now in the bathroom was big enough to make a lumberjack quiver. Time to go, Augustus thought.

"Doyle, you awake?"

Augustus slid the door open another inch to listen. *Harvey had been right, it was this guy Doyle. Was he as dangerous as Harvey said? As far as he was concerned a gang of four men breaking into their guest suite at this hour of the morning meant they were dangerous. Had they followed Harvey? Why would they follow an incompetent hat salesman? To kidnap the Admiral? There were lots of plump kidnap targets staying here at the Del Monte Lodge, but the Admiral would be a primo catch. There is no way they would know about the Admiral – he doesn't exist. If he called in the Calvary, how long before someone would discover that the Admiral was a con?*

He was about to close the door and make his escape good when it occurred to him that he hadn't decided to use the Admiral ploy until he had reached the security gate to Pebble Beach. Second, why would they be taking showers. He listened longer. He didn't hear any high notes when the cold water came on, so they must know there is no hot water.

Harvey was scared, everything was blowing up in their faces. Why was Doyle here? If the cops got involved would he be arrested? Truth was that he was more frightened of Doyle than the cops. Eighteen minutes passed, then twenty. Professor Flimflam had told him to bring help after ten minutes. He left the shadows between two tall shrubs and headed towards the front lobby. As he approached, he saw the reflection of the revolving red and blue lights of a police car parked near the front entrance. A County of Monterey Sheriff's Officer was huddled with the Night Manager, a couple of perturbed guests, and a security guard who had been called off the sports car detail.

Having just become a professional con artist and jewel thief, Harvey's first thought was to cut and run. *God, he hoped it wasn't the same cop that had thrown him to the wolves yesterday.* Too late, his sudden appearance just outside the Grill's garden caused everyone to stop and stare as if he was the one caught doing something illicit.

The night clerk did not know the Admiral by sight, but as he came up behind the younger man in the garden entry, his British accent was unmistakable. "Excellent, excellent, a constable, Johnny on the spot." He stepped past Harvey, who was somewhat flabbergasted to see him. It took Harvey a second to remember that his boss was no longer Professor Flimflam but the Admiral.

The Admiral pretended to catch his breath having run all the way from their invaded guest house. He had fast walked and was in better shape than the slightly older aristocratic Admiral was supposed to be. "My younger companion here managed to wake me just as four armed men broke into our guest quarters. I barely managed to escape through a window, hopping first on one foot then the other as I dressed along the way. Since they did not get what I suspect they were after – me – the cheeky monkeys may well have taken off. Sod's law, if a gentleman can't be safe in a reputable lodge such as The Del Monte, I might as well go back to bloody old England." He paused, looking quite miffed. "Well constable, aren't you going to do something?"

Deputy Sheriff Wynn Owens was, as the Admiral might put it, caught in a binder. He had been called to the lodge because of a reported jewel theft. In most cases, once the thief has struck he is long gone. Now it appeared that there might be four armed men who had broken into the room of a celebrity – which because of notoriety might mean calling in the FBI. His fellow deputies were stretched thin because they were on call for traffic control for the Concours d'Elegance Road Race. The Carmel Police Department would be the next in line and might give him a good response time if he requested a Code 3; i.e., hot response.

He looked at the security guard, who while in uniform, was young and unarmed. *Armed men breaking into a guest house at the Del Monte Lodge constitutes a Code 3*, he decided.

"Is there a service road that will take me directly to the unit?" He asked.

"No, just a gravel path used by the guest and room services. In a police car, you as well run it straight up the edge of the 18th Fairway." The fog had not lifted. God forbid if any of the guests should be on the path they might not be able to see them.

Deputy Owen queried the Admiral. "You are certain that there were four armed men? What type of guns?"

"Revolvers, the type American gangsters carry."

"I'm going to call in additional officers from Carmel, they should be here in about 20 minutes. Meanwhile, I'll drive up as close as I can without being seen – the fog will help. We'll need one more security guard to direct the responding officers to me." He pointed towards the guard. "Get your man, then run up and find me. Your job will be to quietly watch for any guests who might be wakened and herd them back into their rooms.

The guests with wallet and jewelry theft complaints were sent back to their rooms. "As for the Admiral . . ."

"We have some kitchen staff on duty, we'll find a way to accommodate you until this is over." The night manager said. "This way please."

"Bacon sandwiches with builder's tea, never too early

for a proper breakfast. Come along Harvey, perhaps we can manage a window seat and watch the fun."

If there was a remote possibility that they might become suspects in the jewelry theft, he had just handed the police four prime suspects who, according to Harvey, likely had criminal records. If they were determined enough to stick around and use their Chinese fire-drill to rob the reception vault than perhaps he – Professor Flimflam – might find a way to rob the robbers while leaving them swinging with arson charges. The Admiral looked on with a bemused expression on his face. No, better to keep a low profile, it might not be healthy for Harvey, if seen by this Doyle character.

They were seated in the dining room by a window with enough light bleeding through from the kitchen for them to eat their bacon sandwiches. Their view was straight through the garden bar all the way out to the 18th Tee. Once the tea with heavy cream was delivered, the Admiral leaned across the table and whispered, "Tell me everything you can about your friends, Mr. Doyle and Scotty.

I don't know how they chose our guest house, but I'm certain they were not after the Admiral, or to kidnap anyone. They have plans to rob the reception vault during the race tomorrow. If we are clever, then their only rewards for their effort will be a dog's dinner."

"Dog's dinner?" Harvey did not like his hot tea with heavy cream and was beginning to think that the British ate poorly. Most of the pictures he had seen of the British were fat old men who smoked and drank too much.

"A dog's dinner is British slang for making a mess or a fiasco out of something."

The more he learned from Harvey the clearer everything came to the old flimflam man. First, do not under any circumstances let this guy Doyle or any of his henchmen find out who they are, or get a look at them. Revenge was a religion to Doyle, and he would kill them without a second thought. Second, if they did not get arrested in the next hour, then they would go *Full Monty* with their plan to rob the lodge. They would make a mistake; they were low level gangsters reaching for the enviable pot of gold, too heavy for them to lift.

Smokestack found two service carts parked behind the kitchen. The arrival of the sheriff's car changed his plan. He had seen on a posted property map that a second service path ran from behind the kitchen out to the guest houses off the 16th and 17th Fairways. He needed to warn Doyle that there was a cop prowling around and the second path offered the best chance of not being seen. The service cart was almost as quiet as a bicycle on gravel. The fog, great cover, unless he ran into something.

Hector had just come out to relieve Smitty when Smokestack pulled up to the side of the house. He waved for them to follow him as he burst into the front room. "The lodge is swarming with cops."

Doyle stood. "It can't be us, we haven't done anything yet, no one knows we're here."

"We did lift a few wallets," Scotty reminded them. "Maybe we lifted the wrong one – someone important."

"That doesn't bring out the riot squad at this hour of the morning. Damn it! We got no choice, time to get the hell out of here." Doyle pulled open a curtain wide enough to look out. Fog was all he could see - the cops could be anywhere.

"I say we stay put, there is no reason the cops are looking for us." Smokestack stepped out of line by opening his mouth.

Doyle would have smacked him, but he was too busy trying to make out any movement out in the fog.

"How many cops, how many cars? Were they loading their shotguns?" Paranoia was setting in.

Smokestack had to think. "One . . . one car, a sheriff's car. I don't know how many cops were there, I couldn't see inside.

Doyle blew out a gut full of stressed air. He lit a cigarette, thinking that Smokestack would be the first one he'd take care of later. "You don't know?"

"I heard voices, maybe two."

"You get the cart?"

Smokestack nodded. "I came in the back way."

"Okay, here's what we're going to do. Using the fog as cover, we're going to make our way back to the fire station and wait there until it's time to hit the vault. If the cops want to check out the fire station they'll find it locked up nice and tight."

The five left with the service cart from a rear door just as Deputy Sheriff Owens pulled up under cover of the fog, as close as he dared. There was a light on inside, otherwise it was quiet. At this point he would wait for back-up. He wasn't about to take on four armed men by himself if he could avoid it.

Chapter Twenty-Eight

Despite the early hour in the morning Michelangelo sat looking out his bedroom window. There wasn't much to see - except for possibilities.

His legs never itched as much as they did now, anticipating their freedom from his now smelly casts. The doctor had told him that once the casts were off he would have half an hour's worth of water therapy to help get his circulation going. Modern medicine, what would they think of next. After that, he would take a cab to the Archdiocese where he would take off his priestly robes and tell them to go to hell. Perhaps a polite divorce with no hard feelings would be more appropriate. If he were merely taking a leave of absence they would provide him with some sort of allowance with wishes for a speedy recovery. Best not to kick the Arch-Deacon until he got both feet on the ground again. He wasn't worried about his future, something would turn up. He could always return to his family in Grass Valley where everyone would see him as the black sheep who failed as a Priest - not his favorite option.

It had become clear over the glasses of wine and their camaraderie that what mattered to him at this moment in time was this house and the people who made it their home. If the owners sold the house would they be callous enough to throw everyone out onto the streets? The glue that held these wonderful people together was that they were all damaged in one way or another, starting with himself. Betty was a middle-aged woman in a wheelchair without family or means to fall back upon. Michael would always have to struggle in the outside world regardless of his talent as a musician. Mollie had chosen to share Michael's hardships with their marriage. Renata, bless her heart, was old. Oswaldo, a refugee for a crime he did not commit. Harvey, a simple little man who would always stumble over his own feet. And what of Mary Griffin? Like Betty, he had not given up hope that she was still alive. He remembered the way she played the piano; hearing something just once, she would play it as if she had practiced it a hundred times, before it became perfection. After she had mysteriously disappeared, Betty gave the piano to the church, where it now sat as silent as the room that waited for Mary's return. He had never gotten to know Mary who had been quiet and reclusive, her presence in the house her music.

Michelangelo sat and pondered the future, not his as much as everyone else's. There were no bluebirds singing outside his window, only an unusually chilly breeze for August that penetrated the window, foretelling of stormy weather to come.

The house was cursed. Renata knew that to be as true as

the many years that weighed on her soul. She had prayed to the Virgin Mary to take her to heaven rather than move into this house – where evil teased and mocked her. In her prayers, she had been told that she was part of the puzzle that the curse wrapped itself around. Now, in the wee hours of the morning, she felt its presence, rose from her bed, lit a candle, then knelt before the cross she kept on the wall just above her wash basin. In her prayers she asked the Blessed Mother Mary to protect her family from the house's curse. Outside the wind blew oddly cold, and inside she heard a child crying, as if trapped within the walls alone, and very much afraid.

Chapter Twenty-Nine

Deputy Sheriff Wynn Owen was going to have a lot of paperwork to do. Someone had misread the Code – 3, calling in all law enforcement agencies to a critical armed hostage event at the Del Monte Lodge. Everyone knew of the power and influence of the guests staying at the lodge this weekend which elevated the response to the maximum. Wynn, who could hear the multiple sirens responding from all locals, stuck a plug of *Bull of the Woods Chewing Tobacco* between his gums, and bit down. Whoever these guys were, they had just gotten enough lead time to ske-daddle into the woods, and with the mansions in the area, a breaking and entering might just become an actual hostage situation.

As the arriving police agencies closed in, the lights in the multiple guest rooms and houses winked on, until the whole place was lit up. Within minutes six patrol cars, an ambulance, and a fire truck tore up the fairway, braking to a stop near where the Deputy Sheriff held the front line.

The security guard, who had run to his side, was the

first to demand his attention. "What do you want me to do, everyone's coming outside?"

"Gob smacked!" The Admiral laughed. "Our copper, who has been chasing his own tail, has just been caught up in a dog's dinner. The poor man will be the laughing stock of every constabulary from here to Frisco. With all those sirens, your friends will leg it into the woods creating quite a show until race time this afternoon.

Harvey didn't get half of the British words the Admiral threw around. He couldn't help laughing along with him as the cars, sirens screaming, lights blazing, screeched around the lodge tearing onto the golf course with life and death urgency.

While the Admiral appeared to be enjoying himself immensely, Augustus needed to do some quick thinking. Every law agency for miles around was about to become aware of Sir Admiral Stanton Hemphill of Her Majesty's Royal Navy. While no kidnapping had taken place, would the FBI be called in as a precaution? How long before someone thought to call the authorities in England that their beloved Admiral had been under threat only to find out that he was an imposter? Could he and Harvey just leave without someone demanding to know where they were going? Once the race began they would become trapped – so time was of essence. Would the massive police presence cause Doyle to abandon his plan to rob the lodge? If he knew what was good for him, he would.

"Harvey, I want you to dig down and give me your best

guess on how Doyle will react to this sudden threat to his plan to rob the lodge. Will he cut and run – that would be the smart thing to do – or will he stick it out despite the risk?" This he asked in a voice low enough that no one in the kitchen would be able to overhear. He noted that two high ranking police officers had just arrived and were introducing themselves to the night manager. Four additional officers made themselves available nearby. "Quickly, lad, the police are about to start asking questions."

"Doyle runs a petty protection racket and there is no profit to be made in Sausalito. He will risk the lives of his men for a profit this big. I've been told that he is a killer; if true, he is a cruel one without a conscience." He nervously glanced at the police officers now parading in their direction. "Yes, if the police don't catch them before the race, Doyle will go through with it regardless of who he puts at risk."

"You have told me what I need to know. Now, follow my lead, I'm going to deflect all questions the police might have to you. The Admiral knows nothing." A bite of the bacon sandwich gave him a last second stall as the first of the officers arrived at their table.

"Admiral Stanton, Charles Bowden, Chief of Police of Carmel. Are you quite alright, Sir?"

It now became apparent that the four additional officers had been detailed for the Admiral's protection.

The Admiral eyed the Chief with a degree of curiosity and bemusement while chewing thoughtfully.

"The grounds have completely been surrounded

allowing little room for the perpetrators to make good any escape. While you are safe, the FBI has been alerted, and they in turn will be in touch with Interpol."

A sip of tea cleared the Admiral's pallet. "All that, for me? I can assure you gentlemen, that it isn't necessary. Whoever these blighters are, I seriously doubt they are after me. You see, there was a problem with my reservation and the lodge's registration will show that I am not supposed to be here until Monday. My guest house, compliments of the management, is listed as being down for repairs – so you see I'm not really here. That – and I have not seen whoever broke in."

The Chief and the additional high-ranking officer from Monterey cleared their throats as they sorted out the fact that their celebrity victim and chief witness was neither.

"Harvey, my traveling companion, woke me with news that someone had entered the guest house uninvited. While I dressed, he ran to the lodge to summon help. Hearing voices, I escaped through a window and hid long enough to make sure that I had not been seen."

"You did not see any of them, nor identify any one by voice?" The Chief asked.

"No Sir, I haven't a thing that might be of help. Harvey?"

"I heard them come in, then warned the Admiral. I did not see any of them."

Harvey's sincere smile reminded Augustus of a pet beagle waiting to be thrown another stick in a game of fetch.

The Chief had little more to say. "Of course, you will be available should we have any additional questions?"

"Of course, it will be my pleasure. I'll be here, or out watching the race come time. Harvey, please remind me that I've got to talk with management a bit later about being moved to a different room. I don't see how, under the circumstances, we can stay in the current one."

"What's happening at the guest house? Any surprises? The Chief from Carmel asked an officer who had just stepped into the dining room.

The Admiral was not privy to the response to the Chief's question.

Chapter Thirty

Deputy Sheriff Wynn was on the hot seat. He was surrounded by three police chiefs, his boss the sheriff, and the senior management of the Del Monte Corporation, all wanting to know why he had ordered a Code 3. Whatever their intent, it was clear that the Admiral had not been the target. The only crime had been simple *breaking and entering*. The front door had been unlocked, leaving *breaking* into a hotel guest house which was listed as unoccupied due to maintenance issues a moot issue.

Chief Bowden coined the phrase – *'Cold Water Bandits'* - that would soon headline the nation's newspapers. "The way I see it gentlemen, our hands are tied. Since Admiral Sir Stanton Hemphill is involved, even in a minor way – the State Department should be notified as well as the FBI."

"And what do we tell them?" the sheriff asked indignantly.

"That the only known theft by *the Cold Water Bandits* is a guest towel after several of them took showers sometime around four a.m. this morning." His smile lowered the deputy sheriff's blood pressure. "If you want to add the unauthorized use of a bar of soap to the Del Monte's losses, go ahead. At this point it's not difficult to suggest that these Cold-Water Bandits are the likely jewel thieves of a matching diamond necklace and earrings set with an estimated value of . . ." He looked at Owen who had his notebook in hand.

"Forty-five thousand dollars, give or take their value on any given day," he reported.

"Forty-five . . ., why that's more than some of these expensive sports cars cost."

"The owners, a Mr. and Mrs. Sydney Voorhees, own a chain of up-scale jewelry stores in New York and Connecticut," the deputy finished.

The Sheriff looked thoughtful for a moment. "I'll take care of the call to the FBI. These so called 'Cold Water Bandits' may have followed the Voorhees across state lines to steal the jewels. With luck, we'll be able to pass this whole mess on to The Bureau."

"May I suggest that once the room-to-room search has been completed we reduce our presence here to a minimum. We already have enough overtime scheduled for the race in a few hours." The Chief of Police for Monterey was not anxious to provide any more manpower than what was already budgeted for traffic control.

"I'll call in two detectives and add two uniformed officers and have them here before the rest of our troops stand down." Chief Bowden offered.

"And I'll lend you Deputy Sheriff Owen, since he is most familiar with the case." He didn't add that he wanted a deputy on hand for department credit, should they be lucky enough to recover the jewels.

No one at the Del Monte Lodge slept in, everyone abuzz helping to fuel the rumors regarding their early morning show of police to protect them from what horrendous crime someone had in mind. The police were searching each of the guest houses and rooms, one by one, identifying the rightful identity of each guest, checking that no one was harmed, saying nothing more about the reason for their queries. Room service was cancelled due to an avalanche of requests before their normal hours of operation. Unnerved, many of the guests, gathered in the dining room, overflowing to the garden café, where the lodge had no other option than to provide free coffee and pastries. The loss of profit was replaced shortly by a steady supply of Bloody Mary's and Mimosas charged at an exorbitant price most of the wealthy guests didn't even notice.

The Admiral found it all very amusing.

While the police raced towards the guest house, the service cart ambled quietly along the secondary service road until it reached the rear of the lodge where everyone, but Smokestack got off – a service cart designed to sit two was sure to attract attention with five. The in-flow of police made their scamper through the parking lot a challenge, that they were not spotted was a matter of luck. A City of Monterey Police Car did slow down and put a spotlight on Smokestack, who slowed and waved, a white kitchen shirt he lifted from a laundry bin, erasing any suspicion.

Doyle had Hector climb back through the window after pad-locking both doors to the fire station. The cops might rattle the locks and shine lights through the windows but would find nothing out of place. Whatever the cops were looking for, it wasn't them. He and Smokestack had picked a couple of pockets earlier in the day but that was not enough to call out half the cops in California. With luck, they would be able to lay low, out of harm's way, until most of the cops found more important things to do.

He and the boys were tucked into a storage room in the back of the station, the service cart, an expectant silent partner, sat with them. *Oh, the tales it would be able to tell, if only it had a brain.*

"Everyone get some shut eye, no talking, no smoking, no nothing. I'll keep watch. If we have visitors, it will be the firemen. Scotty, you and me, will see to them." Doyle was restless, on the edge of a violent breakdown. Physically, he needed a fix, mentally the same. The beads of sweat that marked his forehead on an otherwise cool morning marked his uncertainty that his plan was fool-proof, that there were so many things that could go wrong. He stared at the boys, placing blame for anything that could go wrong squarely on their shoulders, with hefty penalties promised.

The morning passed without incident, with no arrests, and no suspects unless one counted a couple of the aristo-cratic wives who were ugly enough to be even uglier men

in disguise. By eleven o'clock, the heavy police presence
had dwindled down to five. Two uniformed officers were
posted just outside the front doors to the lodge to assure
the guests that they were still loved and cared for, while
Deputy Sheriff Owen Wynn tagged along with the two
plain-clothed Carmel Detectives. After searching the guest
house for the missing bar of soap and guest towels, they
interviewed the Voorhees and several guests who reported
missing wallets. No one thought to question the Admiral
having been told that he was a *brass only,* VIP contact. If
they wanted suspects, the Garden Bar was full of Bloody
Mary infused know-it-alls who boosted every rumor, the
one getting the most guffaws being that Butch Cassidy and
The Sundance Kid were alive and well, despite reports of
their prior demise.

Detective Sam Churchill and Rod Demers, convinced
that the *Cold-Water Bandits* were long gone, decided that
since they were stuck at the lodge until the roads reopened
they should mix into the rumor mill to listen and see if
anything of interest turned up. The best way to look like
and talk like a local was to down a few Bloody Marys
themselves. No such luck for Deputy Sheriff, and the
two uniformed officers stationed at the front of the lodge,
who soon followed the people that needed protecting
out towards the finishing line. There were two places for
suspects to try to blend in with the crowd, the Garden Bar,
and the finishing line for the Concours d'Elegance.

Augustus, who couldn't risk Harvey being seen by
Doyle, ventured out to his rental car with a policeman

at his side. They were not willing to expose the Admiral to unknown risks. Augustus was not willing to leave the jewels in the car. The officer watched the surrounding parking lot as the trunk was opened and Augustus secured the jewels inside his hat."Dash, I thought I had an extra sweater," he said to the officer. "My luggage has been delayed and hasn't arrived yet."

The Admiral thanked the officer for his protection as he hurried off to join the Deputy Sheriff and his partner out towards the finish line. Augustus – the Admiral – stopped for a moment at the front entrance to the lodge wondering how Doyle planned to pull it off.

Curiosity was part of Augustus' modus operandi.

Patience was not in the Patrick Doyle's gene pool. The quiet unrelenting tick of the firehouse wall clock taunted the boys as they waited - and waited. No talking. No smoking. No card playing. Three aces full, a bluff, and three idiots practically guaranteed a verbal fracas. "You boys just sit there, and think about and do nothing, at which you dunderheads have plenty of practice"He threatened to shoot the clock if it didn't stop its damned ticking.

Scotty, who could feel his bosses' tension rise, wished the clock would either speed up or shut up. Doyle shot him a 'do that again and die' look when he cracked a knuckle.

The noise that stole the clock's thunder was the rattle of a key in the padlock to the sliding fire station door. The men in yellow had come for their boy-toy, their bright and shiny 1934 Ford Sanford Pumper Truck. Virgin for its purpose, the truck, a babied classic, never sullied by soot or flame, was kept pristine by the all-volunteer fire crew, a show-piece they proudly rolled out of the barn for its twice a week facial, massage, and pedicure. Today, with all the classic car aficionados, it was show and tell time for the proud crew.

All six of the volunteer crew, including their Captain, Sylvester Hawke, a retired firefighter, and former stuntman from MGM Studios, entered the station unaware of the menace that awaited them. Their capture was quick and uneventful, with no physical harm done other than their pride. Bound, gagged, and locked into the back room, the firemen could only hope that these ruffians would not scratch nor dent their prized engine.

Sylvester felt the knots securing his wrists, and like the famed Houdini, knew instinctively that they would not hold him. It was the guns that worried him. He had seen two, guessed that all five of their captors might be armed. Like himself, his crew were mostly near or past retirement age. By himself, the big Swedish looking thug could most likely pulverize them without breaking sweat. So, he waited, wrists and ankles bound, for an opportunity to present itself.

The Admiral was thinking that after the massive police presence Doyle and his cronies had gotten the message that their well-laid plan to rob the lodge had become a fool's errand. The odds were against them, but a less daring, certainly brassy plan would be to mix in with the race crowd to pick a few pockets, then scram with some cash for their efforts. Outside of traffic and crowd control there was no real security to protect against such brazen behavior. As he and Harvey wandered among the sports cars on display on the putting green, he contemplated how many wallets could be nicked, with the Admiral under such high public attention. It was time, he decided, for them to make their way out to the 17 Mile Drive and mix with the crowd. The passing of the race cars would allow more than enough distraction to make for a prosperous payday – not to forget the jewels.

"Hey Charlie, the lodge's fire engine was supposed to be here an hour ago. I've got to get this place roped off for crowd control. Have you heard anything from Sylvester?"A man with a clipboard asked one of the security guards as if he might be in the know.

This got the Admiral's attention. There was something in Doyle's plan that involved the volunteer fire department. When he strolled out to the front of the lodge to check on a non-existent sweater in his car, the fire station had been locked up tight – padlocks on all the doors. He had almost missed it. From experience he knew that padlocks were of little hinderance, often an illusion. *The classic fire engine should have been on display an hour ago.* He thought. *Why the delay? Because Doyle and company are in the station and about to make their move? Why a fire engine? Noise, a distraction? To make their getaway? Good God, a fire.* It was all beginning to come together.

"Send someone over to the firehouse and put a bee in

Sylvester's bonnet, will ya?" The man said making a note on his clipboard.

"Sure . . . sure, it's not like I don't have better things to do," bitched the security guard who had been standing idly collecting his hourly pay.

The fire engine was now in front of the station looking as ready as ever to respond to a fire call. Looks were as deceiving as the padlocks had been. The trained crew was hog-tied inside the station, useless for all intents and purposes, as Doyle and the boys tried to look busy and professional as they stared at the dials, gears, buttons, and hoses that made the fire-pumper truck work. There was no operating manual in the glove box.

A phone rang inside the station.

Unable to see where his captors were, Sylvester instinctively worked at the ropes that bound him. All he needed to do was reach the phone – one word "HELP!"

Doyle stared through the open sliding door as the phone rang on the wall, demanding attention. He did not want to answer but anyone around the lodge could see the engine and the firemen busy around it. Not to answer would draw attention. He went into the station, glanced at the fire chief and pointed his finger, his threat a given – "POW" - then answered."Fire station, this had better not be a fire call, we've got the truck polished all shiny and bright for show and tell."

"Put Sylvester on the line." The concierge asked without

his usual jocundity. He was making the call for one of the security guards who was too damned lazy to run across the parking lot.

Sylvester must be the headman, Doyle thought. "He went for coffee."

That's strange, Liam thought, *the fire crew usually helped themselves from the free coffee offered here in the front lobby.* "He'll probably walk through the door soon as I hang up. Just remind him that the engine was supposed to be set up at the putting green an hour ago. Tell him to put a move on it before the show manager has a hissy-fit."

Doyle hung up. That was it, they were out of time, if they were going to move, it had to be now. His gut did a double bender, telling him that he needed to hit the can now. He pushed everything back, this was not the time for shit to happen."Scotty, its time, let's move." He bellowed, not caring who heard as he held his bowels together, quick stepping the best he could out towards the engine. "Everybody had better know their jobs because there isn't going to be a second chance."

Scotty's job was to hang out in the men's room until fire broke out in the lobby. He looked at the boys, knowing they weren't ready, gave them a demanding nod and headed towards the lodge.

Smokestack was to park the service cart loaded with buckets of gasoline between the two front doors. He loaded up the last bucket, sat in the driver's seat, his nerves beginning to fail. Playing with the amount of gas he had in the cart was dangerous.

"That's it, there's no turning back now," Doyle muttered as he pulled on the Fire Captain's gear, sat behind the wheel, lit a cigarette, and turned on the engine. Since they were expecting the fire engine, he would use it to stage the accident instead of the car. They would stash the money in the gear box. When the pumper was dry – or faked – he would pull it back to the station to presumably fill it. That was when they would move the money from the engine to the car's trunk and then get the hell out of Dodge.

It took less than a minute for Smokestack to reach the lodge. Hector and Smitty, dressed in fire uniforms, were to wait at the station until the gasoline caught. Once the fire was set Smokestack was to double time it back to the station, pull on his fireman's costume and race back to fight the fire with Hector and Smitty.

Crap! These guys are stealing my engine, Sylvester thought.

No matter what he tried, he could not free himself. He heard the fire siren start up, grimaced, with visions from his worst nightmares dancing through his head; helpless to do anything to prevent it.

Smokestack stopped the cart right where he was supposed to and splashed a bucket of gas between two of the Eucalyptus trees and the front door. If anyone saw him, they wouldn't have time to do anything about it. A quick glance back towards the fire station scared him witless - trouble was coming at him like a runaway freight train. The fire engine was coming too fast. Any fool could tell that it was time to get out of the way as the truck barreled straight towards the building.

Doyle should have let Scotty drive; he had no idea how to drive a fire engine loaded to the gills with water. He tried to apply the brakes only to find the weight of the water in the pumper only increased his inability to steer. He stood, still trying to drive the rig while yelling at Smokestack to get the hell out of the way.

Smokestack tripped on a loose shoelace, dumping a bucket of gas on his pants as he fell back into the cart. The front of the engine crashed directly into the entryway to the lodge, smashing the two ornate doors before wedging itself firmly in place. Doyle, who had been standing, waving for Smokestack to get out of the way, was thrown across the seat towards the open passenger door.

The terror in Smokestack's eyes froze everything that was happening into one meaningful moment . . . Doyle's cigarette - the whoosh of the gas exploding into a rapidly expanding inferno with Smokestack screaming in the middle. His last sight, the *'Oh Shit'* expression on Doyle's face.

Scotty stopped dead in his tracks just outside the restroom at the sight of the fire engine embedded in the lobby's entrance, the flames roaring, and Smokestack's bizarre death-dance as he twisted and flapped, the flames quickly turning him to char, the fire extinguisher he held useless against the inferno.

Doyle slowly climbed out of the driver's side of the engine, his fireman's helmet missing, hair and forehead blistered. Smoke, heat, burning gas, and the memory of the stench that followed the flame throwers in Okinawa almost paralyzed him.

Hector and Smitty's run across the parking lot wasn't much more than a fast walk as they laughed and joked, boys playing firemen – that the fire was real - only part of the game.

There hadn't been that many people in the lobby. The crash, abrupt and terrifying, woke them from their lazy late-morning malaise, causing them to panic in unison when the fire engine crashed through the entryway. The immediate explosion drove them out through the doors to the Garden Bar and Grill where everyone rose, bursting into their own excited *Tower of Babel,* as the events escalated around them.

As surprised as he had been in the chow hall when the windows imploded from a nearby bomb blast back at Pearl Harbor in Forty-one, Liam, the concierge, ducked and covered. To his surprise it wasn't a second Japanese sneak attack, nor the Koreans - it was the lodge's own fire engine that had brought down the ornate door, the fire already licking at the ceiling.

Two of the three men working behind the reservation desk forgot their emergency training procedures fleeing towards the Garden Grill. Gregory, the Day Manager, kept his composure, dialing the nearest fire station in Carmel as he cringed from the wave of heat and thick smoke that emanated from the fire. It was obvious that the lodge's fire department had just been put out of action. As the phone was quickly answered, he remembered that the roads in and out of Pebble Beach were closed for the race. Outside support from Carmel, or anywhere else, would have a hard time responding. Reporting their situation, he slammed the phone down just as the spray from a fire extinguisher hit him square in the face, blinding him. Scotty vaulted the counter to keep him from closing the vault door. As Gregory wiped the stinging foam from his eyes the extinguisher slammed into his head, instantly shrinking his blurred vision to darkness. Scotty had control of the vault and the money; the hungry fire the unpredictable player.

Steam rose from the blistered paint of the engine's hood as the fire engine's passenger side tire became part of the blaze pumping black oily smoke into the building temporarily forcing Scotty to fall to the floor. For a moment, it seemed as if the fire had taken on a life of its own, mocking, laughing at the greed of mortal men when its appetite was so much stronger.

Hector and Smitty unrolled hoses from the rear of the engine quickly engaging two high pressured streams of water against the fire, the roiling smoke from the burning fire engine limited their effectiveness, the fire spreading deeper into the lobby.

Doyle's plan to get the money out quickly had just vanished. Having survived the crash, he stumbled through the door nearest the concierge desk. The flames had spread from the eucalyptus trees to the roof, the outside air being drawn inside bringing with it more fire, soon to block the second exit. There was now no way to get the cash out the front, and they no longer had the fire engine to stash it in. He could barely see the reception desk as the smoke stole his breath. "Scotty?" This more a cough, a retch, than a recognizable word.

Scotty responded more to the sound of Doyle coughing his lungs out than to the sound of his name. The spray from the hoses pushed the smoke away from them out the rear doors.

Everything was going wrong!

Wide-eyed, Scotty looked at Doyle. "Smokestack?"

"The money?" Doyle demanded to know, the roar of the flames making it hard to hear. Forcing himself to focus, Doyle searched the lobby for a safe exit. They couldn't just wheel the cart stacked with greenbacks through the Garden Bar and Grill. The corridor to the guest rooms was too long and smoke-filled to be safe.

"Smokestack?" Scotty still couldn't believe the younger man had burned alive.

"That's smoke in your eyes, not tears for the bastard. We've got more important things to worry about."

A high-pressure stream of water sprayed the lobby with limited affect. The other hose, wedged, could not reach the farther door. Smitty and Hector now had no way to bring the fire under control.

From the sound of the crash and the first plume of smoke, the Admiral knew that Doyle had bungled his best laid plan. A quick glance through the garden area doors told him that Doyle had boxed themselves in, the only way out being through the Garden Grill and the gardens behind the lodge, which were now crowded with people caught up in the frenzy as the disaster unrolled before them. They would have to bring the money out through the back or leave it to burn; witnesses be damned. *Perhaps they will need some help, for a reasonable fee,* the Admiral mused. He hated to see the magnificent lodge burn, but from all appearances he was about to be handed a royal flush while Doyle was bluffing with a pair of deuces.

Deputy Sheriff Wynn Owen was wondering what the two Carmel Detectives were up to when he saw the fire engine speed across the parking lot. The crash and the flames were almost simultaneous, the front of the lodge exploding in flames. He jumped in his car, turned on his lights and siren, skirting the kitchen side of the lodge to pull up just outside the patio doors to the Garden Bar and Grill where the two detectives were trying to control the panic that was beginning to drive the crowd.

Wynn's first thought was that the fire crew had been killed, leaving no one to fight the fire. Out running his own fear, he ran directly into the lobby where he was confronted by a man with singed hair in a fireman's uniform.

Doyle took a longshot, hoping that the deputy sheriff did not know any of the firemen by name or sight.

"What can I do?" Wynn spit out as he took in the rapidly expanding blaze.

"Get whatever officers you have to push back that crowd. Someone needs to go door-to-door and evacuate the place. We're not going to get outside help on this, and she's out of control." Doyle, his self-control under crisis worthy of an Oscar. He felt more like dropping to his knees and puking his guts out. Somehow, he realized that if he did not regain control now, he never would. All was not lost, as he suckered the officer into aiding his crime. "Pull your car up as close as you can to that door over there – meaning the garden door – there's over a halfmillion bucks in the vault and it's not fireproof. We'll roll it out to you on handcarts and put it in your trunk for safety."

Under the circumstances, that made sense. *If they couldn't save the building, they could save the money. Half a million bucks was a lot of dough.* The deputy moved his patrol car, popped open the trunk, then went after the two detectives to give them directions.

The Admiral agreed, it was a good idea. The patrol car was running, lights still flashing, trunk waiting for the money. He had one chance; with luck everyone was too busy to notice as he outsmarted them all. He gave Harvey the keys to their rental car telling him to take it to the guest house and park it in the back – out of sight. He would be there in a few moments. "Wait, take these," he took off his hat, giving the jewels to Harvey.

Thick, acrid smoke bellowed from the front lobby of the Del Monte Lodge forcing everyone back, coughing, eyes strained and streaming. Hector and Smitty, barely able to keep the fire at their end of the lobby from spreading. They were about to run out of water. Doyle and Scotty each loaded up a cart, racing their loot to the presumed safety of a Monterey County Sheriff's car. The deputy was busy organizing a group to knock on all the doors to evacuate the lodge.

Despite not recognizing the firemen, the concierge jumped in to help unload the cash into the car's trunk. A third and final cart was brought out. Doyle, happy with Liam's help, and very much aware that the lobby was now fully engulfed - even though more cops were arriving -let his greed get in his way as he made one last run through the blistering flames and smoke to the reception desk to empty the cash drawers.

Scotty went to tell Hector and Smitty to drop their hoses and hurry their butts around the kitchen area to where the patrol car was waiting for them.

Standing guard over the trunk, Liam suddenly turned his attention towards the 17th Fairway where the sounds of multiple emergency vehicles could now be heard. "Thank God!"

"You can say that again," the Admiral said as he appeared from out of nowhere. "You go and guide them in, so they don't get tangled in with the car show on the putting green. I'll find the constable and suggest that it's time for him to get his patrol car out of harm's way."

Liam slammed the trunk shut and ran towards the sound of the sirens.

The Admiral looked over his shoulder only once before he sat in the driver's seat, closed the door, turned off the emergency lights, and headed towards the guest house where Harvey should be arriving about the same time.

Barely able to see, breathing labored, Doyle practically collapsed as he staggered from the now fully involved lobby. Scotty, two steps behind him, gave him support as he wheeled the last of the cash, including coins, only a few hundred dollars, towards the sheriff's car.

Only it wasn't there . . .

Deputy Sheriff Wynn Owen shared their look of dismay as they stared at the vacant space of grass where the patrol car loaded with half million dollars in cash had been.

Hector and Smitty screeched to a halt as they saw their boss hovering over a cart with not enough cash to pay for one night at the expensive lodge. "Boss, where's the cop car with the money? We've got to get out of here." Hector said, loud enough for everyone in hearing distance to hear. That included Sheriff Owen and the two returning detectives.

"You stupid . . ." Doyle only had himself to blame, but that was not in his nature. He reached into a pocket of the fire coat.

Scotty tried to stop him.

Two bullets relieved any fear Hector might have had as the searing pain snuffed out his life.

Three shots from the law officers silenced Doyle – a look of acute pain locked on his face as his ulcer exploded in that last second as he recognized that he had gone too far one last time.

In the confusion Smitty got away in the crowd.

Scotty just raised his hands, wondering if he should have committed suicide by cop.

Caesar Augustus Penfield, a.k.a. the Admiral, quietly closed the trunk to their rental car as he watched the multiple fire engines tear up the highly groomed grasses of the Del Monte Golf Course as he waited for his young apprentice to return.

Harvey returned having parked the patrol car, sans cash, in the middle of the 16th Green – all traces of finger prints having been wiped clean. "Where to now, Professor Flimflam?" What he wanted was to go home – a rich man.

The race had been cancelled, the participants stuck at various locations along the 17 Mile Drive. A crowd of thousands descended upon the burning lodge to watch the fire crews limit the damage to the front lobby, with smoke damage to the dining room and various guest rooms.

"Why don't you drive over to the putting green while I see about checking out." Augustus tidied himself as he prepared for one last appearance as the Admiral.

"Check out?"

"While the room has been on the house, we were promised a new room due to our early morning visitors. I don't see that happening now. It would be polite to inquire as to a bill before we depart." He laughed. "They should be properly chastened when they realize how poorly their hospitality has been to Admiral Sir Stanton Hemphill. Better the Admiral be thought a victim than a suspect – don't you agree?" He opened the door to the car waving his apprentice in. "Off you go now, drive carefully, we wouldn't want our first expense to be a traffic ticket."

Augustus, hands in pockets, whistled as he walked back towards the lodge. He doubted he would find anyone with whom he could check out. *There's always good old Liam.*

Poor Sod has had a gob smacked, bloody awful day.

Thinking about Augustus's warning about not getting a traffic ticket, Harvey realized that he now had more than enough money to bail his piece of junk out of the tow yard. "Nah, leave it, maybe I'll get me a nice sports car."

Augustus returned having left the Admiral a character to be spoken about at cocktail parties as part of the story of the great Del Monte Lodge fire.

"Sausalito?" Harvey beamed.

"All in good time. First a little road trip to make sure we aren't being followed. A short stop in Monterey to buy some luggage to store the cash. We'll return the car to the rental agency in San Francisco. Buy a car, its registration to show an address in San Diego. Have you ever been to Yosemite? I hear it's a wonder. After a couple of days, we'll come back to your Sausalito. Do you think they'll have a room for yours truly?"

"Doyle and Scotty just gave notice." Harvey answered with a grin. "I've got to ask, why would you want a room there? It's not exactly a swanky place. Most of us live spoon to mouth. You can afford a lot better."

"All I need is a roof over my head. When you've got the type of money we now have – illicitly earned – you don't want to draw attention to yourself. At least for the moment it sounds just right. You've got the keys," Augustus said. "Perhaps we should have something to eat while in Monterey. I hear the abalone on Fisherman's Wharf is worth the trip."

It had taken some time and the painful loss of two fingernails before Captain Sylvester Hawke managed to work free the rope restraints. Now that he was freeing the fireman next to him, he could feel the painful sting. With the second man freed, Hawke went to the outside of the fire station where the fire engine ought to have been. Earlier he had heard the engine start up and it was more than hopeful thinking that he would find it there safe. As he turned towards the burning lodge, the first thing he saw was their one of a kind engine engulfed in flames beyond any salvage. The gasoline in the engine caught with one mighty air depressing thump, followed by an explosive roar. The front of the lodge where the engine had been wedged rose, towering flames burning, where the roof had once been. Pieces of burning timbers landed across the parking lot, some landing on some of the expensive cars parked there. One after another, plumes of high pressure water rose from the far side of the lodge.

Mixed emotions hit the fire crew, one by one, they witnessed the loss of their engine, along with the bonfire that burned away the heart of the Del Monte Lodge. Their charge had been to protect the lodge, and they had failed miserably; at least that was what their emotions told them.

Captain Hawke rubbed his brow as he took in the momentum of events, prioritizing his small crew's tasks as they stepped into a secondary role from which should have been their job from the start. "Okay guys, we couldn't help not being able to respond. It looks like the bad guys have left one hell of a mess. Other crews have responded via the emergency route across the golf course. Let's hit these fires in the parking lot before any of these expensive beauties makes a bad day worse."

Two hoses were quickly hooked up to the station's hydrant with enough hose to reach across the lot and then some. One hose crew headed towards the front of the parking lot where most of the flaming debris had landed. The second towards spot fires of which there appeared to be five or six, none significant.

Several people tried to stop Smitty as he ran through the Garden Bar and Grill. Most everyone had witnessed the police officers gun down a fireman after he had murdered one of his own. That the fleeing fireman pushing and shoving his way through the crowd was not a real fireman became obvious. Because of the number of guns already drawn no one tied to stop Smitty's flight.

It wasn't until Smitty arrived at their stolen car did it hit him that he was the only one left – Doyle, Smokestack, Hector, all dead. As far as he knew, Scotty too. The thought caused him to shake from head to toe as he dropped to his knees and puked. The powerful explosion of the fire engine brought him back to what was an ugly reality. Straightening up, he pulled off his fire jacket, dropping it to the ground next to the car. He fumbled in his pockets looking for the car keys, which he never had in the first place. "Shit!" He tried the driver's door; to his great relief it was unlocked. While Smokestack had been the king of the pickpockets among the three, Smitty was the car thief. He did one quick look around before dropping down beneath the steering wheel to connect the wires.

Hawke, who was leading a hose team to cover the spot fires, spotted Smitty a second before he dropped out of sight inside the passenger door of the 48 Bentley Mark IV. "There," he pointed towards the Bentley, "that's one of the bastards that hog-tied us." The hose team turned and within moments had positioned the nozzle of the hose directly on Smitty's ass as he fumbled with the wires. Just as the engine clicked, a powerful force of water hit him painfully in his posterior, rolling him, folding him into the passenger's floor space where a full grown human being shouldn't have fit, the force of the water breaking an arm before wedging him in so tight it would take an hour for the emergency crew to pull him free.

Captain Hawke suffered no regrets regarding Smitty as they played their hoses on the smoldering wreck of their prized fire engine.

Chapter Thirty-One

Chief of Police Marc Ganow met the two San Francisco Homicide Detectives early Wednesday morning at his office in downtown Sausalito. Petty larceny and parking tickets occupied the schedules of the four-man police department, and a link to a high-profile heist and triple homicide at a world-famous resort was not something the chief would assign to one of the officers. There hadn't been a high - profile crime in his boring bayside community since the payroll heist at the shipyard back in 1943. That had been before his time and remained unsolved. Who knows, if everything went just right, he might even get his name in the paper.

"Good morning gentlemen." Chief Ganow said. "Can I offer you some coffee before we start out?"

Working with small town cops was a huge ego lift for Detective Schmidt. They treated him as if he were a big deal; one did not become a San Francisco Homicide Detective by being a slouch. The Chief shook Schmidt's hand, not extending the same courtesy to his Chinese counterpart.

"Have you had any prior contact with Patrick Doyle, Scotty McBeth, or any of their associates? McBeth has confessed to being part of a protection racket scam Doyle ran here in Sausalito. A baseball bat found in the car they left at a Colma Cemetery may be linked to a series of brutal murders and assaults in Chinatown. A Rubin Smith – Smitty – a low-life punk who ran with Doyle's gang, has confessed to armed assault, but not to murder. Those were Doyle's doings. He's got quite a history, including a Section Eight from the army during the war." He dropped the file on the chief's desk. "No coffee, thanks."

"Until I got your call yesterday, I hadn't heard of any of these characters. None of my officers have either. Their car is registered to a dead-end address with fourteen unpaid parking tickets – outside of that, nothing."

"And the boarding house?"

"Nothing. Most of the tenets are low income. A while back a young woman disappeared, but we found no evidence of foul play. She probably split because she couldn't pay the rent."

So far, the Chief had not acknowledged Tse's existence.

Tse remained stoic; it was his bad luck to be partnered with Sergeant Schmidt. He wanted to remain in the department and did not need some small town prejudiced cop raising any stink about sending an uppity 'Chink' his way.

"Any trouble with the warrant?" Schmidt asked. The warrant needed to come from a Marin Country judge where

San Francisco had no jurisdiction.

It was a late morning start, the breakfast buffet growing cold, but no one complained. Michelangelo was taking a short walk. His legs, freed from their casts, would take some time to strengthen. A slow trek to the end of the driveway and back about all he could muster. Sarah had piled a breakfast plate high, returning to her room, speaking to no one. Her morning paper she left by the trash. The headlines dominating the front page of the San Francisco Chronicle read: ***WHO ROBBED THE ROBBERS?***

"Over Seven Hundred Fifty Thousand Dollars, taken from the Del Monte Lodge during an arson fire, was stolen from the trunk of a Monterey County Sheriff's car where it had been stored for safekeeping, while authorities were engaged in a gun battle with the original thieves. A spokesperson for the Sheriff's Department said that they were following up on leads in Sausalito where Patrick Doyle, mastermind of the heist, who was shot to death by police, had lived."

The paper was folded as it had been deposited in front of Sarah's door, unread.

Oswaldo and Michael had gone to the junkyard to see

if they could find some lumber that they might be able to use for the stairwell they were working on. Mollie, Betty and Renata chatted about this, that and another thing, their usual morning banter.

Michelangelo had just made it to the end of the drive-way wishing he still had his wheelchair for respite, when the Sheriff's car, followed by a San Francisco Police car pulled up. The sheriff rolled down his window. "Good Morning Padre, good to see you out and about. Can we give you a lift back to the house?"

Michelangelo did not have to be asked twice, while his legs no longer itched they lacked the strength to make him feel as if walking was a good idea. By the time they reached the house, he had heard enough to share what he knew about Doyle; a former priest's observations of a man easily prone to violence, sadistic, perhaps an addict, who rarely spoke or said anything at the community table. He knew that Doyle and Scotty were friends, but surprised that Scotty had been so involved in Doyle's criminal escapades.

Sheriff Ganow showed Betty the warrant, wanting to see both Doyle's and Scotty's rooms, and to interview all the residents who might be present.

Betty was not in the least surprised with the police interest in Doyle and Scotty. Renata had a lot to say. Mollie spotted the newspaper and was busy reading the juicy information as Renata rattled on and on, while Tse took notes.

Betty knocked on Sarah's door saying that there were some gentlemen in the kitchen that wished to speak with her, then returned.

Sarah blanched white at first sight of the policemen, and for good reason. Tongue-tied, afraid that her past had caught up with her, Sarah just stood in the doorway with a guilty smile she tried to hide.

"Sarah Brandt, Sergeant Ralph Schmidt, San Francisco Police – Homicide. We'd like to ask you a few questions about Patrick Doyle and Scotty McBeth."

It was the look of recognition that made Sarah sick to her stomach, felting slightly dizzy, and having to grab hold of the back of a kitchen chair for support. The questions asked were the same as everyone else. How well did you know Patrick Doyle? Did either Doyle or McBeth say or do anything that might have tipped you off to their criminal activities? Did you know they were going to Carmel – Pebble Beach, this last weekend? Were there times they seemed plush with cash? Did they ever mention the names Smokestack, Hector, or Smitty? The questions drew the same answers from everyone including Sarah – they could add nothing of value except the men were prone to violence and to be avoided.

Mollie took the officers upstairs to inspect Doyle's and Scotty's rooms, the officers asking the rest to remain available in the kitchen should they have any more questions.

Schmidt did not at first recognize Sarah, it was her reaction to being questioned that drew his curiosity. *Was she someway in cahoots with either Doyle or McBeth? Lovers? No, not likely.* Then it came to him, she had been a payroll clerk at one of the shipyards in San Francisco during the war. He had been on Robbery at the time. Her name wasn't Sarah Brandt, it was Silvia Brown and a key suspect in the theft of a payroll. There had been another payroll robbery in Sausalito. Silvia Brown had dropped off the face of the earth. The warrant for her arrest might have expired, but more likely just forgotten – by everyone but him. Sometimes, the direct approach is the best way to get a wanted felon to confess. Returning to the kitchen he brought the subject straight up: "Silvia Brown, we have some long overdue business to attend to."

Sarah tried to run, but her guilt tripped her up.

"Silvia Brown, you are under arrest for the theft of the payroll from the San Francisco Naval Shipyard at Hunter's point in March 1944." He brought out the handcuffs. "Chief, I am remanding her to your custody until Navy authorities can be contacted."

"Nice, and I've got a payroll robbery here in Sausalito back in forty-three I think we need to look into."

Everyone in the room was aghast, they had come to investigate one crime, and had resolved two cold cases which otherwise might never have been solved. Sarah – Silvia Brown – looked as angry as she was at herself for being so stupid, and for being caught.

Renata couldn't help but ask. "How much did she get, Officer?"

"As I recall, something in the fifty-thousand-dollar range."

Mollie, who had never see that much money, gasped.

"Fifty-thousand, and you are living here?"

"Yeah, I lived here," Silvia exclaimed, "I bought the place, you stupid cow."

"Moo, to you too," Mollie responded with an unexpected giggle. It was the first time she had ever talked back to the woman; it felt good.

Betty lit up as the Chief took Silvia out to the police car.

"I knew it."

"Well, I'll be damned," Michelangelo said.

"Now that you're no longer a priest, I'd be careful what you wish for." Renata teased. She was having a grand day, Doyle and Scotty were gone, as was Sarah Brandt – the curse of the Bay House had been lifted.

After finding nothing of value other than proof of Doyle's addiction, the police left. Sarah Brandt was arrested on suspicion of being Silvia Brown, a suspect in the payroll robbery. If finger prints did not match up, or former employees of the shipyard could not be found to identify her as Silvia Brown, then they could not hold her longer than 48 hours. Once identified as Silvia Brown a search warrant could be issued for her room.

No one dared think that the inhospitable Sarah Brandt would ever return. Renata was the first to offer up a bottle of wine. Michelangelo agreed that there was much to celebrate. As did Betty, who did not add her concern about the fate of the Bayview House as their fortunes had changed. Sarah owned the Bayview House, and it was up for sale. Perhaps the curse was just beginning?

Work stopped on the stairwell to Michael and Mollie's apartment and the other improvements Betty had thought of. During the day they had nothing to do but speculate. At night they listened to Michael's music and argued their speculations.

It was a nice day with twinkling gems reflecting off the turquoise bay - the sky above infinite in promise, while hope drained away from the residents of the Bayview House as they sat in the shade of an evergreen nestled near the side of the house.

For sale

It had only taken two days for the agent to post the sign since Sarah Brandt's arrest. No officers had returned with a search warrant, leaving the residents depressed and melancholy as they contemplated their future. Each time they heard a car pass by on the street below they half-expected to see either a yellow cab lift dust from the gravel driveway as it returned Sarah to further torment them, or her lawyer with eviction notices for all. Mollie and Renata had served a lunch of iced tea, spam and cheese sandwiches with some potato and dill pickle salad. No one spoke as they ate while looking down the driveway; except Betty who sat in her wheelchair staring at the sign - the two words not quite registering their finality. No one with any business sense would keep a middle-aged woman in a wheelchair to manage what was now a two and a half story residency hotel in need of much repair. She had no family, and no other source of income.

If Michelangelo was forced to leave his parents had a small guestroom above their garage. Their disappointment in his leaving the priesthood would be unspoken but he would always see it in their eyes. What concerned him now was not his own future but that of those who contemplated their bleak tomorrows as they sat pretending to enjoy their lunches in a rare warm August sun.

Renata had outlived her money, as little as it had been, earning her keep with her special talent in the kitchen. He suspected that when the day came to close the Bayview House, she would just lie down on her small bed in her little room at the end of the hall, and just give up; after saying her final prayers, of course.

Mollie had a good chance to become the new manager if that is what the new owners planned to do. Michael faced the same challenges he faced every day of his life, only now he had Mollie. If, somehow, they managed to stay on, he just might be able to continue his night music. If they had to move on, his silence would break Mollie's heart.

The day grew August hot, the fog bank still far offshore, the iced tea tepid, their sandwiches half-eaten, as their eyes all turned toward the street as a brand new 1952 Silver-gray Studebaker Commander Convertible edged its way up the hill.

Michelangelo, who still needed a cane for support rose shielding his eyes against the glare with his cupped hands as the car drew near. Was it the lawyer, or someone thinking of buying and stealing away their home?

The driver honked, twice.

A hand waved from the passenger seat.

Betty was the first to see who had waved. It was not bad neighbor Sam coming to wish her the worst – it was Harvey and a stranger with a very friendly smile.

"You must have sold a lot of hats," Renata said as Harvey got out of the car with a grin as wide and welcoming as the Golden Gate Bridge.

Caesar Augustus Pinfield was introduced as a visiting professor of Ethics and Philosophy on a leave of absence from an unspecified East Coast University.

Michelangelo licked his intellectual chops anticipating many grand conversations.

When asked about a room Betty was honest, telling them that the *For-Sale* sign had just been posted and she did not know anything about the future of the Bayview House. In her heart, she knew that if Sarah could get revenge from behind jail bars, she would.

This took the wind out of Harvey's sails.

"My dear woman, I would be delighted to take accommodations one day at a time until providence suggests that its time to move on. My dear friend Harvey here, has told me so much about you that any other option would be disappointing."

Betty had to think about where to put their new guest. The only room available on the first floor was Sarah's - God forbid she still might return. Doyle was dead, while Scotty faced a long prison sentence. She would have to check with the police to see if their rooms were still considered to be part of a crime scene. The two rooms across the hall were empty but wouldn't that be dreary putting the man across the hall from the ghosts of murders and thieves. That left Mary Griffin's room, but she couldn't give up the idea that Mary would return. It wasn't Mary that she missed so much as it was her music. Mary was practically a ghost even when she had been there.

"It's the right thing to do", Michelangelo said, anticipating what she was thinking. "I doubt that Mary will ever be back, but if you insist on holding a room for her, then move her things to one of the rooms across from Doyle's or Scotty's. Should she return, she will have the morning sun.

Renata winked, sharing a smile of approval.

"Mr. Pinfield, please have a seat here in the shade with us while Mollie makes your room ready. It will be upstairs, Room 10, right across the hall from Harvey. Mollie, move Mary's things to Room 5." Betty relaxed a little having finally made the decision.

"Room 5 will be fine, I wouldn't want to inconvenience anyone." Augustus said, looking most apologetic.

"Like you, professor, Mary Griffin is on a sabbatical. Now would you care for some iced tea?"

"Harvey, you brought some gifts for your friends. I think now would be a good time, don't you? What a marvelous view," Augustus said as he took a comfortable seat to just enjoy the slight August breeze with a view that kept the living alive.

Mollie went up to make Augustus's room ready.

Harvey popped the trunk, retrieving a plain brown paper-wrapped package that he gave to Michelangelo, a larger cloth-wrapped package for Michael, along with a dozen roses for Mollie for when she returned. A woman's small handbag for Renata, which held a lavender head scarf, her favorite color, and from the back seat of the car a new wheelchair for Betty.

Tears filled everyone's eyes with Betty's gift.

He had a hand-held marine telescope for Oswaldo to help him look at the boats that busied the bay. When told of Oswaldo's abrupt departure, he kept the telescope for himself.

Speechless, while wondering where on earth penniless Harvey Freed got the money for such extravagant gifts, each took a private moment to unwrap their own.

Augustus struggled with the weight of a case of good Italian wine, the last treasure besides their luggage hidden in the car's trunk. "Since the sun has diluted your iced tea, may I suggest a bottle of red wine. Augustus said this would be to your liking."

Michelangelo's gift was a thin long-stemmed pipe, English in style, like the actor Bing Crosby smoked in the movies.

Michael's was a new trumpet, the smile that came to his face as beautiful as the music that would soon come from it.

"Mollie told me that you once played the trumpet, that years ago you were forced to hawk it. But when you raised the money to get it back, the pawn shop had sold it to someone else. She said that you always favored a trumpet over the saxophone."

Speechless, Michael tested it, stood facing the city where he and Mollie had first met and played a stirring adaptation of 'And the Angel's Sing', a Johnny Mercer tune. Across Sausalito, people turned and listened, something was happening at the old Bayview House.

"Oh my," Augustus's heart nearly melted at its beauty.

Chapter Thirty-Two

Mollie stepped out onto the platform on the first-floor roof where her husband had first played his night music to look down to where her husband now played. It was the first time he had played when the sun was shining since they had left the Honeysuckle Rose Hotel; not that the sun ever warmed the basement ballroom. She had never heard him on a trumpet – and marveled. The way he played gave her little chills and electric shocks almost as good as when they made love.

Mary had returned to the Bayview House on numerous occasions. She went unnoticed because she wanted it that way - people frightened her. It was Mary's third night away from the Pinetree Institute, her first back home at the Bayview House. The last time she had the attic apartment to herself, which was perfect, because while the doctors told her that there was no longer a reason for her to remain at the Institute, she still had an obsessive need for privacy – to become invisible if that were possible. The doctors had diagnosed her with Avoidant Personality Disorder. Many who suffer from the phobia cannot stand to be around crowds, more extreme cases suffer symptoms when around only one or two people; that was Mary. Mary's was triggered by a fear of being scrutinized by others because of a personal secret – whether perceived or not - she thought that people were trying to unveil her secret to do her harm. When the condition became too much to bear she admitted herself to the Institute – but it was here at the Bayview House that she could truly have her privacy. Over the years she had built secret passageways where she could move about the house without being seen. Without having to confront another person she felt safe, not ashamed of what she was, or who she was. Outside these walls, Bernie mocked and shamed her. Inside these walls, she and Bernie became one living through their music, that was when the Bayview House still had its piano. Here, no one asked questions she refused to answer. At the institute the nurses and interns were always watching her, the kindness in their eyes masking their true cruelty. All she wanted was to be left alone. She checked herself into the Institute when the pressure of the outside world became too much, and she checked herself out when the prying eyes within the Institute became more threatening than those outside. The Institute itself did her little good, it was her 'alone times' in the music room that was the medication she needed.

She had come home in the dead of night, hidden in the trees until the man with the horn stopped playing from somewhere up on the roof and all the lights in the house went dark. Beneath the stairs, just outside the kitchen, she slid a plank aside, to enter a crawl space. After sliding the panel back into place, she lit a penny candle and crawled forward six feet where she found the passageway hidden behind the kitchen walls. The passage was narrow, barely tall enough for her to stand. When needed, she could open a panel inside the pantry that gave her access to the kitchen. There, while everyone slept she could eat, her table a shelf in the pantry, the door closed protecting her from any chance of detection. After eating some leftover chicken, a scoop of potato salad, and some tomato juice, she went back into the passageway, finding her way to the ladder that took her up behind the linen closet to her sanctuary in the attic. Her bed there was oh so much more comfortable than the one at the Institute.

Cupping the candle in her hand, she looked for a second one she always kept on a little table just outside the closet door. It wasn't there. She looked on the floor, the glow from the one she held darting around the room chasing shadows. She couldn't find it, deciding to keep just the one for now – she was tired and started to climb up the ladder to her bed in the loft.

Someone stirred.

She blew out her candle, freezing in place as she listened, the beat of her heart making a horrific racket. There were two people in her bed – a man and a woman.

Michael rolled over in his sleep, placing his arm around Mollie, not aware that there was someone else in their room.

Mary Griffin clung in the shadows to the ladder to the loft bed. A soft snowstorm of muted grays,struggled against the deeper darkness of night, danced through the muted window glass, and the canopies of the trees just outside. What to do? They shouldn't be there. It was her room, her safe place, and now it had been violated. They would have to go! She found herself holding her breath, afraid that she might wake them. She was tired, too tired to think - there would be time enough tomorrow to figure out how.

Above the linen closet, above the attic apartment, there was a small space barely four-foot-wide and seven-foot long. It was dusty, but she fell asleep on the bed made of old flour sacks and linens she had made for just such an emergency.

The tiny ribbon of light that tapped her mind awake reminded her that she was not in her own bed – just like Goldilocks and the Three Bears, someone was in her bed. She became angry as she tried to orient herself in the specks of dust falling through the thin ribbons of light. She had overslept, and she had to pee. All the bathrooms were downstairs. She put her ear to the floor and listened. Certain that whoever had taken her room was gone, she crept quietly to the ceiling panel, slid it aside and lowered the rope ladder. Quiet as a mouse she climbed down into the narrow closet, stepping lightly just in case someone was still there. Her foot touched the closet floor . . .

Mollie heard it first.

Everyone else heard 'the Angels Sing.'

She heard a thump followed by a woman's cry. They all looked up at the sound of Mollie's cry. "Someone's hurt."

Who? Everyone was accounted for.

"That's the curse knocking on the door, or perhaps Sarah has somehow returned."

Renata, I promise you there is no curse," Michelangelo said a bit exasperated with her affinity for the curse.

The thud was loud enough to be heard clearly from the outside.

Michael put down his horn and yelled up to Mollie asking if she was all right.

Renata rolled Betty up the wheelchair ramp into the house where she waited at the base of the stairs as Renata went up to the second floor. Despite his healing legs, Michelangelo was the first to join Mollie at the scene of the accident. What he found was that the floor to the linen closet where Michael and Oswaldo were building the stairs had collapsed, dumping a dazed woman into the linen closet below.

"Mary?" Renata said, as surprised as if they had stumbled upon the legendary curse, instead of a woman feared dead who was very much alive. "Mary? Mary Griffith, how did you . . . never mind . . . are you all right?"

Bewildered, Mary did not recognize Michelangelo without his priestly vestments. Mollie, she did not know at all. These were strangers who were plotting to harm her, their arms reaching menacingly towards her as she backed into a corner of the closet, more frightened of them than the suddenness of her fall. She pushed and slapped at the air in front of her face, madness a barrier against kindness extended. "No! Leave me alone. Go away, you can't see me. No . . ."

"Mary?" Betty covered her mouth with her right hand as if saying her name might change the rotation of the earth. "It can't be? My sweet Jesus, she's alive after all this time. But how? Renata, did you say that its Mary?"

Mollie offered a helping hand, which frightened Mary more.

The young woman was an intruder in her house who was both angry and frightened at the same time, Mary was pushed to her limit - like a frightened cat hissing with no mechanism left but to strike out, claws extended, teeth bared.

Michelangelo was stunned by the blind panic in Mary's face as she launched forward, attacking Mollie, scratching and biting as if her life depended on it.

Mollie shrieked, blood running from several fresh scratches on her cheek, neck, and where she had been painfully bitten on the soft flesh between her left thumb and forefinger as she had tried to protect herself.

Mollie knocked Renata down as she scrambled away from the unexpected vicious attack.

"I'm trying to calm Mary, damn it," Michelangelo swore after receiving a painful bite on his wrist as he too backed away.

Desperate, defending her small space in the closet, Mary searched for an exit. When she forced back her presumed attacks she leaped up onto a closet shelf as she reached for something to grasp a hold of to climb back out the hole she had fallen through. The rope ladder swung slightly in the space above. If she could reach that, she could reach the crawl space above and from there several of her secret passages that beckoned safety and her return to the Institute she now thought of as safe and welcoming. She jumped to a second shelf, which tipped, dumping her back towards the floor only to be caught by a man with a demonic face.

Seeing Michael's face, she screamed and fainted.

Renata, crossing herself, called back to Betty. "It's Mary Griffith. She's alive. She just dropped from heaven into the linen closet."

Mollie looked up through the hole in the upstairs closet floor where she saw a trap door that led from the closet up into the attic where a rope ladder hung down. When Mary had climbed down from her attic hideaway to use Michael and Mollie's bathroom, the closet floor that had been partially sawed through gave way.

The night noises and disappearing food were now explained. It was the ghost of Mary Griffin, who to everyone's surprise was very much alive, desperate, perhaps a bit mad. The question that Mary might be of danger to herself or others hung in the air as Michael carried her into the room Betty had saved for her, placing her gently on the bed.

Renata brought a cold damp cloth, placing it on Mary's forehead. She looked at Mollie and Michael. "Perhaps you should go make some tea. She doesn't know you. Your presence might just frighten her more when she wakes."

She whispered to Michelangelo. "If you have not thrown all your collars away would you – could you – just for a moment become a priest again. Just for appearance sake. She might find some comfort in your being here."

This made Michelangelo most uncomfortable having just freed himself from the Holy Mother Church; his emotions still conflicted.

"Please?"

Betty helped Mollie clean her wounds downstairs in the kitchen. Tears glistened in Mollie's eyes, she was frightened of this violent stranger in their midst, who had just attacked her when all she meant was kindness. "I don't understand?" Betty said, not expecting any rational response. "All this time, Mary couldn't have been up there all this time? Surely, someone would have heard."

"I noticed something when we first moved into the apartment. It was clean, very little dust and no cobwebs. I didn't think much about it at the time. Do you suppose she had been living there?"

"I don't know, it's possible I guess. We'll just have to wait, perhaps she will tell us." Betty said.

The teapot whistled.

"If she doesn't run away," Mollie added as she winched at the touch of a wet cloth as it was dabbed against the scratch on her cheek.

Augustus and Harvey poured themselves a second glass

of wine. Augustus took everything in, wondering if it might not be better to move on. The mysterious woman upstairs might just draw the wrong type of attention. He had more than enough money to do just about anything he pleased. Admittedly, the people intrigued him, especially Michael. What an extraordinary creature, so ugly – frighteningly so – but able to create such beauty at the same time.

Renata lightly held the cold cloth to Mary's forehead as she studied her face. Why she had forced herself into isolation and exclusion from any sense of community or human connection was a question that would have to wait. Right now, Renata's motivation was to calm the troubled girl when she woke, to keep her from lashing out and running away.

"I think I'll make some molasses cookies. Mary always liked my molasses cookies." Betty said, as if she needed to convince herself. Everything was happening upstairs. Just sitting in her wheelchair listening to the voices above where she couldn't go, gave her an uneasy feeling. For the longest time she had held onto the thought that Mary was still alive, that she hadn't been harmed or committed suicide. She had always nursed some deep emotional problems, the closer someone got, if questions were asked, she would drift away into a private fantasy world which she shared with an imaginary friend Bernie. Who was Bernie, someone she had once known, or an imaginary friend? She would play the piano for hours for hours on end. She rarely smiled - when she did it was for some reason only she knew. When asked about Bernie, her answer was angered, perhaps accusatory. "Who is this Bernie, and why do you keep bothering me about someone I do not know?" One thing that Betty was glad for was that Sarah was gone. Mary had always been unreasonably frightened of her. Strangely, there were times when Mary would stare at Sarah as if they shared some unusual bond. She could tell that it was a hate relationship, but there was something more. She reasoned that if there was one thing that kept Mary at the Bayview House it was that everyone - except Sarah - granted her the space she seemed so desperately to need. No one bothered her in her room, or when she played the piano in what had been the parlor. The piano had been Michelangelo's and when the property owner demanded that the parlor be closed to become just another rented room he had donated the piano to the church. It was shortly after that Mary had begun her disappearing acts.

Michelangelo sat in the kitchen watching Betty and Mollie, thinking about everything that had happened; there had been a lot and how it all connected, if at all, puzzled him. There was the revelation that the house was to be sold, the death of Doyle, the arrest of Scotty and Sarah - the surprising arrival of Augustus, a man of some education and means, partnered someway with Harvey, a pauper with little future promise. And now, the mysterious return of Mary Griffin, a very disturbed young woman who for all practical purposes, should be institutionalized, a clear threat to herself and others – or was she?

"Betty, do you know what a savant is?"

"No, I don't think so. Why do you ask?" Betty replied.

Mollie looked up. "Someone who is really smart – I think."

"Not exactly," Michelangelo replied thoughtfully. "A savant is functionally handicapped, perhaps retarded, but has a remarkable skill that most of us don't have. A genius in mathematics whose overall intelligence level is limited to that of a six-year-old,or the ability to memorize an entire novel word for word even though he might not understand the story. If Mary is a savant, it makes her a very complex puzzle. She might never be able to function in a world where she is asked to co-exist with people, but there may be a gifted side where she takes shelter from the world she cannot live in. As a genius savant, she may be able to hear any music and immediately play it on the piano to perfection. At a convent I once visited, there was a girl – sixteen or seventeen – who could translate ancient Latin manuscripts into perfect English; she was functionally illiterate. People, especially women with *Savant Syndrome* are extremely rare, but if I'm right,we might bring a miracle into the young woman's life." He laughed aloud, he had to give up his priesthood before producing a miracle."I think that Mary may be a savant with the ability to hear music of any kind just once and then play it on the piano as if she had been rehearsing it for years."

Betty's eyes flashed recognition. "Yes, remember how she could hear something on the radio and play it on the piano a minute later. Sometimes it was better than it was on the radio. She was fond of classical."

"That was because it was what you liked to hear."

Betty thought of Michael's music. "I wonder if she would like jazz? You don't suppose…"

"I don't see why not. If I'm right, as a savant, she only

needs to hear a tune once, then by golly, she could give Michael a challenge." Michelangelo took out his new pipe and studied it before packing it with tobacco.

"Michael would like that." Mollie added.

"And it might be better for her than sending her back to that awful institution where all that doctors do, is poke and prod, where they have no business going in the first place."

Betty countered with a highly intuitive response. "What if we moved Oswaldo down the hall – should he return, I mean - and put a piano in the room next to Mary's."

"With a connecting door," Michelangelo thought aloud.

Mollie liked having her husband play from the covered balcony by their third-floor apartment. *But if it would help Mary . . .* She touched the still raw scratch on her face. "I'll ask Michael what he thinks." Her response was hesitant, thinking that the woman was unstable and dangerous.

Michelangelo understood her hesitancy. "Why don't you wait, we don't even have a piano yet."

Chapter Thirty-Three

The church was only a few blocks away, the piano had been man-handled there, and could be man-handled back. The archdiocese was selling everything at bargain prices, Michelangelo would leave a dollar in a collection basket for the piano that he had gifted in the first place. He searched his pockets, finding two dimes, opting to take back what was his.

Michelangelo wished Oswaldo was there, right now his strength would be appreciated. The big man had found a job fishing and wasn't due back for a couple more days. Michelangelo stepped out into the yard where he looked with doubt at Harvey's scrawny frame. "Augustus, Harvey, let's go for a short walk, I need your help with something."

"Oh dear, with all the excitement I forgot about Mr. Pinfield's room." Mollie said.

"Why don't you move Oswaldo across the hall, and Mr. Pinfield and Harvey down to rooms five and six." Betty said, anticipating Michelangelo's idea about the piano. Somehow, she knew that he would make it happen.

Mollie hurried off to ready the rooms.

Michelangelo had been given braces for his legs when they tired. It seemed that this might be a good time to put them to use. "Gentlemen, just give me a couple of minutes, I need something from my room."

Augustus had been enjoying the afternoon breeze, soon to be edged out by the cold within the approaching fog bank, as it blurred the Golden Gate Bridge and the nearby Presidio. He wondered what the urgent commotion had been inside the house, bidding his time to inquire.

"I can see why you like it here," he said to Harvey. "While I haven't seen my room, it all seems pleasant enough. I think I'll give it a try . . . for awhile . . . then we'll see. In the meantime, you and I have got to have a talk. You've passed your first test with flying colors and I'm willing to teach you the tricks of the trade."

Harvey swelled with pride, he had never passed any-thing with flying colors, though he didn't have any brag-ging rights because it had been a criminal act. There was one thing he didn't understand; well more than one thing, but he had to start somewhere. "Gosh, I'm flattered, you and me partners; but don't we have enough to last us two lifetimes?" He did not even know what his share was but compared to what he had in the past he was a rich man.

"That we do, lad. The best part of pulling off a good con

is the fun. There's nothing like out witting the other fella and getting paid for it at the same time. You will always remember our great con at the Del Monte Lodge where we out maneuvered the millionaires while they drank their champagne and dip their fat fingers in the caviar. We outwitted the guys who robbed the lodge, coming home with all the goods. There were police all over the place and we took our treasure out in one of their own cars with them none the wiser. That's a tale to tell when you're old and gray and lifting a schooner with the other old men who will enjoy the hell out of the story and not believe word one to be the truth. You will have fond memories of the grand time we had. There might not be the need to pull off another con – except just for the fun of it." He finished his wine as he gave Harvey a wink, allowing the Admiral the last word. "Just for the fun of it."

Harvey popped open the car trunk." I'll put your luggage in your room. It's okay, no one will bother it there." He added, feeling the need to reassure Augustus, because most of the suitcases were filled with money.

"I'm sure they'll be fine. The blue suitcase goes with you," he said giving Harvey a knowing nod.

Betty told Harvey that he would now be in Room Six and Mr. Pinfield would be in Five. Augustus followed, loaded down with two heavy suitcases. Harvey had heard of Mary, never met her, and frankly had thought her to be a figment of Betty's imagination.

"Mary Griffin, I haven't met her, have I?" Augustus asked.

"No, and neither have I," replied Harvey, "I thought she was dead."

"Dead." Augustus had been amused when first meeting his fellow residents of the Bayview House - especially Michael. A dead woman risen heightened his curiosity.

Mollie, who was finishing making up Augustus's room, commented without looking up from her work. "She isn't dead, she just showed up."

Renata peeked in. "She fell from heaven into our linen closet."

Perplexed, Augustus and Harvey's faces showed a disconnect with what they were hearing.

"That's because she was hiding in the attic." Betty added from the bottom of the landing.

Mollie was now concerned because she thought that Renata was with Mary, who still might be dangerous. "Who is with her now?"

"Michael." Renata said. "Do I smell molasses cookies?"

"Michael, do you think it's safe?" Mollie asked remembering that Mary's first sight of Michael had been somewhat traumatic.

"They're fine," Renata replied, helping Mollie with the last tucks of the bedding. "They're becoming kindred spirits."

Augustus put the suitcases in his closet. "I think I need a drink. I know it's early in the day, but damn the clock - you got anything stronger than wine around here?" Not waiting for an answer, he peeked into the room where Michael and Mary were. Determined that Michael was not talking with a ghost, he headed back downstairs. Harvey dropped his suitcases into his closet and followed Augustus downstairs – but not before peeking in on Michael and the mysterious Mary. *So that's what she looks like.*

Renata, who knew where the bourbon was hidden, joined Betty downstairs. Bourbon on the rocks with molasses cookies was always a treat.

Not frightened, Mary was bemused and confused by the man who sat beside her bed. She should have been terrified. Instead she was reasonably comfortable with a strange man in her bedroom. "You're . . ." she started to say.

"Michael."

"I was about to say ugly. I think that's why I'm not afraid of you. I've been afraid of everyone for as long as I can remember." She bit her lip, pulling the sheet tighter, as an older man peeked in the door. He was gone before she could scream.

"Its all-right, no one here will hurt you."

"Yes. They will, it's not safe here, which is why I hid in the attic. But now you and . . . and . . . have my secret place."

"Mollie, she's my wife."

"She attacked me when I fell."

"No one attacked you, but your abrupt arrival did scare

the bejesus out of everyone."

She laughed. There was so much kindness buried behind his hideous face. "I'm ugly too." She once again buried herself until only her eyes and forehead showed above the bedding. "Ohhhh!" This time it was Harvey who peeked in.

Michael got up and closed the door.

They talked and slowly Mary revealed more than she ever had to the brain doctors at the clinic.

Everyone in the house except Michael and Mary sat in the shade eating molasses cookies and sipping bourbon cocktails. There were more cookies than questions, with no one willing to go first, without adding to what a befuddling day it already was. One thing was clear, poor confused Mary Griffin had taken an unusual liking to Michael. If told of this, her doctors would tell them that this level of engagement with another human being was something beyond her capacity. The best thing they could do was just let it happen.

Once the bourbon hit the ice, Augustus lost all interest in helping to move a piano up or down any kind of hill. So did Michelangelo, until an unspoken reprimand recommit-ted him to the task. Harvey, who wasn't fond of bourbon, tagged along. On the way to the church Michelangelo knocked on a few parish doors, rounding up four stout volunteers to guide the piano home.

The piano sat in the shade waiting for Michael's strong back to help get it up the stairs. The volunteers enjoyed the cookies and iced tea, the bourbon a private treat. Finally, to break what was becoming an uncomfortable silence, Augustus sat down and began to play.

'Ol man river

Dat ool man river

He must have sumpin'

But I don't say nuthin'

He just keeps rollin'. . .

His voice was as rich and deep as the Mississippi, almost strong enough to push the fog bank back another day. It seemed to fit with the bourbon and molasses cookies - the bourbon held in check until the volunteers had muscled the piano upstairs and gone their way. As he sang, a window quietly slid open on the second floor. It was Michael. He had placed a chair near the window where Mary now sat and listened. In the closet amongst the tangled linen and in her bed where only her eyes and forehead had really shown, he had never really seen her. He was careful not to gaze at her for more than a moment. Sitting by the window, she wore a melon-pink headscarf that showed little of her hair, which at best guess he thought to be sun-bleached terra cotta; her skin was pale, translucent, having hidden herself from the world, the sun, her fellow human beings. Her hyacinth colored eyes, unusually luminous, made deeper by her pale skin, a clear and vivid purple. Her eyebrows, a darker orange threaded with brown, were unusually thick on such a small dollish face. A long winter coat hid most of her figure. She was perhaps five feet one, petite, light as a feather because she did not eat much or often. Her hands were small, fingers perfectly carved to reach a piano's keys, nails nibbled back to where Michael wondered if they might be tender to the touch.

No one could see her, no one threatened her, as she sang along softly her fingers caressing invisible piano keys on her lap as Augustus continued:

Colored folks work on de Mississippi

Colored folks work while de white folks play

Pullin' dose boats from de dawn to sunset

Getting no rest till de judgment day.'

Michael stole a moment away from Mary to salvage a few cookies from downstairs for himself and his new shadow. Everyone was curious, now was not the time to speculate on any answers. One step at a time. Mary was willing to trust him, one word at a time, as she began to open-up to her gargoyle. They had miles to walk with only the first few steps ventured, two people with two special bonds, their ugliness, and the secret they shared with their music.

Chapter Thirty-Four

The lions of August had come and gone leaving little trace of their passing. That was the way it was in Sausalito, the summer fog making the days as long and cold as February in Vermont.

It was warm with its own special coziness inside the Bayview House, all the bad actors were gone leaving the rest of the community to become a community of friends. The mornings smelled of black coffee, fresh baked bread, and bacon. Augustus and Michelangelo debated the news of the day - trying to find amongst all the printed words that spoke of war in Korea, the Soviet threat, China's revolution, McCarthy and the hunt for Reds and communists working for the government or sitting next to you at the lunch counter at Woolworths, bombs that promised to stop all wars by ultimately eliminating mankind - news that did not speak of doom and gloom. Reading the paper, it was difficult to find something that could bring people together rather than ways to divide them. Listening in Betty, wondered if there would ever be another time when people seemed so distrustful of each other, the drums of discontent stronger than when the world had been at war. The aroma of Michelangelo's pipe helped make their hearth a home, forgetting for the moment that a *For Sale* sign loomed just outside the door. Oswaldo had returned with his rich laugh and heavily accented stories adding one more blessing.

There was a new sound that brought both comfort and joy to the Bayview House from the rise of the first kitchen aromas, when the sun and the fog argued for their place in the world, until the midnight whispers called everyone to their dreams beneath their comforters and cotton sheets. The new sound was Mary finding herself, the music flowing from her soul through the ivories, to be heard in each room, nook, and hallway. Mary never left her private little world which consisted of her bedroom and the music room. Her meals were brought to her by Renata, and for an hour or two each day Michael and she would talk, and then they would bring their music together in the music room - she at the piano and Michael with one of his horns. Now and then, Augustus would lean against the wall just outside the door, adding his rich voice to the music that brought the Bayview House alive; passers-by stopping to look up the hill and listen.

Michael is the only one to know something of Mary's secret. Betrayal of her trust would be a sin without pardon, which he protected, sharing it with no one, not even Mollie.

Michael is ugly and has suffered much pain and exclusion for having been born that way. He can't do anything about that, and the world won't let him be anything but ugly. Ugliness is their secret bond. Mary identifies with his lifelong pain and suffering because she sees herself as ugly. She has chosen to live life as a girl, though she was born a boy. The boy, Bernie, has been pushed back to a point of non-identity, each suffering the other's anguishes, confusion, and pain. As Mary took over, Bernie cried out that he too deserved to live. To Mary, Bernie was ugly, and she would have drowned him like a plague infected rat if she could have. But no matter how hard she tried to hide him he was always there. She was certain that when people looked at her they could see Bernie, and how mean and hateful she has been to him. Bernie, her ugly little secret, screamed to get out.

Michael and Mary's bond were not easy to come by – at the Bayview House no one asked questions, knowing that Michael would not answer them. Mary's trust in her new ugly friend gave her a sanctuary she had never experienced before.

The second week of September, Mollie received a letter which she shared with everyone over dinner.

My Dear Mollie,

I hope this letter reaches you the address I have is outdated, and I have no idea if you and Michael are still in Sausalito. After losing the 'ROSE', Stub, Ivory and I tried to stay together. In May Ivory. took one of his long walks and did not return. His depression, his nightmares from his years as a POW had worsened and we fear the worse for him. Stub has found work, but due to his Tourette Syndrome, has not kept a job for very long. What little I got from the sale of the ROSE Is now nearly gone.

You had written that you had found work in exchange for the cost of a room at the boarding house you found in Sausalito. Do you think there might be a chance that Stub, and I might be able to find a like opportunity there?

Henry is being discharged from the navy and may be back by the time you receive this letter. I do hope that San Francisco will treat him with a kinder heart this time.

Remembering most fondly our wonderful days together at the ROSE - the music and most of all, my Earl. I hope you and Michael are well and that Michael's horn is as hauntingly beautiful as I remember.

Best regards,

Stella.

This led to a lot of questions, Mollie sharing until the wee hours of the morning how she had come to The Honeysuckle Rose Hotel. About Earl Crier, Stella's husband, a blind pianist and crooner whose heart had brought everyone together. How she met Michael. Henry Akita, the Nisei war hero and army medic who Stella had worked with at the Veteran's Hospital - whose clarinet would make Benny Goodman envious. And Stub, the working man's bartender, everyone's favorite uncle, whose arms would fly up into the air tossing drinks all around when Earl played the first notes from 'Stella's Song'. That brought laughter and a desire by all to invite Stella and Stub to join their family. Of course, no one knew what fate faced them now that the *For Sale* sign mocked their aspirations.

Betty promised that the next morning she would call Jacob Fisher, the lawyer, to find out what she could.

"I say, you bring them. I like this Stub fellow very much," Oswaldo said.

Mollie said that she would write Stella back telling her that both she and Stub would be welcome. With Doyle, Scotty, and Sarah gone they had the rooms. She wouldn't say anything about the Bayview House being for sale - why worry Stella. At least for awhile Stella and Stub would be among friends.

That was the first night in months that Michael's music didn't cause the stars to twinkle. He and Mollie held each other and made love as Mary's long thin fingers caressed the piano's keys, bringing her own night music to dance with the night breezes over Sausalito.

Renata's usual routine was to rise early, having the coffee ready with the bread baking before anyone else rose. This morning her quiet time was interrupted by three hard raps on the door. Startled, Renata crossed herself. It was still dark outside; the evil spirits that lurked within the fog that wrapped itself around the house wanting inside. She knew there were no demons in the fog, Michelangelo had told her so. Still, she was alone, and the dark outside voluminous. The unwelcome knocks came again, this time more demanding. The kitchen lights and the aroma of baking bread told whoever was there that a tiny old Italian widow was inside. She carefully raised the curtain to see who was huffing and puffing, threatening to bring the door down - but it was too dark.

Two more determined knocks.

She turned the porch lights on, then unlocked the door.

Their faces flushed from the cold, two Marin County Sheriff's Deputies crowded the doorway as if to suck in what warmth escaped through the portal. They looked down on the surprised tiny woman, who offered no further greeting than the aroma of the coffee and baked bread.

The larger of the two officers spoke: "Sorry to bother you at this early hour, Ma'am. We have a warrant for the arrest of Oswaldo Rafael Cammano, his last address being here."

Renata tried to lie, her eyes betraying her.

Betty, who had heard the knocking, wheeled herself into the kitchen wearing her night robe and a sleepy face. The officers stepped into the house. She blocked the doorway that led to the stairs, looking expectantly for a reason for their being there.

"They've come to arrest Oswaldo." Renata said, tears

coming to her eyes as she feared for the kindly Ecuadorian.

Betty held out her hand, speaking loudly. "You have a warrant for Oswaldo?" By now, everyone in the house was awake, including Oswaldo, who quickly dressed, climbed up to the third floor, found his way in the dark to the rope trolley that dropped him down the back of the house. As the early morning sun lifted the cloak of night he vanished without a chance to say good-by to his American family. The warrant stated nothing about the reason for his arrest, just that he was to be turned over to immigration authorities.

Breakfast went uneaten as everyone felt the immense loss of Oswaldo from their midst. One would have thought that he had died, rather than escape deportation back to his country of birth where he would most likely be executed. No one doubted that they would not see or hear from him again.

Betty thought that he would somehow make his way to the Oregon coast where there were small fishing ports and skilled fishermen were in demand. The belongings he left behind she would set aside, with the hope that one day he would return; Mary did, didn't she.

An abrupt change in their atmosphere of mourning arrived when the first notes from Mary's piano stirred the house. By the second verse everyone looked towards the stairs trying to figure out what was different. Only Mary was upstairs, but it did not sound like her.

Michael went upstairs.

'There's been a sayin' goin' round

And I begin to think it's true

Its awful hard to love someone

When they don't care about you . . .

He stood in the hallway and listened. Mary rarely sang, she had told him that while she liked to sing, her singing slowed down her piano playing, even if she just sang the verse in her head. Now, it sounded as if her singing was setting the tempo with a raffish attitude that just wasn't Mary. He knocked lightly on the door to the music room. "Mary, its Michael, may I come in?"

"Come on in."

That didn't sound like Mary.

'Now I ain't got nobody, and nobody cares for me!

That's why I'm sad and lonely,

Won't somebody come and take a chance with me'.

"Hi ya, guy. Mary was right, you are a fright for sore eyes. Pull up a chair, I've got a river of songs to catch up with and I'm just getting warmed up."

'I'll sing you love songs, honey, all the time

If you will only say you'll be sweet gal of mine . . .

This wasn't Mary who sat at the piano stool, or was it?

"Mary?"

"She took a hike, pal." He swiveled in Michael's direction. "We haven't been formally introduced, Mary was always rude that way. My friends all me Bernie, and since you are the only one I've got, I'm pleased to meet you." He extended a hand to shake, which is something that Mary would never do. Gone was her scarf, dress, and the coat she hid within. Mary . . . Bernie, now wore brown slacks and a shirt Michael was sure belonged to Harvey; neither fit well. His terra cotta colored hair cut short, most likely by scissors, and poorly done. Still milkweed pale, the skin on his face appeared a little tauter, the illusion of a five o'clock shadow - teenage fuzz.

Michael extended his hand, hesitantly. "Bernie, nice to meet you. You know your way around the piano, mind if I play with you sometime?"

"Glad you asked. Grab your horn, I'm not fond of the saxophone, that's Mary's gig. Say, that smells good – bacon and eggs with some hot java. I'm starved."Without hesitation Bernie practically skipped from the room following the breakfast aromas. Mary never left her rooms except to go across the hall to the shared bathroom, and only after making sure she wouldn't be seen.

Oswaldo's departure had numbed them – Bernie now tongue-tied them with his unexpected and exuberant appearance. He was the antithesis of the shy troubled girl they were all struggling to comprehend. Mary hid within her clothing, spoke little, then only to Michael with a word or two to Renata. Working the room, glad-handing all, Bernie was exuberant to the point of being annoying. Locked away for years, his social skills were exasperating at best.

"Say, you're a cutie," he flippantly said to Mollie

caressing her cheek.

"I know you," he said, invading Michelangelo's personal space, "you're the guy who thinks he's smarter than God. You might be right. Heard you're a boozer. That's okay, you're all right in my book, been thinking about taking it up myself."

"You've got one hell of a voice, grandpa." He greeted Augustus as he grabbed a plate, scooping up bacon and scrambled eggs, smearing a piece of toast with butter. Then he stopped, looked at Betty with guilt painted across his face. "I'm sorry, it was Mary who pushed you." Without having taken a bite he set the plate down and returned to the music room without saying another word.

They all looked at each other speechless, having just witnessed the emergence of Bernie. Their stunned silence was interrupted by the sound of Piano Sonata No. 29 in B-flat major by Ludwig Van Beethoven, suggesting that Bernie had returned to wherever he had come from. Mary was back. The piece was known to be one of the most difficult of all the sonatas to play, requiring incredible dexterity and a stunning level of stamina. Classical pianists around the world feared even trying to learn the piece, let alone play it. Upstairs, Mary the savant, played it as Beethoven meant it to be.

"Bravo." Augustus said taking out a cigar, clipping its top, and lighting it while giving a wink to Michelangelo. "Its not too early in the morning for a short one after a performance like that."

"What just happened?" Harvey asked the question on

everyone's lips.

"Dementia praecox," Michelangelo answered. "A savant with multiple personalities, most unusual. Our Mary will turn the psychiatric world upside down. Or is it Bernie?"

Renata passed the plater of bacon, their appetites mysteriously returning.

"Like in the book 'Dr. Jekyll and Mr. Hyde' by Stevenson," Augustus pointed out. "Do you think either Mary or Bernie is dangerous?"

Michelangelo looked through the pall of smoke from his pipe at Betty. "Possibly. Right now, I'm wondering which one is dominate."

Mollie hugged her husband as he stared up the stairs to where Beethoven had just taken residency. She could see in his eyes that for the first time he was frightened.

Betty sat in her chair with tears in her eyes. The question 'had she been pushed' had just been answered - the reason now even more convoluted.

Chapter Thirty-Five

"I hope we are not too early," Stella said. It was the
third time since she and Stub had left San Francisco that
she had voiced her concern. She had often looked across
the bay wondering about what the quaint little community
of Sausalito was like compared to the hustle and bustle of
the bigger city. Several cars behind them on the Golden
Gate Bridge honked for them to speed up. Stub, who was
driving, slowed down.

"We coh . . .coh. . .could sta . . . stop for coffee somewhere first." Stub's stutter had worsened over the last
several weeks as their evictions had drawn nearer. When
Earl, Stella's husband, had been alive he had had the
heart to hire Stub Wilcox as a waiter and bartender at the
Honeysuckle Rose Hotel which he and Stella had owned.
Stub suffered from Tourette Syndrome, with all its unusual
body spasms, stutters, and peculiarities. Rather than an
outburst of uncontrolled vulgar language, Stub repeated
things he heard six times, which is not something you want
when bending a bartender's ears. Neither is throwing your

hands high over your head – which often contained a tray of drinks – when he hears certain musical tones. Regulars at *The Rose* came to think of Stub as everyone's favorite uncle; laughing with Stub, not at him. Stella, a registered nurse, kept Stub near as she tried to adapt to a world absent the love of her life and the family of musicians that had made The Honeysuckle Rose her home.

The cost of a cup of coffee would not break the bank because the bank was already broke. Her letter to Mollie hadn't told the entire truth. She and Stub slept in the car the last three nights after they'd been evicted from a flea-ridden SRO - Single room occupancy hotel - in the tenderloin. Neither had slept well, the drunks and various night creatures curious as to who was sleeping in the car and if there was anything worth stealing. As they turned off the bridge towards the tiny hamlet of Sausalito, they had little more than hope in their hats, their pockets sharing sixteen cents between them.

The fog quickly retreated towards the Farallon Islands as the sun rose brilliant and blinding when they turned onto the still-empty main street. The empty street, store fronts, some with posted for sale or lease signs, did not brighten their expectations. "Oh dear, are we doing the right thing? I mean . . ." Stella said as she tried to freshen her lipstick in the visor mirror.

"No bars, no bah . . . bums." Stub stuttered as he struggled to read the street signs against the sun's morning glare.

And no music scene she thought, knowing how emotionally attached Michael was to his music.

Knock, knock.

The knocks were soft, light, and timid.

"Not again." The knocks on the kitchen door disrupted the comfort that came after a good meal. Above, Mary played with the intensity Beethoven demanded. The thought that the police had returned unsettled everyone, especially Augustus and Harvey who were the only one's with anything to hide.

Renata opened the door.

"Stella? Stub!" Mollie, the morning having been as chaotic as it had been, had forgotten that this was the day that Stella and Stub were to arrive.

Michael turned, a broad smile spreading across his face as Stella, the only mother figure he had ever had, despite the closeness of their age, showed a woman's happy tears as they were welcomed in the door. After hugs all around, Michael grabbed his trumpet, welcoming Stella from his heart.

Augustus knew the song.

'The song a robin sings

Through years of endless springs'

Beethoven fell silent. Bernie stepping in . . .

Starting again, Michael heard and tried to draw Bernie out of his upstairs hideaway.

'The song a robin sings

Through years of endless springs . . .'

The first four notes played on the piano triggered Stub's Tourette, his right arm rising high above his head, then folding slightly, his wrist pointed towards the top of his head as a child might do in *'I'm a little teapot'*.

No one could sing it like Earl had sung it, but Augustus' rich baritone voice brought tears and memories to Stella as he sang her song. Whoever was on the piano upstairs played better than her Earl could ever have imagined. She held Mollie's hand asking, with a finger pointed up: "Who?"

Michael started to say Bernie.

"That's Mary," Mollie answered, "she . . ."

"Fell from heaven into our linen closet," Renata finished.

The pianist overhead played the first stanza hoping for another round.

Stub's arm flew up.

When Michael didn't join in the same keys on the piano tinkled again.

Stub's arm flew up. "That's not funny."

"If you want to play you are going to have to come down and say hello," Michael called up the stairs.

The piano fell silent.

Michael put down his horn. "You've got one hell of a voice. Shall we form a combo?" He asked Augustus.

"We'll need the piano," Michelangelo added.

Michael nodded agreement. "I don't know if Bernie's ready."

"He is if Mary will go back in the linen closet," Renata quipped.

"Renata be nice," scolded Betty.

"She's the one who pushed you," Renata replied.

"So, says Bernie," Michelangelo said. "The question is, can one exist without the other?"

Chopin's Nocturne in E-Flat, Op. 9 drifted down.

"I don't think Mary does the blues. If I were a betting man, my money would be on Bernie to pound out one mean boogie-woogie," shared the ex-priest.

"Is he a savant?" Stella asked. As a nurse she had seen a lot but had only read about savants.

"One and the same."

"A savant, interesting." Stella had a lot of questions which led to coffee, questions, and few answers.

As the morning, passed Bernie remained silent. Mary's playing was intoxicating in its beauty. Stub helped Renata and Mollie with the dishes."Oh dear . . ." Mollie dropped a plate back in the sink splashing soapy water on Stub as her eyes latched onto something out by the driveway.

"This is a day for the record books," Renata said shaking her head. "I'm getting too old for this. I think I'll go up to the linen closet and take a short cut, the trail has been blazed."

Michelangelo did not like the sound of Renata's voice.

It was Harvey who followed Mollie's lead and went to the window. "Jeez. . .!"

The real estate sign outside read: **SOLD.**

Augustus edged Harvey aside. "We may have to take our trio uptown." Augustus said trying to add levity where there was none.

"I don't think anyone will take either Mary or me. We're both ugly."

"Bernie isn't, a little pale perhaps."

Michael gave his wife a meek smile. "It's Mary that thinks Bernie is ugly, that's part of her psychosis." He blanched, having almost said too much.

Stella was beginning to put two and two together. "Both Mary and Bernie are savants. Are you saying that Mary and Bernie are the same person – a savant with multiple personalities?"

Everyone nodded at the same time.

She returned their expressions with a mother's look that had just caught a child trying to pull a fast one. After a moment she said: "I'm a nurse. At the veteran's hospital I saw a good many with mental and emotional issues. Which one should I talk to – Mary or Bernie?"

"Mary isn't talking to anyone but me. Now that Bernie has made himself known, she may become dormant." Michael said. "It's really quite simple. Mary hates Bernie. She is envious of Bernie and can't stand being around people because she is afraid that people will like Bernie better and want to do her harm because of the pain she has caused Bernie. She will talk with me because I am ugly. She thinks Bernie is ugly, thus she is too. I think that about captures it."

"I see . . . so we need to talk to Bernie." Stella cocked her head thoughtfully. "Why is Bernie ugly?"

"Mary told me why, but I can't tell you, because then Bernie would be mad at Mary and thus me."

"And the poor puppy chases its tail round and round because it's there." Renata said. "It all makes perfect sense to me. I say, put Mary back in the linen closet and let Bernie play his piano, that way both can be happy."

"She has a point, " *Sometime the old woman's batty ideas make sense*. Michelangelo thought.

Stub whispered in Stella's ear.

"You are right," she replied. "Stub just pointed out that no one can do anything for Mary or Bernie if they are about to be booted out onto the street. Stub and I were just evicted, and I am dreading to ask if that is what is about to happen here. What does the SOLD sign mean, good or bad news?"

"We don't know." Betty answered.

"Does anyone know anything around here?" Stella asked, a bit bewildered by everything. It was about as confusing as it had been when Earl had bought *The Rose* with no money down and nothing due but a song and a prayer. "Well, here we are then, are we too late for breakfast?"

The bacon had grown cold and greasy, the scrambled eggs had found a worthy home in the trash: Renata made a frittata.

Augustus tapped Harvey on the shoulder. "Come along lad, you and I have an errand to run."

Betty made a phone call to see what the damn *SOLD* sign meant.

Mollie went about her housekeeping while Michael went upstairs to have a musical conversation with Bernie – they really had not had a chance to talk yet – if Mary would let them. In the hallway, outside the music room, Michael began to play. He figured it really didn't matter what, Bernie probably knew it.

Stub and Stella listened, remembering the way music had been the beating heart of *The Honeysuckle Rose Hotel*. They had lost the *Rose*. Were they now about to lose the Bayview House before it could even become their home?

CHAPTER THIRTY - SIX

Jacob Fischer, Attorney at Law, did not return Betty's call. Abraham Bartholomew, the real estate agent, referred her back to Fischer. No answers, and the music played on. "Puppy chasing its tail," quipped Renata, the truth being that she really did not want an answer, fearing what it might be.

Michael danced around Mary, preferring her silent while Bernie now joined them at the communal table, enjoying their company while regaling them with tales that could not possibly be true.

Three days passed.

No one mentioned Augustus and Harvey's absence because it made the waiting that much harder. Harvey had returned two days prior and loaded Augustus's car with their luggage without so much as a 'Good-by and thank you Ma'am.' No one blamed them. Augustus hadn't even had time to unpack his bags before the 'SOLD' sign began to haunt their days. He had money, more than a humble professor ought to, and plenty of opportunities that money could buy. Harvey had found a sugar daddy, not the romantic kind, but a patron who could offer him doors that opened dreams he had never dared dream before. Why should they stick around the old Bayview House and listen to the clock tick waiting for the music to fade away.

The clock ticked. Augustus' rich voice was missed as Bernie and Michael did their best to drown out the neurotic tick-tick-tick.

Renata was in the linen closet trying to figure out where Mary had gone when Augustus' robust voice rebounded throughout the house. "Gather round all, let's not let the evil schemes and plots of sinister witches and ambulance chasers ruin your day." The sound of a popping cork added a twinkle to Renata's eyes as she hurried – almost falling down the stairs.

Michelangelo happily poured.

"I raise a toast to. . .no, I cannot say. . . you must see for yourselves." Augustus announced.

Harvey opened the kitchen door to where two cars waited. Mollie helped Betty. Stella and Stub joined them in Augustus' car while Michelangelo, Michael and Renata rode with Harvey. Bernie, who had become the live wire in the house, refused to leave his home and stayed behind. The windows rolled down on a hot August afternoon, they all heard Bernie playing his version of a bebop blues original; the rhyme both exciting and sad.

Four blocks away, on what had once been the thriving

center of Sausalito, near where the Sausalito Ferry had made its home, was an abandoned hotel the military had used when the shipyard produced merchant ships and warships to save the world. Closed six years, it needed a little paint, otherwise it was in fairly good shape.

"What's this?" Betty asked as Augustus pulled her wheelchair from the trunk.

Michelangelo saw it first, the sign in the front window: *'UNDER NEW MANAGEMENT.'*

"Who?" Renata crossed herself as one does when a miracle has occurred.

"We did," Harvey exploded, unable to contain the news any longer. "Augustus and me, we bought it!" He spread his arms wide. "It's your new home, rent free, that is . . . if you like it?"

"Like it?" Michelangelo could not believe his eyes.

"But how . . ?" Betty held her hands over her heart afraid that she might just die of joy.

"Let's just say that Harvey and I had some luck at the race track and leave it at that." Augustus said, his smile saying: *Don't ask questions I'm not about to answer.*

"The No Name Hotel has thirty rooms, each with their own private bath. There are four floors; the first has a bay view dining room and a bar. I'm told that Dorsey once played here back in thirty-nine." Augustus guided them as they marveled at the décor. "As you can see it is still furnished. The Department of the Navy was very happy to unload it for a song and six-pence. There are three guest rooms on the first floor. One was used by the chef, and the other two for visiting dignitaries."

"Like Dorsey," Stella said.

Towards the rear of the hotel they came to a door. "This one is yours, Betty. And the room next door is yours, Renata. We mustn't have either of you worrying about the stairs. The rest of you pick any room you want, the remaining we can rent out to cover expenses."

"It's so large," Betty sighed. "How can I possibly manage this?"

"I think I can be of some help," Stella said. "It's almost as large as the Rose was."

Betty rolled into her room where she instantly fell in love with the bay window and its view of San Francisco Bay and the city beyond.

Renata found her way to the kitchen where she began to peek into each cupboard and nook, envisioning the dinners to be cooked. They left her singing happily in Italian as they explored the bar where there was an outside deck for sunny days and summer nights, a stage, long bar, and a dance floor.

"Home ahh . . .again, home ah . . .again, jig-itty-itty jig," Stub stuttered. He hadn't had a decent bar to run since the *Rose*.

Michael had his horn in hand when they had all started their mystery trip. He looked around the bar and the dining room, which might seat sixty, then stepping out onto the outside deck, he and Mollie embraced. He then raised in trumpet and began to play a personal favorite: *The Tennessee Waltz*.

The window open in the music room at the Bayview House, Bernie heard his new pal's heart music, and began to play and sing along. He did not know where they had gone, but he had never wanted anything so badly as to be with them right now.

Stella watched as Renata started to climb the stairs. "Where are you going?"

"Looking for the linen closet," She answered as he reached the top of the stairs.

No one had much in the way of personal property, so moving day was a breeze. The piano, last to be moved, was loaded onto the pack of a pickup truck. Bernie, who wouldn't be separated from it, rode standing, while playing a rip-roaring version of 'Little Brown Jug.' It was a silly song choice, but fun and an attention getter. Michael jumped in back, adding his saxophone, while Stella and Augustus belted out the vocals from the cab. It was moving day, and the sleepy little burg of Sausalito would never the same.

'My wife and I lived all alone

In a little log hut we called our own

She loved gine and I loved rum

tell you what, we'd lots of fun

Ha, ha, ha, you and me

Little brown jug, don't I love thee...'

Sarah Brandt sold the Bayview House at a loss, using most of the money for her legal expenses. She got twelve to fifteen years, doubtful that she would ever be paroled early for good behavior.

Mary Griffin was never heard from again.

By the end of September, Henry Akita's clarinet was added to the Michael O'Dea Trio, with vocals by Caesar Augustus Pinfield, and Bernie Griffin on the piano. The new night club was named: *NIGHT MUSIC OVER SAUSALITO,*

Story's end.

And the music begins.